J.A.

JANCE

EDGE OF EVIL

A NOVEL OF SUSPENSE

HARPER

An Imprint of HarperCollinsPublishers

This is a work of fiction. Names, characters, places, and incidents are products of the author's imagination or are used fictitiously and are not to be construed as real. Any resemblance to actual events, locales, organizations, or persons, living or dead, is entirely coincidental.

HARPER

An Imprint of HarperCollins*Publishers*
10 East 53rd Street
New York, New York 10022-5299

Copyright © 2006 by J.A. Jance
Excerpt from *Judgment Call* copyright © 2012 by J.A. Jance
ISBN 978-0-06-195855-7

All rights reserved. No part of this book may be used or reproduced in any manner whatsoever without written permission, except in the case of brief quotations embodied in critical articles and reviews. For information address Harper paperbacks, an Imprint of HarperCollins Publishers.

First Harper premium printing: July 2012
First Avon Books mass market printing: January 2006

HarperCollins ® and Harper ® are registered trademarks of HarperCollins Publishers.

Printed in the United States of America

Visit Harper paperbacks on the World Wide Web at
www.harpercollins.com

10 9 8 7 6 5 4 3

If you purchased this book without a cover, you should be aware that this book is stolen property. It was reported as "unsold and destroyed" to the publisher, and neither the author nor the publisher has received any payment for this "stripped book."

Dedicated to Michael and Sheri;
and to Ernie G. and Patti W.
And in memory of Holly Turner

Prologue

A pair of headlights inched down Schnebly Hill Road, down from the Mogollon Rim toward red rock–rimmed Sedona, eleven treacherous miles below. Had anyone been able to see through the falling snow, they might have thought the vehicle was traversing the sheer cliff face itself. Less than half a mile from the top, at a spot where the road made a hairpin turn back into a canyon, an older model Chevy Yukon came to a stop. With the engine still running, a door opened. Someone stepped out into the falling snow. The door slammed shut quietly, very quietly, the sound muffled by the heavy, wet flakes.

For a few seconds nothing at all happened. And for a while after, it seemed as though nothing would. Then slowly, very slowly, the SUV inched forward. Rather than following the narrow roadway that wound back into the safety of the mountain, the Yukon instead moved forward, straight out and over the edge. The burning headlights cut through the darkness and the falling snow as the Yukon arched downward.

In clear weather the explosion of metal as the vehicle slammed into the first outcropping of rock would have echoed up and down the canyon walls, but on this snowy March night, it was muffled, too. As the Yukon continued its deadly end-over-end tumble, a body flew soundlessly out through one of the smashed windows and landed, limp and lifeless as a rag doll, its shattered arms flung around the base of a scrubby pine. Without its passenger, the Yukon continued on its destructive path, tumbling on and on, down and down. One by one, headlights and taillights were extinguished. When the vehicle finally came to rest, the interior dome light came on briefly. After a few minutes, that too went out. Then there was silence, utter silence.

On the snow-covered track far above, a single person stood and watched, peering through the snow searching for any sign of life coming from the scattered wreckage. Finally, after several long minutes, satisfied that no one could have survived that terrible downward plunge, the coat-shrouded figure turned and trudged back the way the Yukon had come.

Within minutes, the telltale impressions of hiking boots had been totally obliterated. Before long, the tire tracks leaving the roadway had disappeared as well. All that was left was silence and the falling snow.

Chapter 1

When Alison Reynolds left the studio after the eleven o'clock news, she was amazed to find Cliff Baker, the news director, waiting out in the hall. He was usually gone for the day by then, or else he was out in the parking lot toking up.

"Talk to you a minute, Ali?" he said in that clipped almost rude tone of his, one that made his smallest requests come across as issued orders.

Ali was whipped. She had started that morning as the featured speaker for a YWCA fund-raising breakfast. At noon she had MC-ed an American Cancer Society–sponsored charity event. In the process she had driven from one end of LA to the other. She had also co-anchored two evening live news broadcasts—one at six and the other at eleven. She was ready to go home, kick off her high heels, and put her feet up. Looking at Cliff's uncompromising face, she knew he wouldn't take no for an answer.

She summoned a tired but necessary smile. "Sure, Cliff. What's up?"

That's when she noticed Eduardo Duarte, a uniformed security guard, standing off to one side and hovering awkwardly in the background. Ali knew Eddie and his wife Rosa. They had met in a hospital room on a juvenile cancer ward where she had gone to cheer them up while the Duarte's three-year-old son, Alonso, had been undergoing treatment—successful treatment it turned out—for leukemia. Ali Reynolds was, after all, the station's unofficial but very committed one-woman cancer research and treatment spokesperson.

This status had been a natural aftermath of her first husband's death from an inoperable brain tumor at age twenty-four, twenty-two years earlier. His death had left Ali a widow at age twenty-three—widowed and seven months pregnant. Christopher had been born two full months after his father's death. Since then, Ali had been a tireless crusader for cancer research. She walked in Relays for Life, participated in Races for the Cure, and did countless cancer-related public appearances whenever possible. And private appearances as well.

For most of the on-air folks at the station, Eduardo Duarte was just another nameless, faceless security guard who checked IDs as employees came and went through the front lobby. For Ali, Eddie was far more than that. She had been with the Duartes in the hospital waiting room and had held their hands during the dark time when no one had known for sure whether or not their child would survive.

"Hey, Eddie," she said. "How's my man, 'Lonso?"

"He's okay, I guess, Ms. Reynolds," Eddie answered, but he kept his eyes averted. That's when Ali tumbled to the fact that Cliff Baker's hallway ambush meant trouble.

"What's going on, Cliff?" she asked.

Six months earlier Clifford Baker had been brought on board to "fix" things. At least that was the way the story was told to the news team at the staff meeting when Cliff was introduced. But what had been bad then was still bad now. It was hard to win the ratings game when there were too many people out in the parking lot smoking joints before and after their shifts; when there were too many people hiding out in their offices with too many lines of coke going up their noses. And Ali Reynolds long suspected that one of those problem noses belonged to Cliff Baker.

"The ratings still suck," he said.

Ali didn't say anything. She was over forty in a world in which thirty-five meant on-air womenfolk were nearing the end of their sell-by date. Standing there in the hallway, breathing the sweet perfume of marijuana smoke wafting off Cliff's rumpled sports jacket, Ali knew exactly what was coming. There was a certain inevitability to the whole process, and Ali wasn't about to say something that would make Cliff's job any easier. If he was there to fire her, he would have to come right out and say so.

"We've decided to take the news team in a different direction," he said at last.

Presumably without me, Ali thought, but she kept her mouth shut.

"I know this is going to be difficult for you," Cliff continued.

Ali had known from the moment she met the man that he was a cold-blooded bastard. The supposed reluctance he was exhibiting now was all an act—a classic study in self-serving, cover-your-ass camouflage.

"And I'm sure this is going to seem hard-hearted," he went on, shaking his head reluctantly, "but we have to let you go. We'll pay you until the end of your contract, of course, and then I'm sure there'll be some severance pay, but after that . . ." He shrugged.

With the news broadcast ended, there were other people coming and going in the hallway. Ali noticed that they all gave the three people standing outside the newsroom door a wide berth. Ali wondered, *How many of you knew this was coming?*

She had noticed a few sidelong glances of late—quiet conversations that would die away as soon as she came into the room and resume once she left—but in the cutthroat world of television, she hadn't thought them anything out of the ordinary. Now she knew better, but she couldn't afford to think about her spineless co-workers just then. Instead, she remained focused on Cliff.

"Why?" Ali asked. "Why do you have to let me go?"

This was a good journalistic gambit. Go for the *W*s—who, what, why, where, when, and sometimes how. She was never quite sure how the word *how* had been added to the mix of *W*s, or why it was considered to be one, but when taking journalism classes from stodgy professors whose grading meant everything, it's a good idea to avoid questioning the conventional wisdom.

"For the good of the team," Cliff answered at once.

Ali Reynolds came from good Scandinavian stock. She was a natural blonde who could, on occasion, summon a suitably dumb-blonde persona. It was a gambit that had suckered more than one unsuspecting male interviewee into saying more than he intended. Cliff, dyed-in-the-wool male chauvinist that he was, took the bait.

"You know the demographics," he added. "We need to appeal to a younger audience, a more hip audience."

"You're saying I'm too old?" Ali asked.

"Well, not in so many words," Cliff answered quickly.

But, of course, he had said so in *so* many words. Not only had he said the revealing "hip audience" words to Ali, he had made the astonishing blunder of doing so in front of a witness, Eddie Duarte. Ali suspected that the grass Cliff had smoked while waiting for the end of the broadcast had impaired his judgment. Ali glanced toward Eddie, who seemed to be fixated on examining the shine on his highly polished shoes.

"When's my last broadcast?" she asked.

"You just did it," Cliff said.

Ali willed herself to exhibit no emotion whatsoever. She summoned the same strength she had used to get through the noon newscast the day of the Oklahoma City bombing. Her performance that day had been done with enough professional aplomb that it had been instrumental in getting her a job as a "pre"-Laurie Dhue Fox News Channel babe a year later. (Of course, her natural-blond good looks and flawless complexion hadn't hurt, either.) Years later, after Ali had come to LA to assume co-anchor duties there, she had managed to remain dry-eyed and professional during the unrelenting hours of live on-air coverage in the aftermath of the September 11 attacks. She was dry-eyed now, too.

"You're not going to give me a chance to tell my viewers good-bye?" she asked.

"There's no point, really," Cliff said with a shrug. "Come on, Ali. When it's over, it's over. Schmaltzy good-byes don't do a thing for ratings. But that's why Eddie's here. He'll go with you while you clean out your locker and your desk. You're not to touch your computer. Whatever's on your office computer belongs to the station. And be sure to give him your ID card, your elevator pass, and your keys on the way out. Good luck." With that, Cliff Baker turned away and sauntered, down the hall."

"Sorry, Ms. Reynolds," Eddie murmured.

"Thank you," she said.

"Will you be all right?"

"I'll be fine. Come on. Let's get this over with."

She went into the newsroom, where she saw that someone had taken the liberty of placing an empty banker's box on the chair in front of her desk. As she approached it, she noticed that the other people in the room seemed totally involved in other things—studying their computers, talking on the phone. Only one of them, Kimberly Weston—the up-and-coming "weather girl"—came over to chat.

"I'm so sorry to hear about all this," she said.

So the word had been out, Ali realized. And this little twit—the arrogant tiny-waisted twenty-something with her enhanced boobs, the bitch who had masterminded giving Ali a gift-wrapped gag package of Grecian Formula 44 on the occasion of her most recent birthday—had known all about it for God knows how long. Since long before Ali did.

With a swipe of her fist, Ali cleared her son's high school graduation portrait off her desk and slammed it into the box with enough force that only a miracle kept the glass from shattering.

"That's funny," she said, "I only just found out."

"I mean I guess I'd just heard rumors," Kimberly fumbled, clearly uncomfortable.

"Since you seem to be in the know," Ali said, "who's taking my place? Are they promoting from within or importing new talent?"

"Importing," Kimberly said in a small voice.

That figures, Ali thought. *What goes around comes around.*

It was the same thing the station had done to Katherine Amado, the station's previous female anchor, when they brought in Alison. Katy Amado was let go in one day—she was forty-eight years old at the time. The very next day, Ali was down at the station filming promos for the "new" news team.

In far less time than Ali would have thought possible, all of her personal items were summarily dumped into the box. When it came time to leave the newsroom for the last time, no one came near her to tell her good-bye or wish her luck. *Maybe they think I'm contagious*, she thought.

With Eddie shadowing her and carrying the box, Ali ventured back into the darkened studio and retrieved her brush, hair spray, makeup, and mirror from their place in the cubbyhole beneath the shiny wood-grained surface of the news desk. In the women's rest room, she emptied her locker of the two extra blazers she kept there. She also removed the hair dryer and curling iron that she had brought in and allowed other people to use. If someone was in need of a curling iron tomorrow morning, it was too bad. They could get their butts over to Walgreens and buy a new one.

Eddie lugged the box all the way out to the parking lot. He waited while Ali unlocked her Porsche Cayenne, then he loaded the box into the back and closed the tail gate. By the time he finished, Ali had fished out her elevator key and building pass. She handed those to him and then plucked her ID off the strap she wore around her neck.

"Here you go," she said, handing it over. "Thanks for all the help, Eddie. I really appreciate it."

"I heard what Mr. Baker said," Eddie muttered. "About you being too old. He can't do that, can he? I mean, aren't there laws about that kind of thing?"

"He's not supposed to be able to do it," Ali replied with a sharp laugh. "But Clifford Baker doesn't seem to think any of those rules apply to him."

"Will you fight him, then?" Eddie asked. "Will you take him to court?"

"I might," Ali said.

"If you need me to testify," Eddie said, "I'll be glad to tell them what he said—that it was because you're too old."

"You'd do that?" Ali asked.

Eddie nodded. "Yes," he said. "Yes, I would."

"But you'd probably lose your job."

Eddie Duarte shrugged. "I'm just a security

guard," he said. "There are lots of jobs for people like me."

"Thank you, Eddie," she said. "I'll think about it." Then she got in the car and drove from Burbank to her house on Robert Lane in Beverly Hills. On the way, she didn't try calling home to tell her husband what had happened. There wasn't anything Paul Grayson could have done about it. Besides, he usually came home later than Ali did.

When she turned off the 405 onto Sunset, she opened the moon roof and let the wind ruffle her hair. Turning into the driveway, she was surprised to see lights on downstairs. Her son Chris, now a senior at UCLA, lived out back in the guest house, but he often prowled the kitchen in the "big house" late in the evenings in search of food. Ali was surprised to find Chris's Prius missing from its assigned spot in the six-car garage. Instead, Paul's arena red Porsche Carerra was parked at the far end. As Ali walked past it, the ticking of the cooling engine told her that he hadn't been home long.

She found Paul at the bar off the family room mixing himself a drink. "I'm having a Manhattan. Want one?" he asked.

"Sure," she said, kicking off her shoes and dropping into a nearby easy chair. "Make mine a double."

"So how did it go?" he asked as he delivered her drink.

That's when Alison realized that Paul already knew she'd been let go—that he had known what was coming down before she did! He was a network bigwig, and LA was a major market. Naturally they would have told Paul about her firing in advance of their actually doing it. After all, he had been responsible for bringing Alison to town in the first place. Nepotism be damned, he was the one who had finagled his new bride her cushy co-anchor position—a maneuver that had left her open to years' worth of sniping co-workers who claimed she wasn't really qualified. Now, though, Paul would have had to sign off on her being booted out as well.

Somehow she managed to hold the stemmed cocktail glass steady enough that when she took that first sip she didn't spill any of it.

"Cliff Baker fired me," she said quietly. "Tonight. After the news."

"Oh, Ali Bunny," he said. "I'm so sorry. What a hell of a thing!"

She hated it when he called her Ali Bunny.

"I may take them to court," she said calmly.

That shocked Paul, all right—shocked him good. "You're going to what?" he demanded, slopping his own drink down the unknotted three-hundred-dollar tie dangling around his neck.

"It's age and sex discrimination," she said. "The three guys that are left are all older than I am. Randall's got to be sixty if he's a day. Nobody's sacking any of them."

"You can't take the station to court," Paul said. "I mean, how would it look? We're married. I work for the network. What would people say?"

"People would say it's about time somebody stood up for women," Ali replied. "Over forty isn't exactly over the hill."

"If you take the station to court, you'll be blackballed for sure. You'll never work in the mainstream media again."

"All the more reason to sue them, then," she said.

"But think what it'll do to my career!"

Ali took another sip of her drink. "Frankly, my dear," she told him. "I don't give a damn."

Paul stood up abruptly and stalked off to his study, closing the door firmly behind him. Other people might have given the door a good hard slam, but not Paul Grayson. He disdained what he called "cheap theatrics." He considered himself above all that.

But when the heavy door clicked shut, Alison Reynolds heard something else entirely. The sound that echoed down the marble-floored hallway had nothing to do with the locking mechanism on the door and everything to do with the end of their marriage.

Ali sat for a few moments longer. When she and Paul had moved into this house years earlier, she thought herself extremely lucky. After years of being a single parent, she had been glad to have a father figure for her hormone-charged fourteen-year-old son. But things hadn't turned out the way she expected. Paul and Chris weren't close. Not at all. And her happily-ever-after fairy tale romance wasn't what it had been cracked up to be, either. An exciting, whirlwind romance had morphed into a marriage where divergent jobs and interests kept them busy and apart. At times it seemed to Ali that she and Paul were roommates and housemates more than they were man and wife.

Ali surveyed the room, eyeing the opulent leather furnishings that Paul preferred. She hadn't liked them much to begin with, but they had grown on her over time, unlike the art. The splashy modern art that adorned the walls—large pieces with gilt frames, vivid colors, steep price tags, and not much heart—came with enough bragging rights to cut it with Paul's art-snob pals, but they didn't speak to Ali. Not at all.

"I'll miss this chair," she allowed at last, "but the art can go straight to hell."

With that, she knocked back the remains of her drink in one long swallow. Then she stood up, collected her shoes, and headed for bed.

By the time Ali got up the next day Paul was already gone, on an out-of-town trip. It was early Saturday morning. She was pulled downstairs by an irresistible smell. She found Chris in the kitchen, expertly moving an omelet from a frying pan to a plate, folding it with a gentle flick of the wrist just the way Ali's father had taught him.

"You've got to learn to cook, boy," Bob Larson had said. "If you leave it up to your mother, you'll starve to death."

Her parents ran Sedona's Sugarloaf Café, a down-home-style diner that had been started in the mid-fifties by her maternal grandmother, Myrtle Hansen. Myrtle had left the business to her twin daughters, Edie Larson and Evelyn Hansen. Now, with Ali's Aunt Evie gone, Bob and Edie were still running the place, which was usually packed on weekends, especially at breakfast time.

"Hey, Mom," Chris said. "You look like hell. Hungry?"

The double Manhattan had gone straight to Ali's head, but she hadn't slept. She'd lain awake, tossing and turning, and she felt hung-over as hell.

"Yes, please," she said.

"Have this," Chris said, passing her the filled plate. "I'll make another one."

Ali took a seat at the island counter and then watched Chris. "I got fired last night," she said.

Chris whirled in her direction, almost dropping an egg in the process. "You got fired? No way!"

"Yes," she said.

"Just like that?"

Ali nodded.

"When's your final broadcast?" Chris asked.

"Already had it," Ali said. "They pulled the plug on me last night as soon as the news was over."

Turning off the fire under the frying pan, Chris hurried to his mother's side and took her hand. "That's terrible, Mom," he said. "I can't believe they did that to you. Did Paul know about it? Did he know in advance that they were going to let you go?"

"Probably," Ali said.

"And he didn't tell you or try to do anything to stop it?"

Ali shrugged.

"That bastard," Chris muttered.

Ali said nothing. She had arrived at much the same conclusion. Paul Grayson *was* a bastard.

"Which means you don't even get to say good-bye to the people who've watched you for the past seven years?" Chris continued, his voice shaking in outrage.

"Evidently not."

"That sucks!"

"Well, yes," Ali agreed. "Yes, it does."

"Wouldn't you like to let people know what happened—tell them your side of the story?"

Ali laughed. "I don't think that's an option.

"We'll see about that," Chris vowed.

With that, he got up from the counter, returned to the stove, and turned the fire back on under his omelet pan.

Ali spent the day quietly. Once it was two o'clock Arizona time and the Sugarloaf Café was closed for the day, Ali called her parents and told Bob and Edie Larson what was going on—the job part of it anyway, not the marriage part. Bob was as outraged as Chris had been. Edie was instantly sympathetic.

"If you have time off, you should come visit," she said. "You have your Aunt Evie's house to stay in. Come over, relax, and give yourself time to think about what you're going to do next."

Ali had already decided what she was going to do next—track down the names of several wrongful termination attorneys. "Thanks, Mom," Ali said. "I'll think about it."

On Sunday morning, Ali came downstairs and was surprised to find a sheaf of e-mail printouts sitting next to the coffeepot. There were dozens of them, all addressed to her home e-mail account. One by one she read through them.

Dear Ali,

I'm so sorry you're leaving. You seem like a good friend. I'll never forget what a wonderful job you did when our next-door neighbor's son was killed in Iraq. Please let me know where you end up. I'm hoping I'll still be able to watch you.

Mrs. Edith Wilson,
Glendale, CA

Dear Ms. Reynolds,

How can they fire you? You're the only bright spot on that dying news team. I hope you get a good job somewhere else and beat them up in the ratings. They deserve it.

Mac, Sherman Oaks

To whom it may concern:

Since you fired Ali Reynolds, you can kiss my advertising dollars goodbye. You guys don't know a good thing when you see it.

Walter Duffy

Dear Ali Reynolds,

You don't remember me, but we walked together at the Relay for Life in Sherman Oaks. My husband had just been diagnosed with prostate cancer and you told me about losing your first husband when he was only twenty-four and when you were expecting a baby. I just want you to know how much I appreciated your being there for me and for all the other people who are fighting cancer. I wish you all the best.

Millie Sanders

Chris came into the kitchen just then, coffee cup in hand and grinning from ear to ear. "What do you think?" he asked.

"Where did all these come from?" Ali asked.

"From your blog—*your* weblog," Chris answered. "I called it cutlooseblog.com. Me and some of my marketing friends came up with the idea yesterday. I posted a note saying that you'd been fired—that you weren't sick or going into politics or wanting to spend more time with your family. We posted the blog and then we went to the various search engines to make sure it was added. This is what came back."

"But there must be a hundred of them," Ali marveled.

"More than that," Chris said. "These are only the ones I've printed. There are more coming in all the time."

"But how do I answer them all?" Ali asked. "Do I do it one at a time?"

Chris shrugged. "That's up to you. You can answer in a group posting or you can do it one at a time. From the volume, I'd suggest a single posting. Otherwise you'll go nuts."

"But, Chris," Ali objected, "I don't do blogs. I never have."

Chris grinned back at her. "You do now."

Chapter 2

cutlooseblog.com
Sunday, March 13, 2005

My son, Christopher, first laid hands on a computer when he was six. I was given an old Epson from work. I brought it home and gave it to him. Once his fingers hit the keyboard, it was love at first touch—and, yes, he's actually a better typist than I am. It's because of him that I'm writing this today. And not only is this the first time I've visited a blog, this is also the first time I've posted on one.

When Chris created this site, he named it cutlooseblog.com because that's exactly what's happened to me. I've been cut loose and set adrift from a job I loved. There was no advance warning. I didn't see it coming. Chris has already told you that as of 11:30 Friday evening, I was told that my services would no longer be required on the evening and nighttime news. You'll notice that I'm not naming names or going into any kind of specifics here. That's because, come Monday morning, I expect to have an appointment seeking legal advice. With that in mind, the less said the better.

One thing is certain. I wasn't allowed to tell my viewers good-bye, and that made me sad. Now, though, thanks to efforts by Chris and some of his computer-savvy marketing friends at UCLA (Thanks, guys and gals!) I have a chance to tell you good-bye after all.

Through my years on the air I have diligently tried to answer all my own fan mail. But never have I seen the outpouring of kind wishes and words that have turned up in my life today. I can see that there's no way I'll be able to answer them all individually. So let me say a big group thank you to all of you.

Chris tells me that if I really am going to be a Blogger??!!! when I grow up, I'll need to post articles like this one on a fairly regular basis. Since I'm a trained journalist, that shouldn't be all that difficult. I'll try to let you know how things are going for me. I'll also let you know where I next find myself behind an anchor desk because I'd like to think that my career in television news isn't over. I believe I still have a lot to offer.

Again, thank you for writing. I was at a very low ebb this morning when I came downstairs. I was upset. I hadn't slept for the better part of two nights. You have no idea how much your wonderful notes mean to me. If anyone wants to write to me, my e-mail address is listed at the top of this form.

Be well.

Posted: 11:23 A.M. by AliR

Chris left in the early afternoon to go hang out with his friends. Ali more than half expected that her phone would ring with people calling to say how sorry they were, but the people who were friends enough to have her unlisted home phone and her cell stayed away in droves. Either they didn't know or they didn't want to get too close for all the same reasons her co-workers from the newsroom had stayed away on Friday night. Guilt by association.

And so, feeling at loose ends, Ali did what her mother and her Aunt Evie would have done—she cleaned out her closet. Closets, actually. She was surprised by the sheer number of outfits she had. That came with being on television. You had to vary the wardrobe. You couldn't show up night after night wearing the same thing. And Paul never stinted when it came to spending money on clothing for either one of them. He was a great believer in the old adage "Clothes make the man," or woman, as the case might be. He wanted to look good and he wanted his wife to look good too—guilt by association again.

Ali was ruthless. The YWCA had a clothing bank, run in conjunction with a homeless shelter, where women who needed nice clothing for interviews or for new jobs could go and find appropriate attire.

She loaded up three black leaf bags full of clothing and another one of shoes, then she dragged the entire bunch out to the Cayenne and loaded them in the back so she could deliver them the next day.

Her cell phone rang as she came back into the house. "Hi, Mom," she said. "How's business?"

"Not so hot," her mother returned. "We even ended up with leftover sweet rolls."

The very thought of her mother's sweet rolls made Ali's mouth water. Baked fresh every day according to Myrtle Hansen's own recipe, the delectable treats were usually sold out by ten A.M.

"How did that happen?" Ali asked.

"With all the rain and snow we've had this winter—with RVs getting washed down Oak Creek and all—business is way off. In fact, the big storm that came through Friday night dropped five inches of snow right here in Sedona, and a lot more up on the rim. Naturally, with fresh powder, your dad took off from work early so he and Hal Sims could get in some skiing up at the Snow Bowl. On the way, they're going to drop off our leftovers at that homeless encampment just off the freeway up by Flagstaff. You know what a soft touch your father is. He's a regular Loaves and Fishes kind of guy."

That was one of the things Ali loved about her father, and despite the annoyance in her voice, it was probably one of the things Edie Larson loved about her husband as well. Bob may have had a gruff exterior, but inside he was a pushover. He was forever offering a helping hand to anyone who needed it. Through the years Ali had lost track of the countless vagrants—drunks, mental cases, whatever—

Bob had dragged home. He found them clothing and gave them odd jobs to do long enough for them to "earn some moolah and get some traction," as Bob liked to say.

While still a child, Ali had often accompanied Bob Larson on his self-appointed rounds to distribute what would otherwise have been Sugarloaf discards. Sometimes they went to homes where there were children with no food and zero heat. The next day Bob would be on the phone with the utility company trying to negotiate a way to turn the power or gas back on, or else he'd be tracking down some local contractor who, in the process of clearing land, might have access to a cord of firewood or two. Sometimes Bob went looking for homeless people living in parks or camped out in picnic areas. For those unfortunates living rough in cold weather, he often brought along discarded coats and blankets as well as food.

That was what had happened this past year over Christmas when Ali had accompanied her father on one of his mercy missions. With the freeway newly plowed and snow lying ten inches deep, Bob had turned off the I-17 a few miles south of Munds Park and then wandered off the beaten track onto a Forest Service road that was just barely passable with Bob's '72 Bronco 4×4. Twenty minutes later, as soon as Bob stopped the SUV, fifteen or so people had materialized out of the snowbound, thickly forested wilderness and had quickly divested the 4×4 of its mini-truckload of bounty.

"These people live here year-round?" an astonished Ali had asked as they drove back to Sedona.

"Pretty much," her father returned.

"You'd think they'd freeze."

"They've got tents and campers hidden in here in the woods. Believe me, some of these guys have plenty of reason for staying out of sight."

"Is it safe to come here, then?"

Bob grinned. "It is for me," he said. "They're all hungry, and I'm the guy with the food."

"I keep wondering when in the world that man is going to grow up," Edie was saying. "Put him on a pair of skis and he thinks he's twenty again. But I didn't call you up to bend your ear complaining about your father. I'm really calling about Reenie."

Reenie Bernard was Ali's best friend from high school. "What about her?" Ali asked at once. "Is she all right?"

"I don't know, she's missing," Edie Larson answered. She sounded worried.

"Missing?" Ali repeated, as though she hadn't heard properly.

"That's right," Edie said. "Hasn't been seen or heard from since she went to Phoenix on Thursday. I had heard rumors about it yesterday, but you were so upset about your job situation at the time that I didn't want to bring it up until it was actually confirmed. Besides, I was hoping they'd have found her by now, but they haven't. She's officially listed as a missing person."

Ali's head swam. There were times when she and Misty Irene Bernard had gone for a year or two without any more communication than a hastily scrawled note on a Christmas card. The last time she had seen Ali had been at the Sugarloaf Christmas party back in December. Still, despite the years and distance, Ali considcred Reenie to be her best friend.

"What happened?" Ali demanded.

"Nobody knows. One of the detectives from the Yavapai County sheriff's department came in for lunch. According to him, Reenie was supposed to go to Scottsdale on Thursday morning for a doctor's appointment. She left the doctor's office in mid afternoon and hasn't been seen since."

In a matter of seconds the fact that Ali had lost her newsroom job seemed ridiculously unimportant—and selfish.

"That's awful," she said. "How are Howie and the kids doing?"

Reenie's husband, Dr. Howard Bernard, was a history professor at Northern Arizona University in Flagstaff. His and Reenie's marriage was a late-blooming, second-time-around affair for both of them. Their children—Matthew and Julic—were nine and six respectively. Julie had just barely made it in under her mother's self-imposed child-bearing deadline of age 40.

"I don't know," Edie replied. "I haven't called them. I didn't want to be a bother, but I thought you might want to."

"Yes," Ali agreed. "I will. As soon as we get off the phone."

And she did. The moment the call to her mother ended, Ali scrolled through the saved numbers in her cell phone and dialed Reenie's home number. Someone whose voice Ali didn't recognize answered before the end of the first ring.

"It's Bree," Reenie's sister said, once Ali identified herself.

Bree and Reenie's parents, Ed and Diane Holzer, were now staunch, Sunday-go-to-meeting-style Missouri Synod Lutherans—a direct contradiction to their wild and misspent youth. Ed had straightened up enough to join and eventually manage his family banking and real estate interests in Cottonwood. Prior to that, however, he and Diane together had sowed plenty of wild oats. They had named their now middle-aged daughters in the spirit of those psychedelic, free-wheeling days. Reenie, formally dubbed Misty Irene, had spent her school years dodging what she considered a name straight out of the sixties by opting for a variation on her middle name. Reenie's younger sister, Bree—short for Breezy Marie—hadn't fared much better.

Ali's friendship with Reenie hadn't extended as far as Bree, who, as the apple of her father's eye, had been regarded as spoiled rotten and an obnoxious pest besides. All that was years in the past now, though, and Ali was glad Bree was there to help Howie and the kids with whatever was going on.

"My mother just called," Ali said. "Until then I had no idea any of this had happened. How are things?"

Someone in the background on the other end of the call asked Bree a question. "It's Ali Reynolds," Bree answered. "She's calling from California." Then she came back to Ali. "Sorry. Howie can't come to the phone right now. The house is full of people, cops mostly."

"What's going on?"

Bree sighed. "How long since you talked to Reenie?" she asked.

"I saw her briefly over Christmas," Ali replied. "But there were all kinds of other people there. We didn't have much of a visit. Why?"

"Reenie had been having trouble with her back before Christmas," Bree said, "but she didn't get around to going to the doctor until January. She just got a firm diagnosis last week—ALS. She had an appointment to see the doctor—a neurologist out at the Mayo Clinic—in Scottsdale on Thursday. She went there, but that's the last anyone's seen of her. She never came home."

"ALS?" Ali asked. "As in Lou Gehrig's disease?"

"That's right," Bree said. "It's a death sentence—a crippling degenerative neurological disease with no cure. Once you're diagnosed, it's pretty much all downhill after that, three to ten years max. Reenie was devastated when she got the news. How could she be anything else?"

Ali felt sick to her stomach. It was incomprehensible that Reenie, her beloved Reenie, could be dying of some horrible disease, one that would leave her children motherless within a matter of a few years. Why hadn't Reenie called? Why hadn't she let Ali know?

"How awful!" Ali breathed.

"Awful isn't the half of it," Bree returned. "I've been reading up on it. ALS takes away muscle control. People are left bedridden and helpless, hardly able to swallow or even breathe on their own, but their mental faculties are totally unaffected. I think Reenie looked down the tunnel at what was coming and decided to do something about it."

"You mean you think she committed suicide?" Ali asked.

"Don't mention it to Howie," Bree returned. "But that's what I'm thinking. She would have hated being helpless and dependent. That isn't Reenie. Never has been."

You're right about that, Ali thought.

Reenie Holzer had always been a doer, a mover and shaker.

"How are the kids doing?" Ali asked.

"Okay, I guess," Bree replied. "The folks are here right now. They came up from Cottonwood as soon as church was over, so that's a big help. They took Matt and Julie out for pizza. They just got back a few minutes ago."

"Should I talk to them, to the kids, I mean?" Ali asked.

Bree hesitated. "I'm not sure," she said. "Howie's trying to play this low-key, and if everybody makes a big fuss about it . . ."

"What's he told them?"

"That their mom has a disease, that she's gone off by herself to think things over, and that she'll be home very soon."

"I don't blame him," Ali said. "It's bad news either way. And now that you've told me what's up, I think I'll wait a while to talk to Matt and Julie," she added. "That way I won't end up blurting out something Howie would rather I not say."

"Sounds good," Bree returned.

"How are you holding up?" Ali asked.

"All right, I guess," Bree said. "Things are pretty tough, but I'm glad I can be here to help. Howie's taking it real hard."

Howie had always struck Ali as a bit of a prig, but he was a lot easier to tolerate than Reenie's first husband, Sam Turpin, had been. Besides, where was it written that friends had to like their friends' husbands? Truth be known, Ali's own husband didn't care for Reenie or Howie much, either, referring to them as "nobodies from Podunk, Arizona." Ali supposed that made things even.

"I'm glad you're there, too," Ali said. "It sounds like Howie needs all the help he can get."

During the phone call, Ali had made her way through the house and settled into her favorite chair—the oversized one. The soft brown leather was smooth and buttery against her bare skin. It was also solid and substantial.

Looking for comfort—for someone to tell about Reenie, for someone who would sympathize and tell her how awful it was to lose a friend—Ali dialed Paul's cell phone, but he didn't answer. She tried to remember exactly where he was scheduled to go on this trip, but with him doing most of his travel by corporate jet these days, it was hard to keep track. Since it was late Sunday afternoon, however, she could be relatively sure that wherever he was, he was out playing golf. Wherever Paul went, so did his Pings, and once on a golf course, Paul made it a practice—a religion almost—not to take calls, from anyone.

Ali hung up without bothering to leave a message.

Feeling hungry—or was it just a matter of nerves?—she went out to the kitchen and scrounged through the refrigerator. Before the cook, Elvira Jimenez, left for the weekend, she usually made sure the place was stocked with lots of suitable salad makings. Fighting to keep her figure newsroom thin, Ali survived on salads. Right now what she really wanted was one of her father's Sugarloaf special chicken fried steaks. Unfortunately that wasn't an option.

Using the kitchen clicker—Paul had one in every room—she turned on Paul's new Sonos sound system to play a full program of Mozart piano concertos. Then she busied herself at the granite countertop, whacking up lettuce, tomatoes, radishes, cucumbers and onions, as well as a perfectly ripe avocado. She added a few hunks of rotisserie grilled chicken and a thimbleful of dressing. Lots of calories in dressing. Then, she took her salad and a glass of chilly Chardonnay (Paul's current favorite, Far Niente, the 2002 vintage, of course) to the glass-topped umbrella table situated beside the sparkling heated pool with its unobstructed view of the city.

The sweet scent of orange blossoms wafted through the air. The bougainvillea climbing the side of the stuccoed pool house was just starting to blossom. The colorful pots arranged around the patio overflowed with the fat petunias and lush snapdragons that Jesus Sanchez, the gardener, somehow always maintained in wild abundance. Now that the rains had finally stopped, spring had arrived in southern California with a vengeance. Meanwhile it had snowed five inches in Sedona two days ago—the same day Reenie had been reported missing.

ALS, Ali thought. *What would I do if it were me?*

She thought about Reenie's kids, Matt—red-haired, freckle-faced, and serious beyond his years—and about Julie—a bright, blond, blue-eyed, perpetual-motion machine who seemed to dance rather than walk wherever she went. Wouldn't Reenie have wanted to spend every possible moment with those adorable children of hers, or had she made some other choice, one she hoped would spare them the worst of the dread disease that was bearing down on all of them?

That line of questioning took Ali back to a very dark place of her own. In October of 1982 her first husband, Dean Reynolds, had come home from work one night, complaining of a headache. Ali hadn't thought that much about it. He was twenty-four years old, for God's sake. How serious could it be? He had gone to bed. In the middle of the night, she had heard him retching in the bathroom. A few minutes later he passed out. She had heard him fall—a dull thump on the wooden floor of their two-bedroom apartment. Leaping out of bed to help him, she'd had to shove his body out of the way with the bathroom door before she could get inside to reach him. In the confined space of the tiny bathroom, she hadn't been able to gain enough leverage to help him to his feet. Instead, she left him lying on the floor and called an ambulance.

Two days later, in Dean's hospital room, the doctor had given them the bad news—glioblastoma—a word Ali had never heard before and wouldn't have known how to pronounce. She and Dean, holding hands, had listened in stunned silence as the doctor—a resident oncologist—delivered the bad news. The tumor was large, inoperable, and probably fatal within one to two years. They could try chemo they were told, but glioblastomas were aggressive and generally resistant to treatment. A few months later, Dean was dead and Ali was not only a twenty-three-year-old widow, she was also seven months pregnant.

The baby was born on a bright June day two months after Dean's funeral. Ali named her newborn son Christopher Dean Reynolds. Ali's mother had left Bob and Aunt Evie in charge of the Sugarloaf. Even though Edie Larson had never been on a plane before in her life, she had flown out to Chicago to be with her daughter and her new grandson and to help Ali get organized.

Surprisingly enough, Dean's company benefits had provided a fair amount of group life insurance. Their apartment was anything but extravagant. Using the life insurance proceeds and by carefully managing the social security survivor's benefits, Ali had managed to keep the apartment, hire a live-in baby-sitter, and go back to school to finish her Masters. (She'd had to drop out that one semester because Dean was so sick.)

Dean had died in 1983. More than twenty years later glioblastoma was still a grim diagnosis, but there were now some new promising treatments—particle-beam radiation and chemo protocols—that had only been a gleam in some cancer researcher's eye back in the eighties. Ali wondered if there was a chance things were a little more hopeful now with ALS as well.

With half of her salad left uneaten, but with her wineglass empty, Ali stood up. The sun was still shining in the west, but she felt a sudden chill. Dean had fought so hard to live long enough to see his son—to have a chance to be with him. Faced with ALS, surely Reenie would do the same for her kids, for Matt and Julie, wouldn't she?

But as Ali made her way back into the house, she realized she didn't know the answer. The only person who did was Reenie Bernard herself, and she wasn't talking.

After rinsing her dishes, Ali went upstairs to the little study off the master bedroom that was her own private domain. She logged on to her computer and Googled ALS. After spending an hour or so poring over what she found there, Ali finally realized that as far as Reenie and her family were concerned, it could just as well have been 1983.

As Yogi Berra said, "It's déjà vu all over again!"

Chapter 3

cutlooseblog.com
Monday, March 14, 2005

First of all, let me thank you once again for the kind wishes that continue to pour in. I'm astonished by your response. I'll try to answer as many as I can—after all, I no longer have to go to work—but please forgive me if I don't get back to all of you in a timely fashion.

When bad things happen, it's easy to fall in a hole of self-pity and wallow around in it. Losing your job counts as a bad thing, and I would have been wallowing if I hadn't had all those e-mails lifting my spirits.

Tonight, though, when I was channel surfing, I happened to catch a promo for the *new* news team at my former station—a team that now includes my *very* youthful and *very* blond replacement. Seeing her sitting and smiling out at the camera from the anchor chair that used to be mine and flanked by all the guys who used to do the news with me, it would have been easy to turn on the waterworks and go screaming down the street yelling that life isn't fair. But I didn't. Couldn't. Because there are things in life that are lots worse than losing a job—losing a friend, for instance.

Because one of my friends *is* lost. Reenie, my best friend from high school, went missing on Thursday after going to a scheduled doctor's appointment. On the day before I lost my job. No one knows where she is. Her family is baffled. Her husband and children are lost without her.

In the past two weeks, Reenie has received some devastating news about her health. In her forties and with a husband and two young children at home, she's been diagnosed with ALS. Authorities investigating her disappearance have hinted that perhaps she committed suicide rather than endure the bleak future that particularly dread disease holds for all who are stricken with it. I'd like to think she's gone off some place to gather her courage to face whatever may lie ahead. The Reenie I know and love isn't a person who shies away from doing what needs to be done—however hard that may be.

So tonight, unable to sleep, I decided to tell you what's going on in my life because I can tell from the e-mails that have come in that you care. But on the whole, I think you can see that compared to what's happening to Reenie and her family, my problems are pretty small potatoes.

Posted: 1:52 A.M. by AliR

My Sister's Keeper was run by the Sisters of Charity and operated out of a tiny donated storefront in downtown Pasadena. The neighborhood was trendy enough that well-heeled ladies in their late-model Lexus or Cadillac SUVs, or their personal assistants, could drop off clothing discards—things that weren't good enough for consignment stores—without having to venture into some of LA's grittier neighborhoods where the donated clothing might actually be put to use.

The person in charge, Sister Anne, was a tall spare woman with a cascade of braided and beaded hair. In the late eighties, the towering six-foot-seven nun had been known as Jamalla Kareem Williams, a standout player for the UCLA Bruins. Ali had met Sister Anne several years earlier when they had been seated together at the head table for a YWCA fund-raising luncheon. Having spent her whole life watching her father's one-man charitable efforts, Ali knew more than she might otherwise have known about the needs of the homeless. Ali and Sister Anne had struck up a conversation during lunch. Realizing at once that they had a good deal in common, they had stayed in touch.

Dragging the first heavily laden bag into the store that Monday morning, Ali found Sister Anne sorting through a mound of donations. Dressed in shiny blue-and-white sweats emblazoned with

UCLA insignias, Sister Anne looked as though she would have been far more at home on the sidelines of a basketball game than in a convent.

Sister Anne greeted Ali with a gap-toothed grin. "Time to lighten the load?" she asked.

Ali nodded. "There's more where this came from," she added. "It's out in the car."

Sister Anne trailed Ali out to the Cayenne and helped bring in the rest of the bags. "These yours?" she asked. Ali nodded again. "It's always good to get clothes from tall ladies," Sister Anne added with a laugh. "There aren't enough of us to go around."

Once back inside, Sister Anne started pulling items from the first bag. The clothes were mostly still in their separate dry-cleaning bags. After examining several of them, the nun whistled. "These are what I call designer duds," she said enthusiastically. "And they're in really good shape. Are you sure you want to get rid of them?"

Ali had told Chris and her mother about what had happened on Friday night after the newscast, but until that moment, she hadn't confided in anyone else about the fact that she'd been fired. Not Jesus or Elvira—her Spanish wasn't good enough. And for some reason, Charmaine, Ali's personal assistant, hadn't shown up for work this morning. Ali still hadn't heard back from Paul, either, damn him, not since she'd called him the night before. And with Reenie still missing . . .

As Ali screwed up her courage to let go of the words and make her humiliation public, tears were very close to the surface. But Sister Anne beat her to the punch.

"I know about your job," she said. "I saw it in the *Times* yesterday. What's the matter with those guys? Are they nuts?"

Ali looked around the store and was grateful that they seemed to be alone. The news was out, and out in a big way, so at least there was no need for her to go around telling people about it.

She sighed. "That's one of the reasons I wanted to see you this morning," she said, "besides dropping off the clothing, that is."

"What do you need?" Sister Anne demanded.

"An attorney actually," Ali said. "Know any good sex- or age-discrimination attorneys?"

"You're going to sue the station?"

"I'm thinking about it."

"What about using one of your husband's high-powered friends?" Sister Anne asked. "Seems to me they'd be chomping at the bit to take the case."

"That's part of the problem," Ali admitted. "If I go after the station, Paul isn't going to like it, and neither will most of his friends—whether they're attorneys or not. He has a lot of clout in this town, and he isn't afraid to use it."

"Well then," Sister Anne said, "it so happens I do know of one. Her name's Marcella Johnson. We were teammates back in college. Marce is short, only five ten or so, but she was a scrapper, and believe me, she plays to win."

"Winning's good," Ali said.

"She works for Weldon, Davis, and Reed on Wilshire. I've got her cell number. Want me to give her a call?"

Without a word, Ali handed over her phone,

which was how, two hours later, she found herself waiting to meet Marcella Johnson in a secluded corner of the Gardens Café at the Four Seasons Hotel. Even though she thought she was fairly well out of the way, several people glanced in her direction and nodded in recognition as they were shown to their own tables.

Feeling self-conscious and wanting to while away the time, she ordered coffee and then called the Sugarloaf on her cell even though she knew her parents would be up to their eyeteeth in the lunchtime rush by then.

"Any news about Reenie?" she asked.

"Not that I've heard," Edie Larson said. "Have you talked to her husband?"

"He was busy when I called," Ali said. "I don't want to bother him."

"Call anyway," Edie said. "Howie won't be bothered. That's what friends are for. How are you doing?"

"Hanging in," Ali returned.

"You don't *sound* like you're hanging in," Edie pointed out. "You sound upset."

Ali was upset. Strangers from all over southern California somehow managed to know that she'd lost her job, some of them even before the station had made whatever official announcement had ended up in the papers. But none of her friends—make that none of her supposed friends—had bothered to send even so much as an e-mail, and none of them had called to check on her, either. And then there was Paul. Where was he? Why wasn't he calling her back? He sure as hell wasn't playing golf twenty-four hours a day.

Ali sighed. "I am," she admitted to her mother. "I'm upset about Reenie, and I'm upset about my job situation, too. I'm in a restaurant right now, waiting to audition an attorney."

"To go after the station?" Edie wanted to know. "To sue them?"

"Yes."

"Great!" Edie said. "Your father will be thrilled. For the last three days that's all he's talked about, that you should sue their something or other off, if you know what I mean."

Edie Larson didn't say "asses" unless she was referring to the four-legged kind. Bob Larson's language tended to be somewhat more colorful.

"I'm just *talking* to an attorney," Ali cautioned. "It's all very preliminary and definitely not a sure thing. I don't even know if I have a case."

When Marcella Johnson showed up a few minutes later, she was indeed five ten, just as Sister Anne had said. She and Ali were almost the same height. Marcella Johnson, dressed in a black silk suit that showed off every well-toned muscle, strode across the room to the table where Ali waited. An impressive-looking woman, Marce sported Gucci from top to bottom. She had a firm handshake and an easy smile.

"So they fired you, did they?" she asked, settling into her chair.

"They sure did," Ali answered.

"Who's your replacement?"

"I didn't catch her name, but I saw her on yesterday's promos. She's young, very young, and pretty, too."

"Figures," Marce said. "They let you go, but they kept all the old guys, even the pretty one with the terrible rug?"

Randall James was very proud of his hairpiece and thought it looked "natural." Obviously it hadn't fooled Marcella Johnson.

"Even him," Ali said with a smile.

"And what reason did they give?"

"Taking the news team in a new direction is what the news director said. Going after a younger audience."

"With three old guys and a new babe?" Marcella scoffed. "Give me a break."

"That's what I thought," Ali told her.

Marcella removed a slim tablet PC from her briefcase and began scribbling notes with a stylus. "Cliff Baker is the new news director. He's the guy they brought in to fix the ratings, which, as it happens, are still broken."

"I suppose you were alone when he said this."

"Actually, I wasn't," Ali answered. "There was a security guard there, Eddie Duarte. Edward actually. Baker brought Eddie along to look over my shoulder while I cleared out my desk and to escort me out of the building when I finished."

"Having a witness is fine, but a security guard?" Marcella asked. "Those heavy-hitters from the station will mow him down so fast he'll never know what hit him."

"I don't think so," Ali said. "Eddie told me he'd testify if I needed him to, and he will. He and his wife, Rosa, are friends of mine. So's their little boy, Alonso."

Marcella looked intrigued. "You really do know them?"

Ali nodded. "Yes, I really do."

"Their names again?"

Ali pulled her Palm Pilot out of her purse and reeled off Eddie's address and phone number.

"These kinds of cases take years, regardless of whether you settle or go to court," Marcella warned.

"I know," Ali said.

"And since I'm very good," Marcella added, "that means I'm also very expensive."

"Then it's a good thing I brought along my checkbook," Ali said.

"In that case," Marcella told her, "lunch is on me."

And it was a good one. Ali had the heirloom tomato and mozzarella salad. Marcella had the Ahi tuna nicoise. They both had a glass of wine—a Pinot Grigio, which would have been far too lowbrow to measure up to Paul's sophisticated taste buds. Still, wine and all, it was definitely a working lunch. Marcella asked questions and took detailed notes the whole time they were eating, and while they were drinking coffee afterward as well.

On the way home, Ali called Paul's number. He still didn't answer. Why did he carry the thing around with him if he wasn't going to pick up? This time, though, she left him a message, letting him know what she had done. She knew he wasn't going to be thrilled about it, but she wasn't going to sneak around about it, either. After all, her career was on the line. She wasn't about to let it go without a fight.

"Didn't want you to be the last to know," she

said. "I've retained an attorney. I'm going to file a wrongful-dismissal suit based on age and sex."

Back at the house she found that Charmaine still hadn't shown up, but someone—Jesus most likely—had brought in the mail and left it on the entryway table. She went through the envelopes, sorting out the junk from the real stuff. At the bottom was a greeting-card-shaped envelope with no return address, but it took only a single glance for Ali to recognize Reenie Bernard's flamboyant script that was only a smidgeon beneath calligraphy. That had always been Reenie's style. When other people had resorted to e-mail, Reenie had relied on snail-mail to stay in touch. She always seemed to have a supply of just the right note cards readily at hand.

Maybe I'm right, Ali thought hopefully. Maybe Reenie's just gone off somewhere to think things over.

The postmark on the envelope said, "Phoenix, AZ Mar 10," but that didn't mean much. Yes, it was the day Reenie had gone to the Phoenix area. The envelope could have been mailed from there, but it could also have been sent from Sedona or any other small town in central Arizona. Ali knew that mail from smaller towns often wasn't postmarked until it reached a more centralized processing center in one of the larger cities. Still . . .

Eager to read Reenie's message, Ali tore open the envelope, leaving behind a jagged edge of paper and a tiny paper cut on her index finger. Inside was one of those black-and-white greeting cards, the ones that feature little kids in old-fashioned clothes. This one showed two cute little girls, a blond and a brunette. Four or maybe five years old, the two girls sat side by side, with their arms slung over one another's shoulders and with their smiling faces aimed at the camera. Inside the card said, "Some friends are forever." Written on the opposite side of the card, again in Reenie's distinctive penmanship, were the following words:

"I think I'm in for a very bumpy ride, but I'm not ready to talk about it yet. I'll call you next week. R."

A bumpy ride, Ali thought. Only Reenie, wonderful Reenie, could look at something as appalling as ALS and call it a "bumpy ride." But then, studying the note more closely, she noticed subtle differences between this and Reenie's usual handwriting. Here the letters were rushed, and a little sloppy, but then maybe she had been in a hurry. Putting aside the note, Ali checked her land line answering machine. There was no message from Reenie, but there was one from Chris.

"Hi, Mom," he said. "I read your post, and I can't believe it. Is it true Reenie's sick and missing? Call me on my cell and let me know what you've heard. Oh, and by the way. I looked at the number of hits you're getting on your site. For a brand-new blog, there's a lot of traffic."

Traffic on the blog didn't seem very important right then. Instead, Ali picked the card back up and studied it again. When her mother had first told her about Reenie's diagnosis, Ali had been hurt that Reenie hadn't told her directly. Knowing that she simply hadn't been ready to talk about it made Ali feel better, but it hurt her to think of Reenie going off on her own to wrestle with her situation. Rather than dealing with it alone, wouldn't she have wanted to be with her family, with Howie and the kids?

Ali's cell phone rang just then. The number in the display told her that the call was coming from the Sugarloaf Café. Ali knew that by now the customers would be long gone and Bob and Edie and their waitress in chief, Jan Howard, would be cleaning up the restaurant in preparation for the next day.

"Ali?" her father began as soon as she answered.

That was unusual. Generally speaking it took an act of God to get her father to talk on the phone at all. He preferred conducting his calls by relaying information through his wife, a habit that drove Edie to distraction.

"What's up, Dad?" Ali asked warily. "Is something wrong?"

"Yes, baby, it is," he said. "I'm afraid I have some bad news. Your mother wanted me to make the call because she doesn't want to make a fool of herself on the telephone."

Ali's heart skipped a beat. "It's about Reenie, then?" she asked.

"They found her car late this morning," Bob Larson said. "She went off Schnebly Hill Road probably during that snowstorm we had the other night."

Ali walked as far as the leather chair in the family room and sank into it.

"She's dead, then?" Ali managed.

"Yes," Bob returned sadly. "Yes, she is. She was thrown from the vehicle as it fell. They don't know for sure yet, but they're assuming she died instantly. That's what we're hoping, anyway. They found the car this morning long before they found her. I talked to Detective Holman at lunchtime. You remember Dave Holman, don't you? Wasn't he in your class?"

A vision of a tall scrawny kid passed through Ali's head. Dave had been a year older than she was, and a big man on campus due to his being smart and an all-around athlete as well, lettering in football, basketball, and baseball. She'd been such a nobody by comparison that she doubted they'd ever exchanged so much as a word.

"A year older," she said impatiently. "But go on. Tell me about Reenie."

"Her SUV was white, so until some of the snow up there melted this morning, it was impossible to spot. It had also rolled so far and so hard that it's mostly nothing but a ball of smashed sheet metal. Besides, no one thought to look for her up there. I mean, what the hell was she doing on Schnebly Hill Road in the middle of a snowstorm? What was that girl thinking? The gates on Schnebly Hill were closed at both ends, so she must have opened and closed the upper gate behind her."

Schnebly Hill Road was a treacherous eleven-mile dirt track, barely one car wide in spots. Narrow and sometimes studded with rocks, the road clung gamely to the cliff face as it threaded its way down from the top of the Mogollon Rim and into Sedona far below. Back in Ali's day, driving up and down Schnebly Hill had been a required rite of passage for every newly licensed teenaged driver—Ali included—who had managed to survive Mr. Logan Farnsworth's Driver's Ed class at Mingus Mountain High.

Ali understood that Schnebly Hill Road was dangerous under the best of circumstances. The idea of Reenie being on it alone in the dark and snow made her shiver. But with an ALS death sentence hanging over her head, it seemed likely that Reenie might not have been particularly concerned about either road conditions or bad weather.

What a terrible, lonely way to die, Ali thought.

"Anyway," Bob continued, "according to Dave, both the Coconino and Yavapai County sheriff's departments are investigating. The car was spotted early this morning by a jet flying into the airport. The wreckage was in steep, rough terrain, though. It took hours for a rescue crew to reach it. Then when they realized she'd been thrown free, they had to bring in a couple of search-and-rescue teams with dogs. It was one of the dogs that finally found the body a little before noon."

Unable to respond, Ali digested the terrible news for the better part of a minute.

"Ali," her father said finally. "Are you still there? Can you hear me?"

"I'm right here," she answered. "Any word on when the services will be?"

"Not yet. Dave says it's way too early to even think about things like that. There'll have to be an autopsy first—toxicology reports and so forth. The body can't be released for burial until after that."

How many times as a reporter and anchorwoman had Ali Reynolds discussed countless accident and homicide victims in those cold and oh-so-scientific terms—autopsies, medical examiners, toxicology reports? But this was Reenie, Ali's own beloved

Reenie. It broke her heart to hear her father now applying those very same harsh but journalist-approved words to what had happened to Reenie. For some reason Ali couldn't understand, she didn't cry—not a single tear. That surprised her.

"I'll come home." Ali made the split-second decision as she spoke the words. "I'll throw a few things in the car and head out. It won't take that long. It's only five hundred miles. I can be there in under eight hours."

"But I just told you," Bob objected, "no one has any idea when the services will be. It might be the end of this week or even the first of next."

"Doesn't matter," Ali told him. "I'm not working, remember? I'm free as a bird, and since I have my own place there, I can stay as long as I like. Paul's out of town anyway. He won't mind."

"All right, then," her father said. "If that's what you want to do, I'll go up to your place and check things out—make sure the heat's on and none of the pipes are frozen. I did that the other morning—checked the pipes—so they should be fine. Do you want me to put a few groceries in the fridge?"

"Thanks, Pop," she said. "For the pipes and the heat, but don't worry about food. I'll probably be spending a lot of time up in Flag. When I'm not there, I'm sure I'll be able to scrounge enough Sugarloaf grub from you and Mom to keep from starving."

"Okay," Bob said dubiously, "but you drive carefully. And call once you get here."

"It'll be too late," Ali objected. "It'll wake Mom."

Edie Larson rose every day at four A.M. and

walked from their little apartment at the back of the lot to her kitchen in the restaurant that fronted on the highway. That's what it took to have the sweet rolls up and ready to go when the first early-bird Sugarloaf breakfast customers came through the door at six.

"Call on my cell phone," he said. "I'll keep it with me out in the living room. Once Edie turns off her hearing aid, she can't hear a thing. She's deaf as a post."

"All right," Ali agreed. "I'll let you know when I get there."

Just then the back door slammed open and shut. "Mom?" Chris called from the kitchen. "Are you here?"

"Gotta go, Dad," Ali told her father. "See you tomorrow." Then to Chris she added, "In here. In the family room."

He came as far as the doorway, munching on a fistful of Elvira Jimenez's freshly baked cookies that he'd pilfered off the counter. Chris stopped cold as soon as he caught a glimpse of his mother's stricken face.

"Reenie's dead, isn't she," Chris said.

Ali nodded wordlessly.

"What happened?"

"She went off Schnebly Hill Road sometime over the weekend. They didn't find her until a few hours ago. I just got off the phone with Grandpa. I told him I'll come home to Sedona as soon as I can load things into the car."

"I'll go with you," Chris offered at once. "It's a long trip. I can help drive."

"But you have school," Ali objected.

"Not really," Chris said. "It's the end of the quarter. I have one class tomorrow and two on Wednesday. Then I don't have anything more until finals. The first one isn't until next Monday. If I talk to my professors and tell them what's happened, it won't be a big deal."

"You're sure?" Ali asked.

"I'm sure," Chris said.

She stood up, went over to her son, and allowed herself to sink into the comforting grip of one of his weight-lifting-powered bear hugs.

"Thanks, Chris," she said. "Thank you so much."

The tears came then, and she let them. Having someone hold her as she cried made all the difference.

Chapter 4

As Ali and Chris finished loading the Cayenne, Chris paused next to the ski rack. "Should I bring 'em?" he asked.

Ali shrugged. "Why not? After that big storm, I'm sure there's plenty of new snow up at Flagstaff, and you know how much Gramps loves to ski, especially with you."

"Are you sure? I mean, with Reenie and everything . . ."

Ali nodded. "Reenie's my problem, not Dad's. Besides, remember how he was when Aunt Evie died? Practically useless. We'll be better off with him skiing than we will be with him under hand and foot twenty-four seven."

Obligingly, Chris loaded the ski rack and the skis onto the Cayenne's roof rack. And when they left the house, Chris drove while Ali rode shotgun, managing the MP3 player. Wanting to think about song lyrics instead of what had happened to Reenie, Ali scrolled through the index, selecting one musical after another, songs Chris had culled from Aunt

Evie's personal CD collection and added to the playlist.

Her mother and Aunt Evelyn had shared more than just their birthdays and a lifelong partnership in the Sugarloaf Café. Together they had adored musical scores, everything from *Showboat* to *Cats*; and from *Carousel* and *Oklahoma* to *Evita* and *The Lion King*. Aunt Evie had collected them all. To celebrate their sixtieth birthday Ali had convinced her mother and aunt to get passports. Then, as a surprise and using some of Paul's and her own accumulated air miles and credit card points, the three of them—Ali, her mother, and Aunt Evie—had flown first-class to London for five days of wonderful first-class hotels and nonstop theater productions. It had been great fun, and they had done it just in time, too. Only a few months later and with no advance warning, Aunt Evie had succumbed to a massive stroke.

While listening and riding, Ali glanced over at Chris. He drove with both hands gripping the wheel and with his eyes constantly focused on traffic. As she watched him, Ali was at once both startled and gratified to realize how old he was and how competent. Christopher was twenty-two—a grown man now—only two years younger than his father had been when he died. And a close-but-not-quite carbon copy of his father—Chris was taller and heavier than Dean had been.

For the past seven years, living with his stepfather's money and privilege and with his mother a staple on the nightly news, it would have been easy for Chris to lose track of who he was. An atmosphere of poisonous privilege and ready access to drugs had blighted many of his classmates. That he hadn't fallen into those traps was due primarily to the way his mother had raised him prior to Paul Grayson's appearance on the scene.

For years it had been just the two of them—Ali and Christopher. There had been a song in Aunt Evie's collection that spoke to that as well—Helen Reddy's poignant "You and Me Against the World." And now, driving eastward on I-10 and in heavy traffic, it was true again. But with Chris grown—in another two months, he'd be graduating from college—this might well be the last road trip they'd take together, riding along and listening to Aunt Evie's music. She wondered if, as Chris grew older, hearing some of these old familiar songs would bring him back to this long sad trip.

They drove onto the 10 at the beginning of rush-hour traffic, so it took them the better part of three hours to make it to Palm Springs. They had just passed Rancho Mirage, Ali mindlessly humming along with "Adelaide's Lament" from *Guys and Dolls*, when her cell rang. She saw at a glance it was Paul.

"What's wrong with you?" he demanded the moment she answered. "How come you're talking to an attorney? I thought we agreed that you wouldn't start any proceedings against the station."

There was no mention of what had happened to Reenie. No explanation of why it had taken him so long to get back to her. No, just an instant all-out verbal attack.

"I don't remember any such agreement," Ali re-turned.

"Come on, Ali," he said. "I told you very clearly the other night that, with me as a network exec, we couldn't afford to get mixed up in any kind of legal dust-up. We just have to take our lumps and move on."

"Our lumps?" she asked. "What do you mean our? I'm the one who got fired, not you."

"And you sure as hell better hope it isn't catching. What if you piss them off and they end up firing me, too? Then we'd be in a hell of a mess. We can get by without what you make, but we can't get by without what I bring home. Now tomorrow, I want you to go see that attorney and give him . . ."

"Her," Ali corrected.

"Her then," he conceded. "Give her whatever she needs to drop the case. If you just talked to her today, she can't have done very much. If she wants to keep the retainer, fine. Let her. Just be sure the case gets dropped. I don't want it to go any further than it already has, understand?"

Ali understood all right. Paul was handing down orders, and he expected unquestioning obedience. That's what he required of all his underlings, and the salary comment made his wife's standing pretty clear—it was in the lower echelon of the chain of command. Why did he have to be such an overbearing jerk at times?

"I can't," she said quietly.

"Can't?" Paul shouted into her ear. "What do you mean you can't?"

Ali looked at her son. Chris seemed intent on the road and traffic, but she knew he was listening.

"Just what I said. I can't," she told him. "Chris

and I are on our way to Sedona. Reenie died over the weekend—in a traffic accident. I want to be there to help Howie and the kids."

If Ali expected a word of sympathy about what had happened to her friend, none was forthcoming.

"Call the damned attorney from Sedona, then. You can do it over the phone if you have to. I just want to be sure it's stopped before there's any more damage."

"As in damage to your career?" Ali put in.

"Yes," Paul said. "Of course. What did you think I meant?"

"What?" Ali said. "What did you say? I can't hear you. You're breaking up. Hello? Hello?" She closed the phone and slipped it back in her pocket.

Chris gave her a sidelong glance. "That call wasn't really breaking up," he observed. "I checked the last time I drove through here. There was good service with plenty of signal from here all the way to and from. What's going on?"

Chris and Paul had never gotten along. Paul had disapproved of almost everything his stepson did, from the clothing he wore to his choice of school. He had been particularly offended by Chris's stated intention of squandering his fine arts training by hoping to become a teacher. Paul Grayson wasn't the least bit altruistic and had no patience with people who were. Ali, on the other hand, had been inordinately proud.

"Your stepfather doesn't like it that I consulted with an attorney about filing a wrongful dismissal suit against the station," Ali admitted quietly. "He thinks I should just shut up and take my lumps."

"Are you going to?" Chris asked.

"No," she said. "I'm not. No matter what Paul wants, I'm going to take them on, and it won't just be for me, either. It'll be for every woman in the television news business who's in danger of being put out to pasture because she's past forty and isn't interested in joining the Botox nation. Meanwhile the guys can stay on the air until they're doddering old men and need guide dogs to drag 'em around. No one says a word to them. They're still viewable."

"Good," Chris said. "And what about Paul?"

"What about him?"

"He's a jerk. And with everything else that's going on . . ."

At first Ali thought Chris meant everything that was going on with Reenie, but then she looked at the grim set to her son's jaw and realized there had to be something more.

"What everything else?" she asked.

Chris shook his head. "Come on, Mom. You know what I mean. There's no point in talking about it."

"No, I don't know what you mean. I don't have any idea. Tell me."

Not wanting to answer, Chris compressed his lips and shook his head. "Why do you let him treat you like that?"

"Like what?"

"Like crap."

Ali wasn't thrilled to be discussing her troubled marriage with her son—or with anyone else, for that matter. After seven years of playing peace maker and running interference between Paul and Chris, Ali's first ingrained response was to attempt to minimize whatever had been said, in both directions.

"He's opinionated," she commented. "And he's upset that I'm going ahead with the wrongful dismissal suit. You know Paul. He's used to having people jump to do whatever he says."

Chris drove in silence for several miles before saying anything more. "You do know he's screwing around on you, don't you?" he said at last.

"He's what?" Ali demanded. She felt as though a bucket of icy water had been flung in her face.

"He's got a girlfriend. More than one actually."

Ali could hardly believe her ears. Chris was her son. Surely she couldn't be having this conversation with him.

"I don't know," Ali managed stiffly. "And if you do, maybe you should let me in on it."

Chris gave his mother a questioning look. With his attention momentarily diverted, a gust of wind, blowing through the mountains behind them, sent the Cayenne wandering across the lane-edge warning bumps along the shoulder of the freeway.

"You really don't know?" Chris returned.

Years of sitting in front of a camera reporting on all kinds of catastrophes had taught Ali Reynolds how to master her own emotions and maintain control. She did that now.

"Tell me," she said.

"April Gaddis, Paul's new administrative assistant, is the older sister of a friend of a friend," Chris explained. "That's how I heard about it, sitting around having a beer with the guys after a basketball game. The brother asked me if it was true you and Paul were getting a divorce. According to him, April is telling all her friends that they'll be married by the end of the year."

There was a long pause. At last Ali found her voice. "Well," she said, "if that's the case, he'll have to get a move on, won't he. From what I hear, there's no such thing as an instant divorce in California."

"Don't joke about this, Mom," Chris said, his voice tight with concern. "It isn't funny. And then there's Charmaine."

"Charmaine?" Ali repeated stupidly. "You mean my Charmaine?"

Charmaine Holbrook, an intently cheerful young woman, had been Ali's personal assistant for the past three years. She had come through a temporary staffing agency and had turned into a permanent employee. Ali would have trusted Charmaine with her life.

Chris nodded miserably.

"What about her?"

"One Friday night, I had a few too many beers and one of my buddies gave me a lift home. I went inside to take a nap. You were at work. When Paul came home, my car wasn't in the garage and my lights weren't on. He must have assumed I wasn't home, either. A while later, I heard them carrying on out in the pool. That's what woke me up. He and Charmaine were both in the pool naked, but swimming isn't all they were doing."

"Why didn't you tell me at the time?" Ali demanded. She felt betrayed, as much by her son's silence as by her husband's infidelity.

"I thought you knew, Mom," Chris declared.

"I swear to God. I figured you must have decided to make the best of a bad bargain. Lots of women around here do that, you know. They find out what their husbands are up to, but, for one reason or another, they decide to just put up with it instead of throwing the bum out."

"I had no idea," Ali murmured.

"I know that now," Chris said. "And I'm sorry, but hearing him ordering you around like you were some kind of servant . . ."

"How many people know about this?" Ali asked suddenly.

Chris shrugged. "Lots, I suppose," he answered. "I mean, if I know, then other people must know, too. They probably haven't taken out an ad in the *Times*, or anything like that, but . . ."

Ali's phone rang. Paul's number showed in the display. "It's him," she said. "I'm not going to answer."

And she didn't. The cell rang five times before it went to message. A few seconds later, the lights started flashing, indicating she had a voice mail waiting.

For ten miles or so, Ali did nothing; said nothing. Finally, she reached for her phone.

"Don't call him back," Chris pleaded. "Please don't."

"Don't worry," she said. "I'm not."

Instead, she picked up the phone and scrolled through the called numbers until she located the one for Marcella Johnson's cell phone. Marcella answered on the second ring.

"Hi," Ali said. "It's Alison Reynolds, your newest client."

"Did you change your mind?" Marcella asked.

"Why would you ask that?" Ali returned.

"I just came from Leonard's office—Leonard Weldon, the senior partner. He called me in right after your husband called here."

"Paul Grayson called you?" Ali asked.

"Oh, no. He didn't call me. He called Leonard and hinted very strongly that we should think about returning your retainer. That if we did, he'd make sure some of the network's very lucrative business got thrown in our direction."

"That underhanded son of a bitch!" Ali muttered under her breath.

"Yes," Marcella said. "That more or less covers it."

"So I suppose I need to go looking for a new attorney."

"No," Marcella said. "Not at all. I believe Leonard pretty much told him to stop throwing his weight around and put a sock in it."

"He did?"

"Leonard told me he was in the same foursome with Paul Grayson at a charity golf tournament a number of years ago, and Paul kept shaving strokes. If there's one thing Leonard Weldon can't tolerate, it's someone who cheats at golf!"

Among other things, Ali thought.

"So if you're in, we're in," Marcella continued. "Weldon wants us to pursue this case to the bitter end."

"Oh, I'm in all right," Ali declared.

"So what did you need, then?" Marcella asked.

"Does anyone at your firm handle divorces?" Ali asked.

"I don't," Marcella said. "Not personally. But we just brought in a lady named Helga Myerhoff."

"Wait a minute,"Ali said. "I've heard of her. I seem to remember she specializes in high-profile divorce cases. Don't people call her Rottweiler Myerhoff?"

"That's right," Marcella laughed. "Or Helga the Horrible, depending. Most of the time, though, the only people dishing out those names are Helga's opposing counsel *after* she takes their clients to the cleaners. Her clients praise her to the high heavens."

"She works with you, then?" Ali asked.

"That's right," Marcella said. "Three months ago, Helga's long-term partner retired. She and Leonard Weldon went to law school together a hundred years ago. When Helga decided she didn't want to be a sole practitioner, she came knocking on Leonard's door. But who's looking for a divorce attorney?"

"I am," Ali said in a small voice. "At least I think I am."

"Do you want me to have Helga call you?"

"Not right now. My son and I are driving to Sedona. At the moment, we're in the middle of the desert between Palm Springs and nowhere. Have her call me tomorrow."

"Will do." Marcella hesitated. "I don't know you very well, but you sound down. Are you going to be all right with whatever's going on? If you want me to call her right now . . ."

"No," Ali said. "Tomorrow will be fine. As I said, my son's with me, and he's been a brick."

"All right then."

"So I'll need to send another retainer?"

"Talk to Helga first," Marcella advised. "Then you can decide, but if you're talking to an attorney about this, you should probably also get in touch with your banker. You could find yourself up a creek without a credit card and without a checking account, either."

"I think I'm okay there," she said. "I've got my own checking account and my own credit card as well."

"Good," Marcella said. "Lots of women don't."

Ali closed the phone and put it in her pocket. When she looked over at Chris, he was grinning. "You're going to hire Helga Myerhoff?" he asked.

"Why?" Ali returned. "Do you know her?"

"I've heard of her. Remember Sally Majors, the girl I took to the senior prom?"

Ali remembered the photo her son had given her that year. He had stood in front of someone's massive fireplace decked out in a white tux, pale pink shirt, and cranberry-colored cummerbund and tie. Standing beside him, dwarfed by his size, had been a tiny girl in a full-length cranberry gown that screamed designer label. Ali had always been struck not by the beauty of the gown, but by the unremitting sadness in the girl's eyes.

"I remember her," Ali said.

"Her father's a worm," Chris said. "He was getting ready to ditch his wife. Same thing. Younger woman. He was hiding assets, doing all kinds of underhanded crap. Sally's mother hired Helga, and she nailed him. I ran into Sally at Starbucks a few months ago. She told me all about it."

"Go Helga," Ali said. But her heart wasn't in it.

After that, she turned up the music and subsided into silence. As the miles rolled by, she was surprised that she didn't feel more. Maybe, with all that had happened in the past few days, she was simply beyond feeling anything at all. That turned out to be wrong, however. Because when she finally did start feeling, what hit her first was anger—with a capital *A*.

"How old is this girl?" she asked finally.

"April?" Chris returned. Ali nodded. "A little older than I am," he said. "Maybe mid twenties."

"Oh," Ali said.

So this was all part and parcel of what had happened to her on Friday night. If you were forty-five and female, you were expendable—professionally and personally. Over the hill. Useless. And nobody, not the people at the station and certainly not Paul, expected her to stand up on her own two feet and fight back. Well, they were wrong—all of them.

Chris pulled off I-10 in Blythe for gas and for something to drink, then they forged on. They stopped for a Burger King on the far west side of Phoenix before they turned north on Arizona 101. Chris downed all of his Whopper and more than half of Ali's.

It was well after midnight when they turned off I-17 and headed toward Sedona. By then they were close enough that Ali figured it was okay to call her dad. When he answered the phone, it was clear he had been sound asleep.

"Okay," she said. "We're here."

"We?" he mumbled.

"Chris drove me over."

"Good then," Bob Larson said. "If I had known he was coming along, I wouldn't have worried."

Another put-down from the male of the species, Ali thought. "Thanks, Pop," she said. "See you in the morning."

As they drove up Andante to Skyview Way, the waning moon was just starting to disappear behind the looming presence of the red rock formation known as Sugarloaf. When Chris stopped the car and they stepped outside into the graveled driveway, the air was sharp and cold, and their breath came out in cloudy puffs. With one accord they both glanced up at the star-spangled sky.

"I always forget how beautiful it is here," Chris said. "I always forget about the sky."

"Me too," Ali said.

"You go unlock the door, Mom," he said. "I'll bring the luggage."

Inside the heat was on. Lamps were lit in the living room and in one bedroom. There was a note on the fridge in her father's handwriting. "Tuna casserole is ready for the microwave."

Tuna casserole was Edie Larson's cure for whatever ailed people. If there was a death in the family or if someone wound up in the hospital, that's what Edie would whip up in her kitchen and dispatch her husband to deliver. Ali opened the refrigerator door and glanced at her mother's familiar Pyrex-covered dish. Seeing the scarred turquoise blue veteran from some long ago era left Ali feeling oddly comforted.

Chris turned up behind her. "Your luggage is in your room," he said. He reached past Ali and grabbed one of the sodas that had also miraculously appeared on the shelf. "What's that?" he asked, pointing toward the covered dish."

"Tuna casserole," Ali answered.

"Great!" Chris exclaimed. "I love that stuff." He grabbed it out of the fridge. "Want me to heat some for you?"

"No thanks," Ali said. "I'm not very hungry. If you don't mind, I think I'll go to bed."

Chapter 5

cutlooseblog.com
Tuesday, March 15, 2005

It's five o'clock in the morning. When I typed the date and saw it was the Ides of March, I realized that it really is a time for bad news.

I know you've been writing to me. There are 106 e-mails in my in-box. From the subject lines, I know they're not spam, either. No one is offering to sell me low-cost prescription drugs. No one is advertising Viagra. They're all e-mails to me, and I'll get around to reading them in a little while. I may even finally have a chance to answer them, but first I need to tell you what's happened because, since you've been reading the posts, you deserve to know what's going on.

My friend Reenie is no longer lost—she's dead. Her vehicle went over the edge of a cliff during a snow storm. Her body was thrown from the wreckage. Neither she nor her SUV were located until late yesterday morning. I wanted to come here, to Arizona, to be with her family—her husband, her two young children, her parents, and her sister—and to help them as they face this grueling ordeal. I'm under no illusions that my presence here will change anything, but that's what friends do—they come and they sit or they talk or they do nothing or everything. Sometimes friends just are.

Yesterday afternoon my son, my wonderful twenty-two-year-old son, took time away from his classes at UCLA to drive over to Sedona with me. We arrived after midnight at the home my Aunt Evelyn left me two years ago. When we arrived, the heat was on and so were the lights. There was tuna casserole, milk, and sodas in the fridge and coffee in the canister on the counter next to the coffeepot. (Have I mentioned that I also have wonderful parents? They run a diner just down the road, and when Chris wakes up, we'll go there for breakfast.)

Over Christmas Chris installed a high-speed Internet connection here, and he also hooked up a wireless network. That means I can take my laptop and work anywhere in the house, so I'm working at the dining room table with my coffee cup near at hand.

The sun is up, and the view across the valley is beautiful. Because of the recent rains, everything is green and that makes Sedona's red rocks that much more visible in contrast. It's a lovely scene, but I'm not looking forward to being out in it. I'm sure this is going to be a long day and a tough one. I don't know what I'll say to Reenie's husband or to the rest of her family. I've already heard hints that the authorities are exploring the possibility that Reenie committed suicide rather than face up to the awful reality of dying of ALS. I can't accept that. I won't accept that. Reenie was a fighter. Her daughter is only six; her son is nine. No matter what, I can't believe that she would choose to turn away from spending every possible moment with her precious family. Ill or not, I can't imagine she would abandon them even one single instant before she had to.

Bottom line, I suppose, is that I can't accept that she would willingly abandon me, either. How's that for being selfish?

But it's not just selfishness on my part either. The last communication I had from her was a handwritten note she mailed last week, postmarked on the day she disappeared. In it she said she was in for a bumpy ride. To me that sounds like someone saying she knows it's going to be tough but that she's signed on for the duration. It doesn't sound like someone who was looking for an easy way out. Reenie is one of those people who always did things the hard way—from staying too long in an untenable first marriage to finishing college long after all her contemporaries had graduated. Yes, everything I've read about ALS says it's a daunting adversary with no cure and very little going for it in the way of treatment options, but my friend Reenie Bernard has always been a scrapper and a fighter. She's never been a quitter. Why would she turn into one now?

Posted: 6:03 A.M. by AliR

As Ali read through her comment before posting it, she was struck by how similar the process was to writing in a diary—particularly the pink and blue one with the locking clasp that she had received for her twelfth birthday and had kept religiously for the better part of that week. The sentence, about Reenie's abandonment of Ali, would have been as appropriate in a junior high schooler's diary as it was here. The big difference was, the diary had been written for Ali's eyes only. This was bound to be read by any number of strangers.

She was tempted to cut the whole thing. It seemed too personal; too private. Instead, she clicked on SEND and shipped it off into the ethers. And even as she did it Ali was smart enough to realize that, by concentrating on what was going on with Reenie's family, she was able to avoid thinking about what was going on in her own. The cell phone, left in the bedroom, was still blinking the "message waiting" signal, but Ali still hadn't listened to Paul's message from the night before, and she hadn't bothered to call him back, either. Turnabout was fair play.

Ready for breakfast, Ali rousted her reluctant son out of bed. While he showered and dressed, Ali scrolled through and answered some of the accumulated e-mails. Lots of them still dealt with her sudden disappearance from the small screen. Others concerned her emotional post about Reenie's going missing. Two e-mails in particular touched her:

Dear Ms. Reynolds,

I always liked seeing you on TV. And then you were gone. My grandson is letting me use his computer so I can see what you've written. I just wish I could see your face again. You have a nice smile. My grandson has one of those new-fangled telephone cameras, the ones they show in the commercials. Maybe your son could use one of those video phones to put your picture here as well.

Velma Trimble, Laguna Beach

To: Alison Reynolds
From: Carrie Fitzgerald

I know how your friend Reenie feels. My older brother is in the final stages of ALS. I am fifty-five. I don't have any symptoms yet, but I do have the gene, so it's only a matter of time.

I'm praying for Reenie and for her whole family. You didn't say your friend's last name or where she lives, but that doesn't matter. God knows exactly who she is.

Yours in Christ,
Carrie Fitzgerald

Please pray for me as well.

Chris, his hair still damp from the shower, sauntered into the kitchen and helped himself to a cup of coffee. "What are you doing?" he asked.

"Reading the things people have sent to me," she said. "Some of them are very nice." She pushed the computer in his direction long enough for him to see the screen. Then he scanned through the list of the messages Ali had yet to answer.

"Couldn't we just post their comments automatically?" she asked.

Chris shook his head. "Nope," he said. "Somebody has to go through and edit them. If you leave a portal open like that, pretty soon the blog will be flooded with offers for Viagra and on-line gambling."

His fingers worked the keyboard with lightning speed. "But if you'd like to have a spot to post comments, I can put one in. What do you want to call it?"

"A comment section?" Ali asked. "From other people?"

Chris nodded and Ali thought for some time before she replied.

"How about The Forum?" she asked.

"Sounds good," Chris said. Several minutes later he handed the computer back, open to the blog page where there was now a section called The Forum. "I've added a caution that says, unless otherwise stated, comments may be posted. You shouldn't post any comments that were sent before the caution went up. But here's how you do it."

After a few minutes' worth of practice, Ali had the comment-posting issues under control.

"Great," Chris said. "Now, what's for breakfast?"

"I don't know about you," Ali told him, "but I'm having one of my mother's world-famous Sugarloaf Café sweet rolls. I don't care what the scale says tomorrow morning."

"Let's go then," Chris said. "I'll drive."

Several other vehicles had beaten them to the punch by the time they pulled in at 6:30 A.M. to the sugarloaf parking lot.

Myrtle Hanson, Ali's grandmother, had started the Sugarloaf in what had once been her husband's gas station when she was a recent widow with twin four-year-old daughters to support. Though she lacked formal training and business experience, she'd had loads of grim determination and a killer sweet-roll recipe. In fact, it was a plate of those sweet rolls, delivered by her daughters to a local banker, that had launched the Sugarloaf in the mid nineteen-fifties. After tasting the sweet rolls, Carter Sweeney had ignored Myrtle's inexperience and had given her the loan that allowed her to go into her business.

By the time Myrtle passed on, the Sugarloaf's humble roots were no longer quite so apparent. Myrtle had left the thriving business along with the sweet-roll recipe to her grown daughters. Situated at the bottom of the distinctive rock formation that shared its name, the Sugarloaf had been a Sedona-area hangout and its sweet rolls a local staple for fifty years.

In high school, Ali had been more than slightly ashamed of the humble Sugarloaf with its gray Formica countertops and down-home atmosphere. Now that she was older, however, Ali had some grasp of the courage, grit, and fortitude it must have taken for her grandmother to start and keep the business running. She had also come to value the loyalty and determination of her parents and Aunt Evie in keeping the place going.

On this crisp March morning, the moment Ali stepped out of the Cayenne, the smell of freshly baked rolls beckoned across the parking lot and across the years. And stepping into the warm, steamy atmosphere was almost like stepping into a gray-Formica and red-vinyl time machine. For Ali, the Sugarloaf seemed forever unchanged and unchanging.

As soon as Chris appeared in the doorway, a smiling Edie Larson darted out from behind the counter and clasped her grandson in a fierce hug. "Look who's here!" she announced to the restaurant at large. Then to Chris, she said, "I told your grandfather to make sure there was nothing at the house for breakfast. I was hoping that way we'd get to see you bright and early."

Edie let loose of Chris and turned him over to Jan Howard, a waitress who had come on board after Aunt Evie died. Jan was a red-haired, bony, seventy-something widow, who called all her customers either "Honeybun" or "Darlin'." Jan's false teeth tended to click when she talked, and her apron pockets always bulged with one or more packets of unfiltered Camels. She was also hardworking and utterly dependable.

"Christopher, Christopher, Christopher!" she exclaimed. "If you aren't a sight for sore eyes."

Meanwhile, Edie turned to her daughter. As she did so, the look on her face changed from joy to sadness. “I’m so sorry about Reenie,” she said, hugging Ali close. “Come in, come in. Sit right here at the counter. That way I can talk to you between customers.”

Before Ali could slip away to the counter, she, too, had to endure a smoky-haired hug from Jan as well. Meanwhile, from the kitchen, Bob Larson saluted the new arrivals with a raised spatula as he placed a steaming plate up in the order window and pounded the bell to produce two sharp dings, letting either Edie or Jan know it was time to retrieve an order.

Unasked, Edie poured coffee for both Ali and Chris and pushed the cream pitcher in her grandson’s direction.

“Your father’s off his game this morning,” she continued. “Stayed up too late waiting for you to call. He’s already botched two orders. If I were actually paying the man, I suppose I’d have to dock him. How come it took you so long to get here—I thought you were leaving at two? And what’ll you have, besides sweet rolls, I mean?”

Chris ordered ham and eggs. Ali ordered a roll along with one egg and two strips of bacon, then she turned around and surveyed the room. In the old days, Edie and Aunt Evie and the other waitresses had worn black-and-white uniforms. Those had now given way to blue-and-white Sugarloaf Café sweatshirts (available for purchase at the cash register), tennis shoes, and jeans.

Ali’s sweet roll arrived huge and soft and oozing icing. She had just picked up the first sticky piece to put in her mouth when her cell phone rang. She glanced at it, saw it was Paul, and didn’t answer.

"Still playing hard to get, I see," said a male voice close to her shoulder.

Ali turned to look. The man seated on the next stool, unlike every other man in the place, was dressed in a long-sleeved white shirt and a colorful and properly knotted red-and-blue tie. He was broad-shouldered and bull-necked, and his salt-and-pepper hair was definitely receding.

"Excuse me?" she said.

"I'm sure you've forgotten me long ago," the man continued. "But nobody around here is allowed to forget you. Your mother won't stand for it."

Pointing, he indicated the wall behind the cash register. Plastered there, right along with the business license and the fire-department plaque for maximum occupancy, were a dozen or more professionally produced publicity shots. Some of them dated from Ali's early work in Milwaukee. Others came from her time at Fox News. Most of them, taken for whatever reason, came from Ali's long stint as anchor on the station in LA. All of them testified to Edie Larson's unstinting motherly pride in her daughter's accomplishments. Seeing them there together made Ali blush with embarrassment.

"I'm afraid you have me at a disadvantage, then," she said. "You know who I am, but I'm sorry to say, I don't know you."

"Dave Holman, Class of '77, at your service," he said. Grinning, he held out his hand. Ali brushed as much of the icing off her fingers as possible before placing her still slightly sticky hand in his. "Detective Dave Holman," he added. "Good to see you in person again after all these years."

Ali returned to her sweet roll. "Obviously my parents keep you up to date on what's going on with me. What have you been doing in the meantime?"

Holman shrugged. "Spent some time in the military—the Marines—and I'm still in the reserves," he answered. "Graduated from college. Got married; had kids; got divorced. All the usual stuff. Now I'm a homicide detective with the Yavapai County Sheriff's department. But back at Mingus Mountain High, Billy Garrett was a good buddy of mine. Remember him?"

Ali tried to reconcile this powerful-looking, middle-aged man—this Dave Holman—with the tall scrawny boy she remembered from high school. As for Billy Garrett? She recalled him as an even skinnier but much shorter kid—a regular smart-ass—who, his senior year, had mustered up enough courage to invite Ali to the prom. And she had turned him down. Not because she was playing hard to get, as Dave Holman seemed to assume, and not because Billy Garrett wasn't tall enough, either.

Finances had been tight in the Larson household the last two years Ali was in high school. Remodeling the restaurant had taken more time and cash than anyone had anticipated. That was the reason Ali had graduated from high school with no class ring to show for it and with no yearbook for those two years, either. She had helped out at the restaurant during the summer and on weekends, but she had done so without pay, and her tips had gone into the family coffers to help keep things afloat. An academic scholarship to Northern Arizona University was the only reason she'd been able to go on to college.

But right now, with her mother standing there behind the counter, smiling and waiting for Dave Holman to place his order, Ali couldn't very well tell Dave the real reason she had spurned Billy Garrett's prom invitation—she simply hadn't been able to afford a dress.

"The usual?" Edie asked Dave. He nodded. Edie hurried away, jotting down his order as she went.

"I never have been big on dancing," Ali said. "Not then, and not now, either."

"Too bad," Dave said, shaking his head. "Broke poor Billy's heart. He went straight out and married the very next tall blond he ran into. Her name was Doreen, I think. She was a handful. You could have spared the poor guy all kinds of grief and at least one really bad marriage if you had just said yes our senior year instead of no."

At that point, though, the corners of his mouth went slightly upward, and Ali realized Holman was teasing her—most likely for the benefit of several other Sugarloaf regulars who were listening in on the conversation with avid attention.

"Billy didn't really marry that woman because I turned him down for the prom, did he?" she asked.

Dave grinned. "Makes a great story, though. And Billy's fine, by the way. He's a professor of philosophy somewhere in Colorado, and his second wife is great."

For the next few seconds, Ali tried to imagine Billy Garrett either studying or teaching philosophy. It just didn't compute.

Meanwhile Dave Holman turned serious. "You're here because of Reenie Holzer?" he asked.

It was always easier to remember girls from high school by their maiden names rather than by their married ones. Ali nodded.

"I'm sorry," he said. "I remember the way the two of you were in high school—always together. One tall, one short. One blond, one brunette. One thin and the other"—he paused—"well, rounder," he concluded diplomatically. "Reenie always had way more curves than you did."

By mentioning Reenie's name, Detective Holman had given Ali an opening, and she took it. "Are you making any progress finding out what happened?"

"Some," he said.

"I'm planning on going up to Flag later this morning to see Howie and the kids and to find out if there's anything I can do."

"I'm guessing he'll be pretty busy this morning," Dave said.

"How come?" Ali asked.

Dave set down his coffee cup and lowered his voice, although by then most of the people who had been eavesdropping on Ali and Dave's encounter had resumed their own breakfast conversations. "I talked to Lee Farris last night. He's my counterpart in homicide in Coconino County. He's planning on bringing Mr. Bernard in for questioning this morning."

"Howie?" Ali asked. "They're going to be questioning Howie about this?"

"We have to talk to everyone," Dave said. "That's how you get to the bottom of what really happened."

"But you're not saying he did it, are you?"

"I'm saying we have to talk to everyone," Dave repeated firmly. "At this point it could be an accident, but no one's ruling out suicide, either. If you start down Schnebly Hill Road in a snowstorm, you're pretty much asking for trouble. And considering what she was looking at, with spending the next few years dying of Lou Gehrig's disease, who could blame her if she did choose a shortcut? I sure as hell would."

"But what about her kids?" Ali objected. "From what I understand, she had just been diagnosed and was still in reasonably good health. I know her better than that. She wouldn't just abandon her kids like that, not before she had to."

Dave shrugged. "She might," he said.

Bob Larson emerged from the kitchen carrying Chris and Ali's orders. He set the plates down in front of them. "Morning, Dave," he said. "See you've already met my grandson, Chris."

Dave shook his head. "I haven't, actually. I've just been jawing with your daughter." He reached in front of Ali and offered his hand to Chris. "Glad to meet you," he said. "Your mother and I go back a long way." Noticing Chris's UCLA sweatshirt he added, "Think the Bruins will make it all the way to the Final Four this year?"

Chris responded with an enthusiastic affirmative. Chris, Dave, and her father wandered into a spirted discussion of which teams were likely to make it to the championship and which ones wouldn't. Meanwhile Ali was left to consider how easily men's conversations—regardless of whether the participants were friends or strangers—immediately devolved into sports talk. It was one of those annoying male traits, an auto-cloaking device designed to keep each of them from knowing anything personal about the others.

Right now mindless chatter was keeping Ali from learning more about what really mattered—whatever it was that had befallen her friend Reenie.

"Hey, sport," Bob said to Chris. "What say we hit the slopes for a while this afternoon, assuming your grandmother will give me time off for good behavior."

Chris glanced questioningly at Ali. "It's fine with me," she said. "I'm on my way to Flagstaff. I have no idea when I'll be back."

"Your grandfather can have the afternoon off," Edie agreed, "but only if he gets his tail back in the kitchen and finishes up the rest of breakfast."

Waving his wife's good-natured nagging aside, Bob retreated to the kitchen. Meanwhile, Ali's phone rang once more. She could see from the display that Paul was calling again. Leaving her place at the counter, she went out to the parking lot to take the call.

"What?"

"What?" Paul repeated. "Not even hello? Not even good morning? Why didn't you call me back?"

"April," Ali said bluntly. "I believe her name is April."

"My administrative assistant," he said. "What about her?" He was cool, wonderfully cool.

"I hear she has plans to get married soon—to you," Ali told him. "And then there's Charmaine as well—something about your skinny-dipping with

Charmaine. Tell her she's fired by the way. I don't think I want to have anything more to do with her."

Paul paused but only for a moment before going on the counterattack. "Who've you been talking to?" he wanted to know. "What kind of nonsense is this?"

"It doesn't matter who my unnamed sources are," she returned. "And it's not nonsense."

"I asked you to talk to that attorney of yours—Marvella or something like that. Did you do it?"

"Marcella," Ali corrected. "And, yes, I talked to her all right. She told me that you'd made some pointed suggestions to one of her firm's managing partners about what kind of good things they could expect if they convinced me to drop my wrongful dismissal case. But I'm not dropping it, Paul, and they're not dropping me, either. If the old guys at the station get to stay on the news desk, then the old girls should get to stay on as well. What's fair is fair. Now let's talk about April and Charmaine."

"Come on, Ali," Paul returned. "Forget them. They're not important. Those women mean less than nothing to me. You should know that by now."

"Actually," Ali returned, "I don't know anything of the kind. 'Those women' as you call them may not mean anything to you, but they do to me. What they're saying is that it's over between us, Paul. Totally and completely over. I'll be consulting a divorce attorney later on today—a lady who's associated with Marcella's firm. Her last name is Myerhoff; first name is Helga. You may have heard of her."

There was a pause. Helga Myerhoff's name packed some weight in certain circles. Ali knew beyond a doubt that Helga had handled divorce proceedings against more than one of Paul's philandering pals.

"Ali Bunny . . ." he began.

"Don't call me that!" she snapped.

"Ali, be reasonable. We can fix this. Or if we can't we can do this amicably. There's no need to . . ."

"I don't want to fix it," she interrupted. "And I've no intention of being amicable. The way you work, I'm quite certain that wouldn't be in my best interests."

Much to Ali's surprise, she remained amazingly dispassionate. She should have been in tears. She should have been devastated. But there was part of her that felt nothing but relief.

"Look, Paul," she said. "It's clear that our marriage has been on its way out for some time now. Maybe I was too busy to pay attention and figure out what was really going on. But I'm not too busy now, because, as you may have noticed, I've recently lost my job. That means I have the luxury of paying attention and I'm not liking what I'm finding—April and Charmaine included.

"And don't hassle me about not returning phone calls. You didn't return mine over the weekend until you were damned good and ready. Was April off with you wherever you were? Or was it Charmaine, since she didn't bother to come to work on Monday? Is that why you didn't call me back?"

"Be reasonable," Paul insisted. "I'm sure we can get to the bottom of all this."

"Get to the bottom of what?" she demanded. "The fact that you've been going around with your pants unzipped and screwing everything in sight?"

Paul sighed. The sigh was supposed to mean that she was being unreasonable. And demanding. "Just tell me when you'll be home," he said.

"You're not listening to me," she returned coldly. "I won't be coming home. My friend Reenie is dead. I came to Sedona to be with her family and with mine. I plan on staying as long as I want to."

"But what about . . ."

"You have April and Charmaine," she said. "I'm sure you'll be just fine."

Chapter 6

Ali had hung up the phone and was about to step back inside, when the blaring headline in a newspaper vending machine for the *Flagstaff Daily Sentinel* caught her eye: LOCAL WOMAN DIES IN SNOWY CRASH. Searching through her coat pocket she came up with enough change to purchase a copy.

> The Coconino County Sheriff's Department is investigating the death of Misty Irene Bernard, age forty-five, Executive Director of the Flagstaff YWCA, who died over the weekend when her Yukon plunged off Schnebly Hill Road and rolled several hundred feet. Ms. Bernard, who was not wearing a seat belt at the time of the accident, was thrown from the vehicle.
>
> Ms. Bernard was reported missing late Friday, twenty-four hours after she failed to return home from a doctor's appointment in Scottsdale. Coconino County Sheriff's Office investigators have been trying to trace her activities from the time she left Flagstaff on Thursday until her body

was located near the wreckage of her vehicle on Monday.

Investigators tracing Ms. Bernard's movements have so far been unable to determine why she would have attempted to drive the little-traveled treacherous route between Flagstaff and Sedona during a snowstorm so severe that it forced brief nighttime closures on both I-40 and I-17.

People close to the investigation who spoke on the condition of anonymity suggested that, after receiving a dire medical diagnosis, she may have committed suicide. Evidence of both drug and alcohol use were found at the scene, but toxicology reports won't be available for several weeks. An autopsy is scheduled for sometime later this week.

Married to NAU history professor, Howard M. Bernard, the dead woman is survived by her two young children and her parents, longtime Cottonwood residents, Mr. and Mrs. Edward Holzer. Bernard, an NAU graduate, had worked for the YWCA for the past ten years and had served as executive director for the past five.

Funeral services are pending.

Ali recognized the cold journalese of the article. It was impartial. It gave the facts. It said both too much and too little. It did nothing to capture the wonderful resilient character Reenie Bernard had been. It did everything to dismiss her—turning her into a statistic by implying that she had died primarily because she had failed to fasten her seat belt—as if a plunge off Schnebly Hill Road were in any way survivable.

Offended, Ali hurried back into the restaurant. She almost ran into Chris who was on his way out, grinning and dangling a set of car keys in one hand.

"What gives?" she asked.

"Since you're on your way to Flagstaff, Gramps is lending me his SUV so I can run a few errands," Chris said. "I'll see you later tonight, after we finish skiing."

Ali was surprised. Her father had purchased the Bronco new in 1972. He had babied it along for more than thirty years and over 300,000 miles, and he hardly ever relinquished the keys to anyone else. "You must be pretty special," she said. "Whatever you do don't wreck it."

Ali went inside and back to her spot next to Dave Holman. By then he had finished his breakfast and was in the process of pulling several dollar bills from his wallet. She dropped the newspaper in front of him.

"I don't care what the newspaper says," Ali told him, "I still don't think she committed suicide."

Dave shrugged. "Suit yourself. Just because something's in the paper doesn't make it true or false. You of all people should know that."

"What's that supposed to mean?" she demanded.

"Look," he said. "You're a journalist. I'm a police officer. That means most likely we'll never be pals. Let's just leave it at that."

"Sounds good to me," she told him.

Leaving both his money and the bill on the counter, Dave got up and walked away. Edie Larson came back over to where her daughter was sitting. "More coffee?" she asked.

"No, thank you," Ali said. "Are your customers always that obnoxious?"

"Which customers?"

"That one," Ali said, pointing at Dave, who was getting into his vehicle outside.

"Dave? He's a little surly on occasion," Edie said. "His life hasn't exactly been a bed of roses lately. Don't take it personally. What about you? Are you all right? You look awfully pale."

Ali had no desire to discuss the contents of her phone conversation with Paul. And she didn't want to mention being chewed up and spit out by Dave Holman, either. Instead, Ali shoved the newspaper with its visible headline across the counter to her mother. Edie glanced at it and nodded.

"Oh, that," she said. "I read it this morning while I was waiting for the rolls to rise."

Ali stood up. "I'm going to head on up to Flag," she said. "I want to see if there's anything I can do to help."

"You do that," Edie said. "And be sure to let Howie and the kids know that we're thinking about them."

Back outside, Ali slipped off her coat. The sun was warming the chilly air, and the Cayenne's heated seats—a laughable accessory in southern California—would keep her more than toasty. Standing there, next to the car, she looked at the mountains on the far side of Sedona. First came the layers of red rock formations standing out against the more distant green. But higher up, much closer to the rim, the landscape was still shaded white with snow. And there, snaking down the side of the mountain, as thin as a gossamer thread from a spider web, was the line that Ali knew to be Schnebly Hill Road. The place where Reenie had died.

Shivering, but not from cold, Ali climbed into the Cayenne and turned on the engine—and the heated seat. Then she took her MP3 player out of her pocket and scrolled through the playlist.

She searched through the index until she found "Tell Me on a Sunday," one of Andrew Lloyd Webber's less well-known shows, but one Ali had seen on the trip to London with her mother and Aunt Evie.

It had been a one-woman show—ninety solid minutes of music masterfully sung by a former BBC television news presenter turned actress—the irony of that similarity wasn't lost on Ali now. Nor was the similarity in content. The play had consisted of a litany of songs, telling the story of one heartbreaking romantic breakup after another.

"And here's another one," Ali said aloud as she turned on the music and headed for Flagstaff. There was one song in particular that hit her hard when one of the character's supposed friends shows up eager to spill the beans about her partner's latest indiscretion, to which she responds, "I knew before."

But I didn't, Ali thought. She had assumed that she and Paul had both been working hard on their careers, building something together. With that erroneous assumption now laid to rest, Ali wondered how much else in her life was little more than a mirage—smoke and mirrors and special effects. Unfortunately, she and the lady singing the songs about dashed hopes and dreams had all too much in common.

To an outsider it might well seem as though she had made up her mind to call a divorce attorney too hastily in the overwrought and emotionally charged atmosphere of having just heard about April and Charmaine. In actual fact, Ali had been thinking about just such an eventuality for a very long time, and well before her trip to London, which was one of the reasons the musical had affected her so much when she first heard it on stage. And now that it was time for Ali, too, to take action, she was surprised to find herself clearheaded, calm, and focused. She would deal with Paul and with the station's firing her all in good time, but for the moment she would do what she had said she would do—she would be there for Reenie's family for as long as needed.

The route to Flagstaff up through Oak Creek Canyon was only twenty-nine miles long, but with road crews out in force sanding the icy spots, it took Ali over an hour to arrive at Reenie and Howard Bernard's unremarkable ranch-style house on Kachina Trail. It was a newer house, with one of those towering front-entry facades that had little to do with the rest of the house and everything to do with needing to use a ladder whenever it was necessary to change the bulb in the porch light.

The last time Ali had been to Reenie's house had been Christmas two years ago. Back then the entire yard had been covered with a layer of new-fallen snow and the whole place had been festooned with strings of red and green chili-shaped Christmas lights. There had been lights and decorations everywhere, including a beautifully decked-out ten-foot-tall tree in the middle of the living room window.

Ali parked behind a bright red Lexus with Arizona plates. There was snow in the yard this time as well, but it was several days old and turning gray. Near the corner of the front porch an armless, featureless snowman had dwindled away to sad, shapeless lumps. His forlorn appearance seemed a harbinger of what Ali could expect once she entered the house.

She was making her way up the icy sidewalk when a snowball flew past her ear and smacked harmlessly into the trunk of a nearby tree. Following the snowball's trajectory, she went around to the side of the house where she found nine-year-old Matt, bareheaded and in his shirt-sleeves, forming another snowball in red, cold-roughened hands.

"Truce," she called when she saw him. "It's not fair to hit someone who's unarmed."

Matt dropped the snow in his hands and came toward her. In the past, he would have thrown himself enthusiastically into Ali's arms. This time he approached her cautiously as if unsure of his welcome. He stopped several feet short of where Ali stood and observed her with a silent but penetrating look. "Did you hear about our Mom?" he asked.

Ali nodded. "Yes." she said. "Yes, I did. Your Aunt Bree called me. That's why I'm here."

"What did she tell you?" he asked. Seeing the hurt in Matt's eyes was almost more than Ali could stand. He was only nine—far too young to be carrying around this kind of heartbreak.

"She told me your mother died in a car wreck,"

Ali said. "That the car she was driving went off Schnebly Hill Road in the middle of a snowstorm."

"Dad said it was an accident," Matt said after a pause. "But I read the newspaper. It said she probably killed herself. Do you think that's true? Dad said she was sick—that she was starting to get sick—but she wouldn't leave us like that, would she? I mean, if she killed herself, does that mean she didn't love us anymore?"

Those were questions Ali could answer with absolute honesty. "I don't think your mother would leave you on purpose, either," Ali said. "She wasn't like that. And of course she loved you, Matt. She loved you very much."

"But if it isn't true, how can the newspaper say it, then?" Matt asked.

By being irresponsible, Ali thought. "We have to let the investigators do their job," she said. "So should the newspapers."

"But what if Julie finds out?" Matt asked. "What if someone tells her?"

"I won't," Ali declared. "You don't have to worry about me. I would never tell Julie anything of the kind.

Matt heaved a sigh of relief. He came to her then, leaning his small frame against her and letting Ali comfort him. He was cold, and his hands and feet were soaking wet. "You're freezing," she said. "We need to get you inside."

"No," Matt said. "Aunt Bree's in there, braiding Julie's hair. She's not very good at it, and Julie keeps crying and crying. That's how come I came outside—to get away. I didn't want to listen anymore."

"That's understandable," Ali said. "Let's sit in the car, then. It's warmer in there than it is out here."

Nodding, Matt walked toward the Cayenne. Once inside, Ali had no idea what to say next. The last she had known, Howie Bernard had been soft-pedaling his wife's disappearance in an effort to protect his children. That ruse wasn't going to work much longer.

"If it wasn't an accident, and if she didn't kill herself, maybe it was something worse," Matt said softly.

"What do you mean worse?" Ali asked.

"The cops came by a little while ago and took Dad away. What if they arrest him?"

"Did they put handcuffs on him?" Ali asked.

"No, but they put him in the back of a cop car and everything. What if they think . . ."

Ali had uncovered another source for Matt's pain.

"Don't give that another thought," Ali said. "I talked to one of the deputies down in Sedona. He said that officers up here would be talking to your father today, but I'm sure it's nothing to worry about. Just routine questions. That's what they do when someone dies. They ask questions. They try to find out who last saw the person who's dead. They want to find out what was going on, whether or not anyone had had a disagreement."

"A disagreement?" Matt asked.

"You know," Ali said. "A quarrel. An argument."

Matt turned his face away from Ali, but not before she caught sight of a single tear coursing down his cheek.

"Had there been an argument?" Ali asked.

Without answering, Matt shook his head and then angrily swiped the tear away with the back of his hand. Before Ali could ask anything more, there was a sharp rap on the passenger window next to Matt's head. When Ali looked past him, all that was visible through the steamy glass was a distorted masklike face. As soon as Ali rolled down the window, Bree Cowan's face came into view, her features distorted by a fit of anger—or worry.

"Matthew Edward Bernard, where in the world have you been?" she demanded. "I've been calling and calling. I want you inside right this minute!"

Obligingly Matthew climbed out of the Porsche. "And you came outside without even so much as putting on a jacket?" Bree continued. "Don't you think I have enough to deal with right now without your catching cold on top of everything else? Grandpa and Grandma will be here any minute. Now go inside and get into something clean and dry."

Only after he trudged off toward the house did Bree turn to Ali. "You have no idea how glad I am to see you," she said. "These kids are driving me nuts. Julie's been crying her eyes out ever since her father left, and Matt . . . Well, I guess he's just being Matt."

Ali had never cared for Reenie's baby sister. She had always seemed brusque and opinionated, and Ali liked her even less that minute.

"He's upset," Ali said. "And who could blame him?"

"Of course he's upset," Bree returned, following Matt and leading the way into the house.

Everything about the house was so like Reenie, that Ali had difficulty staying focused on what Bree was saying.

"So am I," she continued. "We're all upset. Losing Reenie like this is a terrible shock, but I still need him to do what I've asked him to do. I want the kids ready to go to Cottonwood when the folks get here. I'm already late for my meeting. Howie called a little while ago and asked me to come over. The cops needed to take him in for questioning, and with the kids out of school because of what's happened . . ."

"I could look after them for you," Ali offered.

"Really?" Bree returned. "The folks will be here soon. Howie asked if they'd look after the kids for a couple of days, but if you'd watch them until my parents get here, it would be a huge favor."

"That's what I'm here for," Ali said. "To help. You do whatever you need to do."

"Are you sure?"

"Yes, I'm sure. Go."

Bree glanced down the hall toward the spot where Matt had disappeared. Then she came across the room and gave Ali a quick hug.

"You're really a lifesaver," she told Ali. With that, she gathered up a coat and purse that had been flung over a chair just inside the door and hurried outside.

Moments later, a red-eyed and tearful Julie emerged from the hallway. "Hi, Ali," she said matter-of-factly. "Did you know Mommy's dead?"

Ali hurried over to the child and scooped her up. "I know, sweetie," she said. "I heard. That's why I'm here."

"And the cops took Daddy away a little while ago. Did you know that?"

Ali nodded. "Matt told me that, too. They probably just need to ask him a few questions. I'm sure he'll be back in a little while."

"I don't think so," Julie said, shaking her head hard enough that the barrettes on the ends of her braids clattered together. "I think they arrested him, and they're going to put him in jail. That's why Aunt Bree is making us go to Grandma's house."

"Aunt Bree has an important meeting," Ali said. "And someone needs to look after you. Now, are you all packed and ready to go?"

"I don't *want* to go there," Julie whined. "I want to be here. With Daddy."

"With everything that's happened, your daddy has far too many things to take care of right now without having to look after you," Ali said. "Besides, I'm sure your grandparents are thrilled to have you."

"But how long do we have to stay?" Julie asked.

"Just for a couple of days."

"Are you sure? What if Daddy goes to jail? What if they don't let him come back home?" Julie asked. "Will we have to stay in Cottonwood forever? And what about Sam?"

"Sam?" Ali repeated. "Who's Sam?"

Matt came into the living room and dropped a bulging backpack onto the couch. "Our cat," he said. "Samantha. We can't leave her here."

"Why not?" Ali asked. "Isn't there someone who could come by and look after her? A neighbor? A friend? Your Aunt Bree lives here in town. Maybe she . . ."

"Sam doesn't like Aunt Bree," Julie interrupted. "She and Uncle John have dogs. Poodles. Sam definitely doesn't like dogs. That's why she's hiding."

Clearly Ali's arguments were going nowhere. She and the kids spent the next half hour searching the whole interior of the house. Ali had concluded that the cat must have escaped unobserved through an open door when Matt found her, curled up and sleeping on a stack of folded bath towels in the far reaches of the linen closet.

All through the search, Ali had envisioned finding some cute and helpless little kitten-like puffball. When Matt dragged Sam from her hidey-hole, she turned out to be a fifteen-pound heavyweight tabby cat with a raggedy torn ear and one missing eye. She may have been ugly as sin, but she purred mightily once Julie hefted her onto the couch and let her curl up in her lap.

Mindful of the fact that Sam didn't like strangers, and not wanting to provoke another disappearing act, Ali stayed on the far side of the room. "Does she mind riding in cars?" Ali asked.

"She hates it," Julie said.

Great! Ali thought.

"But we have a cat carrier," Matt offered. "Mom uses it when she takes Sam to the . . ." Looking stricken, he stopped suddenly when he realized what he'd said and knew that his mother wouldn't be taking Sam anywhere ever again. "It's out in the garage," he finished lamely. "I'll go get it."

Straightening his shoulders, he headed for the kitchen and the door that led to the attached garage. Watching him fight back tears and struggle to maintain his dignity as he walked away, Ali felt her heart constrict.

I'm in way, way over my head! she told herself. *What on earth am I doing here?*

When Reenie's parents showed up, Ali was shocked by their appearance. Ed and Diane had to be about the same age as Ali's own parents, but they seemed far older and, when it came to Ed, far frailer as well. Remembering what Bree had said about Ed having had heart bypass surgery, Ali wasn't too surprised when Diane directed her gray-faced husband to have a seat in the living room while she oversaw getting Matt and Julie and their possessions loaded into the car.

"Your children aren't supposed to die first," Ed Holzer said, repeating a sentiment Ali had heard from her first in-laws. Ed wasn't looking at Ali when he spoke. He seemed to be addressing the universe in general.

"No," Ali agreed. "They're not."

"You were her friend, Ali," he said quietly. "Do you think Reenie killed herself?"

The question caught Ali by surprise." No," she answered. "I don't think she did."

"Why?" he asked.

"Because I don't think she'd drive herself off a cliff without telling her kids good-bye," Ali answered.

"Neither do I," he said. "Everybody else says I'm way off base here—Bree, Diane, Howie, the cops—but I don't think she'd just give up that way without a fight. And I don't think she did."

Ali waited for Ed to say more, but he didn't.

"How long did the doctors say she had?"

Ed shrugged. "All she ever told me was two to five years after diagnosis."

"And her diagnosis was when?"

"She just got a final confirmation last week," Ed said. "Evidently her back started bothering her late last fall, but I had just had my heart bypass then, and she never mentioned it to anybody. She just toughed it out. She didn't want to do anything that would upset the holidays. She finally went to the doctor sometime in January."

"So this was early, then?"Ali asked.

Ed nodded. "Way early," he replied.

"Has anyone talked to her doctor?" Ali asked. "The one she saw before she disappeared?"

Ed shrugged. "I'm sure Howie has," he said. "And probably the cops have. Why?"

"I'd like to know what exactly he told her," Ali replied. "Maybe her ALS was progressing faster than anyone knew."

"Maybe," Ed agreed. "But still . . ."

He seemed ready to say something more, but thought better of it.

"Still what?" Ali asked.

"Nothing," he replied. "It doesn't matter."

About then the loading process came to a screeching halt. Matt stomped back into the living room, shouting over his shoulder in his grandmother's direction, "I didn't want to go in the first place. If Sam can't go with us, I'm not going either!"

Diane followed Matt into the house, trying to reason with him. "Look, Matt," she said. "You know very well that your grandfather's allergic to cats. Under the circumstances, I'm sure your father is capable of taking care of Samantha."

"No, he isn't," Matt insisted. "He doesn't even like her. The only way Mom convinced him to let us keep her was if we promised to take care of her so Dad wouldn't have to."

"This is different," Diane said. "I'm sure he won't mind."

"Besides," Matt added stubbornly. "Why do we have to go with you anyway? Why can't we just stay here with Dad?"

"Because your father wants you with us," Diane returned. Her voice was firm, but she also sounded tired and exasperated.

"I'll take care of Sam," Ali offered. The words were out of her mouth before she even considered what she was saying.

Gratitude flooded Matt's young face. "Would you?" he asked. "Really."

"Sure," Ali said. "No problem."

Chapter 7

Once Ed and Diane Holzer finished loading the kids and took off for Cottonwood, Ali stuck Samantha and her cat carrier into the back of the Cayenne. The moment the carrier hit the floorboard, Sam started screeching bloody murder. Ali wanted to wait around long enough to talk to Howie, but with everyone gone, there was no way to hang around the house. Feeling at loose ends and with no real purpose in mind, Ali drove to Reenie's old office.

The Flagstaff branch of the YWCA was located in part of a strip mall on South Milton Road just south of Northern Arizona University. NAU, hungry for useable real estate, had gobbled up the YW's previous location, and Reenie had masterminded the move to a more modern space that included a day-care center, an exercise room, and a complex of conference and counseling rooms as well as administrative offices. There were children and teachers visible inside the building, but the brightly colored playground equipment, sitting in a fenced side yard and covered with dingy snow, looked abandoned and forgotten.

Seeing all Reenie had accomplished put a lump in Ali's throat. Reenie was responsible for all of this. When the creaky old building had been sold, conventional wisdom had said that the YWCA in Flagstaff should probably fold its tent and disappear as well, but Reenie Bernard was too much of a fighter to simply close up shop. Instead, she had masterminded a major capital fund-raising campaign that had, in a few short years, made this new building and all its programs possible.

But is it solid enough to continue without her? Ali wondered. There was no way to tell that right then.

Walking inside, Ali found Andrea Rogers, Reenie's receptionist, staring blankly at her computer screen. "I thought I'd come by and check on you," Ali said. "How're you doing?"

Ali had met Andrea on previous occasions. She was a frumpy, never-married woman in her late fifties who had worked for the Flagstaff branch of the YWCA all her adult life. She had been Reenie's right-hand helper for years.

Andrea reached for a nearly empty Kleenex box sitting next to her keyboard. "It's all so awful that I still can't believe it," she said tearfully. "I have to come in and keep the doors open. I'm so sick at heart that I'd rather be home in bed. But I can't. The day care has to stay open and so do we, but I can't imagine how we'll get through this." She paused and took a deep breath. "How are Reenie's kids?"

"Not too good," Ali said. "Reenie's parents took them to Cottonwood for a few days."

"And Howie?" Andrea asked. "How's he?"

"I haven't seen him yet, but I think he's okay," Ali told her.

"Have they found a note?"

"Not that I know of."

"They'll find one," Andrea said confidently. "They're bound to. She wouldn't do such a thing without saying something to the people she was leaving behind."

"So had she talked to you about her . . . situation?" Ali asked.

Andrea nodded. "Of course," she said. "As soon as she got the diagnosis she told me about it. She said we needed to make a plan, and to start looking for someone to take over as executive director."

"Had she found anyone?" Ali asked.

"In a week?" Andrea returned. "Are you kidding? Of course she hadn't found anyone. Where would we find someone willing to work as hard as she did? I'm not sure we'll even be able to keep going, although I know she'd want us to." Andrea blew noisily into a tissue, tossed that one and reached for another.

"All I can think of," she continued, "is that her doctor down in Scottsdale must have given her some really bad news. But why didn't she say something to me when she called. I couldn't have done anything to help—nobody could—but at least I could have been there for her, could have listened to her and talked to her. She wouldn't have been so alone, and maybe . . ."

It struck Ali that Andrea's comment about Reenie taking her own life without a word of warning to anyone was the workplace equivalent of Matt's plaintive "Didn't she love us anymore?" That was Ali's complaint as well, and it took a moment for her to process the rest of what Andrea had said.

"You talked to her after her doctor's appointment?" Ali asked.

"Yes," Andrea replied. "She told me she was stopping by the bank and then she was on her way back here."

"To the office?"

"That's what she said, but she wasn't here when I left. I assumed she'd changed her mind and gone home instead."

"Which bank?" Ali asked.

"She didn't say. That's what the cops wanted to know, too—which bank? I told them I didn't know. I think they use Bank of America, but I have no idea which branch. Detective Farris said he'd be able to find out. He said she probably needed to cash a check or something, but if she was going to drive herself off a cliff, why would she need money?"

Good question, Ali thought. "So you have spoken to the cops about all this?" she asked.

"Over the weekend," Andrea said. "The first time was on Saturday afternoon. They came to my house. Then they came here again on Monday, after they found the body. They wanted to know if Reenie was upset about anything. Talk about a stupid question. With that kind of diagnosis, who wouldn't be upset? Still, she acted more relieved than anything."

"Relieved?"

"She'd been feeling sick for months—just not herself—and no one could tell her what was wrong. But once what was wrong had a name—even though it was awful—at least she knew what she was up against and nobody could call her a hypochondriac."

"Somebody called her that?" Ali asked.

Andrea nodded. "Her sister. Sometime around Christmas. So once Reenie knew it was ALS, she was gung-ho to fight it. At least that's what she told me. That she was going to research it, find out everything she could, and see if there were any programs she might qualify for—you know, experimental things that might help."

"She said that?" Ali asked. "That she was going to try to be accepted into one of the ongoing protocols?"

"That was just a few days ago," Andrea added. "What would have made her change her mind?"

Ali shrugged. "I can't imagine," she said.

Walking past Andrea's desk, Ali took a step toward the doorway of what had been and still was Reenie's private office. The office space itself was modern enough, but the furniture was old-fashioned wooden stuff that had come from the other building. Given a choice between purchasing new playground equipment for the day-care center or new furniture for Reenie's office, there had been no contest. Playground equipment had won hands down.

Lots of people decorated their offices with framed degrees and plaques—walls of honor. None of Reenie's degrees were on display. Instead, most of the walls were papered over with a colorful collection of greeting cards in all shapes and sizes. Scattered among the cards were pieces of childish handmade art.

"She did love cards," Ali observed.

"Isn't that the truth," Andrea agreed with a sigh. "She went through more cards than anybody I ever knew. She sent cards for big occasions, little occasions, and no occasions at all. With her gone, that Hallmark store out at the mall will probably end up going out of business."

Ali thought of the greeting card Reenie had sent her—the one that had arrived after Reenie's death and was still in Ali's purse.

"She couldn't stand to throw any of them away," Andrea continued. "When Detective Farris came by for the computer, I asked him if it was okay if I took the cards down, boxed them up, and saved them for her kids. He said not yet, that I should stay out of her office until they gave me the all clear. So that's what I'm doing—leaving things as is."

And that was how the office looked—as is. Files lay scattered here and there on the desk as though Reenie had just stepped out and expected to return to her work at any moment.

"Detective Farris took her computer?" Ali asked.

"He said he was looking for a note. He said if she wrote one it's probably still out on the mountain somewhere and they haven't found it yet. He thought she might have written it on her computer. I told him she wouldn't have, that she'd have found a card—just the right one, too. I tried to tell Detective Farris that, but he looked at me like I was nuts, so I shut up."

"She sent me a card that day," Ali observed.

Andrea looked at Ali eagerly. "On Thursday? From Scottsdale?"

Ali nodded. "It was a cute card—a friendship card.

She said she thought she was in for a bumpy ride. I don't think she was talking about driving off a cliff."

"That's all she said?" Andrea asked. She sounded disappointed.

Ali nodded. "That's all."

"Maybe she was talking about Howie," Andrea suggested softly.

"Howie?" Ali asked. "What about him?"

Chewing her lower lip again, Andrea stalled. "Nothing," she said.

"Tell me," Ali insisted

"I think she and Howie were having marital difficulties," Andrea answered reluctantly. "She came storming into the office a couple of weeks ago and said, 'Remind me again why I got married?' And I said, 'Well, you probably wanted to have kids.' She shook her head and said, 'Kids aren't the problem. Husbands are.' And then she came in here and slammed the door. Reenie wasn't like that, you know. She didn't do temper tantrums. She spent most of the morning on the phone that day. I know she made an appointment to see Mike Hopkins."

"Who's he?" Ali asked.

"An attorney here in town. He specializes in divorces."

"She was going to get a divorce?"

Andrea shrugged. "I'm not sure," she said. "I do know she made an appointment to see him. Then when the diagnosis came in, she canceled it. I guess she figured that with everything else that was going on, there wasn't much point in going to the trouble of getting a divorce—that she'd just put up with whatever was going on for a while longer."

"Do you know what was going on?" Ali demanded.

"It's just gossip. I probably shouldn't have mentioned it."

"Tell me," Ali prodded.

"I heard Howie has a girlfriend," Andrea said in a small voice. "I think she's one of his students."

Out in the car, Ali could barely contain her outrage. Reenie had found out she was dying and that her husband was having an affair all at the same time. That was more than a mere "bumpy road." She drove by the house on Kachina Trail on her way out of town. She wanted to confront Howie. She wanted to ask him whether or not it was true. Fortunately, he wasn't home. Still. And maybe that was a good thing, she reflected, as she headed on down the road toward Sedona. Reenie was dead. So what if Howie was having an affair? What business of it was Ali's? Besides, how much of the anger she felt toward Howie should have been directed elsewhere—at Paul, for example, for being a two-timing clod? Or at herself, for being stupid?

She was so distressed on the way back to Sedona that listening to Samantha screeching from the backseat was a welcome diversion. Once back at the house, Ali stowed Samantha's cat carrier in the corner of the living room and the litter box next to the washing machine in the laundry room. She filled the water dish and put that and the food dish on the kitchen floor. Leaving the door to the cat carrier open, Ali went to her computer.

For a long time, she sat with her fingers poised over the keyboard. There was a part of her that wanted to go off and lob incendiary bombs in Howie

Bernard's direction. But there was enough old-fashioned journalism still flowing in Ali's veins that she couldn't rant about something that was nothing really but unsubstantiated rumor, especially since it made no difference.

Finally, mastering her emotions, she forced herself to write something else.

cutlooseblog.com
Tuesday, March 15, 2005

My friend is dead. Two young children have lost their mother forever. Their lives are in total disarray. The children are with their grandparents who don't even live in the same town. They've been pulled away from school, from their friends, and from everything familiar to wait for a funeral that will happen eventually, but at some unspecified time and place. (Funeral arrangements can't be made until the medical examiner releases the body, and he has yet to say when that will happen.) In the meantime, their cat is here with me.

I don't like cats. Never have. The idea of what I'm going to have to do with the litter box that is even now lurking in my laundry room is more than I want to consider—and probably way more information than you want to have, either. But the truth is, there wasn't any choice. Sam (short for Samantha) had nowhere else to go. With their father preoccupied, the children needed to know that someone would look after their beloved pet. Since the kids are with their grandparents and since their grandfather turns out to be highly allergic to cats, that job fell to me.

Sam is not a beautiful animal. She's huge. She's missing an eye and a big part of one ear. (I would have thought that male cats did more fighting than female ones do, but maybe that's the reality behind what men like to refer to as "cat fights.") Even though I left the carrier door open, she's still inside it and glaring at me through that one good eye. I don't think she likes me any more than I like her, and I'm afraid once she leaves the carrier, she'll disappear somewhere here in the house and I'll never be able to find her again.

The kids had warned me in advance that Sam hated riding in cars. Now I believe it. The drive back to Sedona from Reenie's place in Flagstaff only takes half an hour, but it felt much longer with Sam in the car because she cried the whole way. Make that SCREAMED!! AT THE TOP OF HER LUNGS! It made me wonder how fifteen or so pounds of cat could make that much of a racket. I was afraid people in other cars could hear her, too.

I keep reminding myself that I came here to help. For today, taking care of Sam is what needed doing for Reenie and for her family. So, uneasy though Sam and I may be with our current arrangement, the cat is here.

My life is in almost as much turmoil at the moment as Sam's. I seem to be getting a divorce, not because I necessarily wanted one but because I have it on good authority that my husband has not one but two girlfriends. Two! Maybe he picked them up at Costco. Isn't that where you always have to take two of everything, whether you need two or not?

That would be his case—he didn't really need them. Considering he already had a wife, me, I should have thought he didn't need any girlfriends at all. But it must have seemed like a good idea at the time. For him.

It's not a good idea for me, however, so I'm telling myself it's probably time for me to move on. One of the two girlfriends is evidently busy telling everyone who gets near her about her plans to marry the man who is currently my husband. That being the case, I've decided to take the hint, get a move on, and let her have him. I'm not interested in sharing him and I certainly don't want him back. If she does marry him, she'll know in advance that he'll be as likely to cheat on her as he did on me.

But at least I *can* move on. For me moving on is possible. With any kind of luck, I'll be able to pick myself up (again), dust myself off (again), and see where the road of life will take me. My friend Reenie can't do that. I don't know everything that was going on in her life. I know she was having health issues. There could have been other stresses at work in her life as well. If there were, she didn't mention them to me.

The general consensus, however, is that, for whatever reason, the burden of living had become too much for her. The authorities continue to search for a suicide note. As much as I don't want to believe that my friend took her own life, I'm more than half hoping such a note will be found. I'm hoping that whatever is written there will offer both answers and closure for the people who are grieving her loss. That it will put an end to the speculation and help us understand why Reenie might make the choices she did—why she might choose to be gone when the rest of us weren't nearly ready to let her go.

But I'm not at all sure closure exists. Everybody talks about it, but maybe they're all pretending. Maybe closure is no more a reality than the Easter Bunny or Santa Claus. Still we all maintain that once the remains of a loved one are put to rest or once the criminal is sentenced in a court of law or a murderer is put to death that there's "closure" for the grieving survivors. I'm worried that it's a fabrication—an emotional crutch we all cling to in hopes that some day we'll feel better than we do right now. And I suppose that, as far as Reenie Bernard is concerned, that's the only hope we have.

As for me? I think it's time I gave myself a swift kick in my self-pitying butt. Reenie Bernard has lost everything. So have her children. Compared to them, I'm a wimp.

Posted: 2:20 P.M. by AliR

For a while Ali read through the surprising number of comment e-mails that had come in since Chris had posted the notice about The Forum. She read through them, posting them as she went.

Don't be so selfish. Your friend didn't abandon you. She spared her family and you from having to see her go through what was coming. I have ALS, too. It's not that bad yet, but I know it will be. I don't have the same kind of courage your friend had. I would never be brave enough to drive myself off the edge of a cliff. Instead, I've saved up some sleeping pills, enough, I hope, to do the job.

The trick will be knowing when to take them. Swallowing is already getting difficult. I'd like to live long enough to see my daughter graduate from high school next spring, but I know that if I wait too long, I won't be able to take the pills on my own and I'll lose the ability to have my own say in the matter.

Please give your friend credit for leaving on her own terms. It was her choice.

Anna

Ms. Reynolds,

Suicide is a mortal sin. It is wrong. No matter what! Your friend is going to hell. I'm sorry.

Midge Carson

The next comments referred to Ali's absence from the newsroom:

Dear Ali Reynolds,

Please come home. The kid they have sitting in your spot at the news desk needs a high chair. And a haircut. She looks like she's fresh out of high school and just stuck her finger in an electrical outlet. I'm writing to the station saying that they need to take you back. If not, I'll watch my news somewhere else.

Bob Preston

Dear Ali,

If they were going to fire someone, why not that tedious windbag with the dreadful toupee? When you get hired on another station, please let me know where. I hope it'll be one of the stations from around here so I can still see you from time to time. You are the best thing that ever happened to the Evening News.

Wanda Carmichael

Dear Ms. Reynolds,

Someone is selling an autographed picture of you on e-bay. Do you think it is real. Will it be more valuable now that you're fired. How much do you think I should pay. Please answer back right away. The online auction is supposed to end tomorrow morning.

Also if you ever want to buy Beenie Babies I have a lot of those and some of them are very rare. I would give them to you at a good price now that you're unemployed.

Sylvia

Ali was still puzzling over that one and wondering if she should laugh or cry when the phone rang. "You're home," Edie Larson announced. "How are things?"

It was a simple question with no easy answer. There was so much Ali needed to tell her mother—so much she had yet to tell her—that she had no idea where to start. Just as she had in the blog, Ali avoided the land mines by using Samantha for emotional cover.

"Matt and Julie are down in Cottonwood with Reenie's folks. They asked me to look after their cat, so Samantha is here with me."

"You don't even like cats."

"Exactly," Ali agreed. "But somebody had to do it."

"How are the kids holding up?"

"They're dealing with it," Ali replied. "Matt had read the paper. He's aware the cops suspect Reenie committed suicide. Matt's big worry is that Julie's going to find out."

"They'll be better off if someone comes straight out and tells them," Edie said. "Howie should do it, or else Reenie's parents."

"But is that what happened?" Ali objected. "Somehow I just can't get my head around the idea that Reenie would kill herself. No matter what."

"You and I haven't walked in her shoes," Edie said. "It's easy to say she wouldn't do this or wouldn't do that, but until you've actually been there . . ."

"According to her secretary, Reenie was going to fight," Ali returned.

Edie sighed. "She probably changed her mind." "Look, Ali," Edie added. "It hurts like hell to lose someone you're close to. Your Aunt Evie may have been my sister, but she was also my best friend and my partner. When she was gone out of my life all of a sudden, I didn't know how to cope. Something would happen and I'd want to tell her about it. Or I'd wonder what she'd think about it. And I still miss her every day. You just have to get through it, that's all. And one way to do that is to take care of yourself. Did you have lunch today?"

That was vintage Edie Larson. Caring but utterly practical, and bent on providing food for the body as much as food for the soul.

"No," Ali admitted.

"I didn't think so. Chris and your father left for the Snow Bowl a little while ago. I know how much Chris loves pot roast. I'm cooking up one of those because I know it'll hold until they get home, whenever that is. The only question now is, do you want to come down here for dinner or should I bring it up there?"

Ali glanced at the cat carrier. Sam obliged by staring balefully back with her one good eye. "Maybe you should bring it up here," Ali said.

"I'll be there about dinner time. We'll break into your Aunt Evie's wine cellar and offer a toast to her and to Reenie Bernard as well."

"Sounds good," Ali said.

But she didn't mean it. At that very moment, the last thing she felt like doing was drinking a toast to anyone, not to Reenie and not to anyone else.

Chapter 8

They had barely hung up when the phone rang again. "Alison Reynolds?" asked a deep voice Ali didn't recognize.

"Yes." Ali answered warily. The land line phone number was still listed under Aunt Evie's name, and Ali didn't like the idea of some strange man having access to it.

"My name's Helga Myerhoff, with Weldon, Davis, and Reed in LA. One of my associates, Marcella Johnson said you might be interested in speaking to me. Is this a convenient time?"

A smoker no doubt, Ali concluded once she realized the male-sounding voice actually belonged to a woman.

"Yes," Ali said. "Talking now would be fine."

"I've taken the liberty of doing a little checking on you," Helga continued purposefully. "Which is to say, I know who you are, how long you've been married, that kind of thing. I don't do run-of-the-mill divorces, you see, Ms. Reynolds. I prefer to handle ones that are worth my while, so to speak. Let me ask you then, is there a pre-nup?"

"Yes," Ali said.

"Figures," Helga said. "Women who fall in love with high-powered men also fall for prenuptial agreements. It's just the way things are."

"So that's bad?" Ali asked.

"That depends. You were married seven years ago, but county records show that the house you and your husband live in, the one on Robert Lane, was purchased only six years ago. Is that correct?"

"Yes. Paul always loved that house, but it didn't come on the market until after we were married."

"Excellent," Helga said.

"But we bought it with his funds," Ali objected. "I never could have afforded—"

"Doesn't matter," Helga interrupted. "He purchased it after your marriage. It appears to be held as community property now. And you say your husband loves the house?"

"Adores it."

"That's nice to hear. It should give us a bit of a bargaining chip. Generally speaking, the more the other side likes something, the better it is. So what brought you to this pass, Mrs. Reynolds? In my experience people don't go to the trouble of consulting with a divorce attorney unless they've already pretty much decided the marriage is broken."

"It is broken," Ali said, but she was thinking of Reenie breaking her scheduled appointment with the lawyer in Flagstaff. "And my name is Ali," she added.

"Very well, Ali," Helga corrected. "So tell me. What went wrong? Domestic violence, drugs, girlfriends, or boyfriends?"

"Girlfriends," Ali said. "His, not mine. They've

been around for a while, I suppose. For a long time I turned a blind eye to how 'busy' he was with work and put up with them, but now that one of his 'projects' is telling people she and my husband are going to get married . . ."

"I understand you lost your job last week," Helga asked.

"That's true."

"Isn't that station an affiliate of the network that employs your husband?"

"Yes."

"And isn't he some kind of network bigwig for them?"

"That's right."

"Did he know they were going to let you go?" Helga asked.

"Probably," Ali said. "I can't imagine that they wouldn't have told him. According to them, it was all ratings. Paul lives and breathes ratings."

"Did he happen to mention any of that to you in advance? I mean, did he give you any kind of a heads-up?"

"No," Ali said. "He didn't."

Helga clicked her tongue. "There are some cases I like better than others," she said. "From what you're telling me, Mr. Paul Grayson sounds like a not so nice man who needs to be taken down a peg."

Ali laughed in spite of herself. "Yes," she said. "I suppose he is."

"If that's what you want," Helga said, "it would be my pleasure to take him on. Do you happen to have a fax machine where you are? That way I can fax over some forms for you to fill out. Don't worry about all the gory financial details. I'll be able to get all that. I have a forensic accounting firm that I hire to track down financial dealings that unsuspecting spouses often know nothing about. My guys are expensive," she added. "But they're very, very good."

"Can you just e-mail them to me?" Ali asked. "I have a printer but no fax."

"Sure," Helga said. "No problem. What's the address."

Ali gave it to her. After ringing off, she sat for a long time, watching Samantha watch her. "Well, Sam," she said at last, "it looks as though both our lives have changed. Before I was just *talking* about getting a divorce. Now I'm really doing it."

Turning back to the computer, Ali looked for Helga's e-mailed forms. Scanning her in-box she was surprised to find that several new e-mails had arrived in response to her last posting a short time earlier:

Dear Ms. Reynolds,

What's the matter with you? Why don't you like cats? Are you one of those people who only likes dogs? I was bitten by a dog once when I was little. I have NEVER been bitten by a cat.

Janelle

My mother had ALS. She told my father that she didn't want to live that way. She asked him to fix it for her and he did. The judge sent him to prison for twenty years. He has never seen his grandchildren. I lost both of my parents. It is so unfair.

Phyllis

Dear Ali,

My husband had plenty of time for his girlfriend and his big screen TV and no time at all for me. When I left, I gathered up every clicker in the house and dropped them into his other baby, his 250-gallon aquarium. The clickers were still glowing like pretty little lavender goldfish when I left, but I bet they didn't glow for long.

Tami

Wish I had thought of that, Ali told herself silently with a rueful smile.

Dear Ali,

Maybe everybody is calling it a suicide, but I bet the husband did it—that he killed her and only made it LOOK like suicide. I know. I have a sixth sense about these things. Please be very careful when you are around him. He could be a danger to you and the children.

Maxine

PS When the husband goes to jail for murder, will you take care of the kids and the cat? Somebody has to do it, and the grandparents are most likely too old.

That one sent a chill down Ali's body. From the beginning, Ali had objected to the idea that Reenie had committed suicide. And an accident seemed unlikely. Who in their right mind would attempt to drive Schnebly Hill Road in the middle of a snowstorm? Ali had never consciously allowed herself to consider the logical alternative—homicide—but now she did. There was some part of her—some dark place she hadn't ever encountered before—that knew Maxine was right—that Reenie Bernard had been murdered. But how? And was Howie responsible?

Possibly. Maybe he and his girlfriend weren't interested in waiting around long enough for ALS to run its inevitable course. Or maybe there were insurance policies to take into consideration. Certainly there would be far more money left over for Reenie's beneficiaries if her death came suddenly rather than as a result of a long debilitating illness complete with staggering hospital bills. And speaking of insurance, how much was there? And did it all go to Howie? Who else? And if Maxine was right, and Howie went to prison for murder, who would take care of the kids?

Ali reached into her pocket, pulled out a business card Bree Cowan had pressed into Ali's hand earlier that morning, and called.

"Thank you so much for taking care of Sam," Bree said as soon as Ali reached her on her cell. "From what my mother says, she and Dad wouldn't have been able to pry Matt out of the house if you hadn't come to the rescue."

"Sam's no trouble," Ali said. And that was true.

The cat had yet to set paw outside the open door of her cage.

"What can I do for you?" Bree asked.

Ali wasn't sure where to start. "I was just wondering if you knew anything about Reenie's insurance situation?"

"Life insurance?" Bree asked. "I know she has some, if that's what you mean. Dad saw to it that we had life insurance, and our husbands, too. I heard Jack and Howie joking one time that as soon as they got home from the honeymoon, Dad set them up with his insurance guy."

"Do you know how much insurance is in force?" Ali asked.

Bree paused. "Not exactly, but I'm guessing it'll be fairly substantial amounts. I'm sure Howie and the kids will be well provided for, if that's what you're worrying about."

"What about guardianship?" Ali asked.

"There's no question about that, of course," Bree replied. "None at all. Matt and Julie go to their father."

"And if something were to happen to Howie? Then what?"

"Then Matt and Julie come to Jack and me," Bree said. "But let's hope to God that never happens. I always suspected I wasn't motherhood material, but this morning was proof positive. I almost lost it with Matt outside in the snow and Julie bawling her eyes out while I was trying to braid her hair. I know my limitations. It was awful."

"You were fine," Ali assured her. "There was a lot going on. The kids were upset."

"Thanks for saying that."

"What do you hear from Howie?" Ali asked.

"Nothing," Bree said. "Why do you ask?"

"I went by this afternoon before I came back to Sedona, and he still wasn't home. I was wondering how the interview went."

"If I hear from him, should I have him call you?" Bree asked.

"No," Ali said. "Don't bother." She started to hang up, then changed her mind. "One more thing," she added. "What bank did Reenie use?"

"Bank?" Bree returned.

"Yes. I was talking to Andrea at the YW, and she mentioned that Reenie was planning on stopping by the bank on her way home from seeing the doctor. I was wondering if you happened to know which one she might have used."

"Why?" Bree asked.

"I don't know," Ali said. "Maybe I'm way off base here. I just wanted to talk to someone who may have talked to Reenie after she saw the doctor. Just to know how she was, is all. Does that sound crazy?"

"No," Bree said. "Not crazy. It sounds like someone who cares about what happened. I'm pretty sure they use Bank of America. That's where we all ended up once the mergers finished. I have no idea which branch she would have used. There must be dozens of B of A branches between the Mayo Clinic in Scottsdale and Flag. She could have stopped at any one of them. It won't be any trouble for Howie to find out which one, though. All he'll have to do is contact the toll-free number and ask about recent activity on his account."

"Thanks, Bree," Ali said. "I'll ask him the next time I see him."

If I don't punch his lights out first.

By the time Ali got off the phone, Helga's e-mail had arrived. Ali downloaded the forms, printed them, and began filling them out, but she couldn't concentrate. Her mind kept being drawn back to the responses that had come in earlier.

She had written one thing and, within minutes, other people had replied, adding their own frame of reference or perspective to what Ali had written before. They wrote personal things. Private things. They wrote about feelings they might not have mentioned to their own family members. How come? What caused that?

Obviously what had happened in Reenie's family was a tragedy. Unfortunately, it wasn't nearly as unique as Ali would have hoped. The same was true of Ali's own marital misfortunes. And the anonymity of the Internet, the very thing that made Ali free to say what she wanted, was also what gave her readers permission to send back their own private thoughts and comments.

It was, Ali thought, a bit like driving past a car wreck and being incredibly grateful that it had happened to someone else and not to you. Even though you tried to keep your eyes averted and give the unfortunate victims some privacy, you couldn't help but peek and you couldn't help but be grateful that it wasn't your car wreck—it was somebody else's. And maybe that gratitude was part of the reason people felt compelled to write.

At the station there had always been a delayed

response between what was said and what the viewers said back. This was far more immediate. It was also far more personal. Putting her fingers to the keyboard, Ali wrote an additional post of her own. She had to.

I spent lots of years in the news business, most of it in television news and sitting at an anchor desk one place or another. When it's time to film a new set of station promos, news anchors usually resort to saying something trite about having "conversations" with their viewers. This is actually a lie. The word "conversation" implies dialogue—as in talking back and forth. What anchors do is deliver "monologues" to their viewers. By their very nature, monologues are far less inclusive than "conversations."

What I'm having right now on cutlooseblog.com is an actual conversation. I put up a post at 2:20 P.M. Within minutes there were several responses from people who weighed in with their own opinions.

The one from Phyllis is heartbreaking. Her family lost both of their parents in a situation not too different from Reenie's. As a result, Phyllis's entire family was destroyed. Her e-mail makes me wonder. Shouldn't people who are ill and dying have some say in what's going to happen to them and how their last days on earth are to be lived? Shouldn't there be some allowance made for self-determination when it comes to last wishes?

Tami and her drowning clickers made me laugh. It's something I wish I had thought to do. I could have. My husband had clickers everywhere.

And then there's Maxine. Even though everyone else seems to be convinced Reenie committed suicide, Maxine is concerned that she was murdered. She's also worried that I, too, may be in danger. Thank you for worrying about me, Maxine, and rest assured that I'll be keeping a sharp eye out.

And finally there's Janelle. She's not worried about me or about the kids. Her concern is for the cat, Samantha, who's still sitting here in her cage, regarding me with that one huge yellow eye of hers. But Janelle wouldn't even know Samantha existed if it weren't for the Internet and for the powerful way it connects people and brings them together.

I have no idea where Phyllis, Maxine, and Janelle live. They could be right here in Sedona or in some distant corner of the country. Or the world. I just want to say to all of them, and to anyone else reading this: Thank you for sending your responses and comments. They make me feel like I'm less alone. They make me understand that even people who never met Reenie are capable of caring about her.

Thank you.

Posted, 4:35 P.M. by AliR

After that, Ali took a long dip in Aunt Evie's pride and joy, the soaking tub in the master bath. Lying there amid a mound of bubbles Ali realized that her Aunt Evie's home, complete with all its upscale bells and whistles—wine cellar, soaking tub, and all—wasn't what members of the media elite and Paul Grayson in particular had in mind when they talked derisively about mobile homes and trailer trash. They had no real concept of what the homes were like and very little connection to the ordinary people who lived in them.

She was back in the living room and slowly making her way through Helga's multipage form when Edie Larson arrived at the front door, carrying a steaming Crockpot and bringing with her the mouth-watering aroma of cooking meat. After setting the dish on the kitchen counter and plugging it into a wall socket, Edie returned to the living room and bent down to study the open traveling crate Samantha had yet to abandon.

"She still won't come out?" Edie asked.

"Nope," Ali answered. "I took a long bath and left her alone for the better part of an hour, but she still hasn't budged."

"In that case," Edie said. "It's time to take the bull by the horns."

She reached into the crate, grasped the startled cat by the nape of her neck and pulled her out. At first, Sam struggled and tried to escape, but Edie didn't let go. She held the animal firmly against her chest and then eased herself down onto the sofa with the cat still in her arms. Within a matter of seconds, Sam settled down against her, purring loud enough that Ali could hear her all the way across the room.

"You always did have a way with animals," Ali said.

"Being married to your father made that a necessity," Edie said with a smile. "And Sam will be fine now. She just needed to know she was welcome here. Which is more than I can say about you. You don't look fine at all. It's hitting you pretty hard, isn't it."

Nodding, Ali looked at her mother. Edie's naturally silver hair was pulled back in a French roll that was held in place by a collection of antique combs. She had worn her hair that way for as long as Ali could remember. So had Aunt Evie.

"I can't believe Reenie's gone," Ali said.

"I wasn't talking about Reenie," Edie said. "What about Paul? Were you ever going to tell us about that?"

Edie had her there. Ali had done her best to avoid the issue of her broken marriage. Now she was stuck. "I just wasn't ready to talk about it, but I guess Chris spilled the beans."

"He didn't have to," Edie said.

"What do you mean?"

"I mean Evie and I had Paul Grayson figured out a long time ago—before we went to London even. It was clear to everyone early on that it wasn't working—everyone but you, that is."

"I wanted it to work," Ali said.

"Of course you did," Edie agreed. "And why not? You're not the first mother who spent years making the best of a bad bargain in hopes of maintaining some kind of financial security for her kids. And, if you weren't your father's daughter, you would have been out of it years ago."

"What does Daddy have to do with this?" Ali asked.

Edie smiled. "Have you ever heard the man say he was wrong? And you're exactly like him, Ali. Spitting image. First you let Paul Grayson sweep you off your feet, and then, because you didn't want to admit you'd made a mistake, you tried to make the best of it—for years, and at a great cost to yourself, I might add."

Edie eased Sam out of her lap. Once on the floor, the cat shook her paws—as though the carpet somehow didn't measure up to her expectations—then she stalked off to the far corner of the room and curled up in a corner next to the drapes.

Ali gave a rueful laugh. "So is that what you've been doing down at the Sugarloaf ever since I left this morning—you and Dad and Jan and Chris and anyone else who happened to come in the door—discussing me and my marital difficulties?"

"No," Edie returned. "We didn't, but I'm here to discuss it now. I think it's about time you and I had a heart-to-heart chat. It sounds like you could use one."

Considering the circumstances, it turned out to be a very nice dinner. Ali cracked open a bottle of Aunt Evie's Seven Deadly Zins to accompany Edie's pot roast. And they talked. Or rather, Ali talked and her mother listened, all the while passing tiny tidbits of roast to Sam who had positioned herself next to Edie's feet under the table.

In the presence of her mother's unconditional

acceptance, Ali felt her own emotional wall crumbling. Tears she had somehow held in abeyance for days came on with a vengeance as she spilled out the whole tawdry story. Between Monday and now she had shed plenty of tears for Reenie Bernard. The tears she shed that evening were for Alison Reynolds.

When eight o'clock rolled around, Edie stood up. "I've got a four A.M. wake-up call, so I'd best head home."

After Edie left, Ali sat on the couch thinking. Her parents were absolutely grounded. They clearly loved one another and they also loved Ali. So how was it that, coming from such a stable background, Ali had managed to make such a mess of her own life? How could she possibly have mistaken Paul Grayson's phony promises for the real thing, and how could she have convinced herself to settle for whatever crumbs he was offering? *Maybe I only think I'm from Sedona*, she told herself. *Maybe I'm really from Stepford.*

Ali was half asleep when a ringing telephone startled her awake. "Mom?" Chris asked.

She could tell from the quake in his voice that something was wrong. "What is it?"

"It's Grandpa."

"What's happened? Is he hurt?"

"Yes, he's hurt. Some hotshot snowboarder crashed into him from behind and sent him flying. The ski patrol just got him down off the slopes. They're loading him into an ambulance right this minute to take him to Flagstaff."

"How bad is it?" Ali asked.

"Pretty bad," Chris said. "At least one broken leg, maybe two. And a broken arm as well. I just got off the phone with Grandma. She's on her way."

"So am I," Ali said. "Where are they taking him?"

"Flagstaff Community."

"I'll be there as soon as I can."

Chapter 9

All the way from Sedona back to Flag, Ali should have been worrying about her father. Instead, she thought about Howie Bernard. Had he murdered his wife? The idea of a mild-mannered history professor suddenly turned killer seemed unlikely. Still, Ali knew that extramarital affairs and the possibility of collecting sizeable sums of life insurance proceeds had turned more than one otherwise law-abiding citizen into a murderer. And in a town where university professors carried a fair amount of social clout, would the cops charged with solving the case give Howie Bernard any more than a cursory glance?

Somehow Ali doubted that would be the case. The detective who had collected the computer from Reenie's office had taken the machine, but Ali had seen no evidence that they had dusted for prints. They were still focused entirely on the suicide angle. The fact that it might be something worse than that seemed not to have occurred to them. But it had to Ali, and the more she thought about it, the more she wanted to talk to Howie. Alone. And preferably unannounced. She wanted to catch him off guard and see if he might say something to her that would tip his hand.

Speeding all the way, Ali arrived at Flagstaff Community Hospital far sooner than she should have. Even so, Edie beat her there. By the time Ali walked into the waiting room, Bob Larson already had been rolled away to surgery. A subdued Chris sat quietly off to one side while Edie Larson fumed and paced.

"That man doesn't have a lick of sense," she raged. "If I've told your father once, I've told him a hundred times, he's too old for snowboarding!"

"Snowboarding!" Ali exclaimed. "I thought they were going skiing."

"That's what he *said* they were going to do," Edie replied. "But Bob's a great one for telling me what he thinks I want to hear rather than what's really going on. And if he got hit by a snowboarder, I'm guessing that's what he was doing, too, snowboarding, the bird-brained dim-bulb."

Ali looked at her son who shrugged his shoulders in silent confirmation of his grandmother's worst suspicions. He and his grandfather had indeed been snowboarding.

"And of all the weeks for him to pull a stunt like this!" Edie railed on. "Why didn't he just haul out a gun and shoot himself?"

"Calm down, Mom," Ali said. "What's so different about this week?"

"With everything else that's been going on, we haven't had a chance to tell you, but your father and I are thinking of retiring. We've got a potential buyer who's supposed to come look at the restaurant sometime this week. We'll be able to hold out for a lot more money if we're selling the place as a going concern. If Dad's laid up and the buyer thinks your father's on his last legs—or on no legs at all, from the sound of it—it'll be a lot tougher to make the kind of deal we want to make."

"In other words, you can't shut the place down just because Dad's in the hospital."

"Of course I can't shut the place down," Edie snapped. "I can't even afford to open up late. It needs to be business as usual. In fact, I should be home in bed right this minute so I can be up at four to start baking sweet rolls. When the restaurant's actually open, I can cook every bit as well as Bob can, but where on God's green earth does he expect me to find someone to fill in for me out front? I'll never be able to find someone dependable on such short notice, and Jan's too old to manage the whole place on her own. It'll be a disaster."

"I could do it," Ali suggested. The words were out of her mouth without her necessarily thinking about them, just as they had been when she had offered to look after Samantha.

Edie stopped in mid rant. "You?" she asked in disbelief. "Come on, Ali. It must be twenty years since you last waited tables."

"It's probably a lot like riding a bicycle, isn't it?" Ali returned. "Once you learn, you never forget how. Besides, as far as I can tell, you haven't changed the menu. Looks like the same old same old to me."

"But—" Edie began.

Ali cut off her mother's objection. "Look, Mom,

if I can look after Matt and Julie's kitty, I can certainly help you out. At least until you find someone better."

"I just thought . . ."

"You think I'm too good to wait tables?" Ali asked.

"Well, yes," Edie admitted.

"I'm not. Your owning and running the Sugarloaf was good enough to keep a roof over our heads when I was growing up and when I was going to NAU. Helping you and Daddy out now that you're in a pinch is the least I can do. Besides, the station's still sending me a paycheck until the end of my contract. That'll make me the highest-priced waitress the Sugarloaf has ever seen."

"But shouldn't you be out looking for another job?"

"You mean shouldn't I be looking out for me instead of looking out for you?"

"Well, yes," Edie agreed reluctantly. "I suppose that is what I mean."

Ali went over to her mother and gathered her into her arms. "You and Dad raised me better than that, Mom. This is payback."

When Edie emerged from her daughter's embrace, her eyes were bright with tears. "All right, then," she said. "You're hired. But only for the short term and only until I can find someone else. Assuming I manage to open the restaurant tomorrow morning, you can start then."

They settled in to wait for Bob to return from surgery. Being back in a hospital setting made Ali uncomfortable. It brought back too many bad memories of the days and weeks she'd spent with

Dean, and her waiting skills were shaky at best. She tried to sit still, but couldn't. She kept looking at her watch, twitching, and willing the surgery to be over so she could leave. Finally Edie lost patience.

"Look, Ali," she said. "There's no sense in both of us sitting here fidgeting. Go for a walk or for a ride or else bring Chris something to eat. Doing what you're doing is driving me nuts."

"I could do with some Kentucky Fried Chicken," Chris said. "I saw one not too far from here."

They drove through the cold, clear night to a steamy and almost deserted KFC. After the man behind the counter took their order for one bucket of Original, Ali changed her mind and ordered a second.

"Mom," Chris objected. "I'm hungry, but I'm not that hungry."

"I want to stop by Reenie's place to check on Howie," she said. "There'll most likely be a crowd of people there who'll be as happy to see some KFC as you are."

She dropped Chris back at the hospital and then headed for Kachina Trail. Once outside the Bernard place she was surprised to find that the expected gathering of friends and neighbors hadn't materialized. There were no other vehicles parked anywhere nearby—not in front of the garage and not out on the street, either. The windows were uniformly dark. The only sign of occupancy was a single porch light burning on the front porch.

He's probably not even home, Ali told herself. *I should have stayed at the hospital.*

Grabbing the fragrant bucket of chicken, Ali

made her way gingerly up the icy sidewalk past the dwindling snowman. The afternoon sun had diminished him even more, and now the snowman was little more than a knee-high ghost in the reflected glow of the porch light.

Sure she was on a fool's errand, Ali rang the bell. Seconds later, though, a light came on somewhere in the interior of the house, followed shortly thereafter by a lamp in the living room. The dead bolt clicked. When Howie opened the door to let Ali in, he was holding a cordless phone to his ear. He smiled in welcome and drew Ali inside before shutting the door behind her. He swayed slightly on his feet as he turned to go back into the house. His ungainly walk and the smell of liquor on his breath told Ali that he'd had at least one drink and probably several more than that.

"Your mother's friend Ali is here," he said into the phone. Then, after a pause, he added. "Just a minute. I'll ask her. It's Matt. He wants to know how Samantha is doing." The words slurred slightly and ran together.

"Tell him she's fine," Ali said. "She's out of her crate and making herself at home."

Without waiting for directions, Ali took the bucket of chicken out to the kitchen and set it on the counter. She and Diane Holzer had cleaned up the breakfast dishes earlier that morning. It appeared that the kitchen had remained unchanged since then. That probably meant that no one else had stopped by to visit with Howie, which struck Ali as odd. People usually rallied around bereaved spouses—even unfaithful ones—no matter what.

When she returned to the living room and took a seat on the couch, Howie was finishing up his phone call. "You be good now," he was saying. "Don't give Grandma and Grandpa any trouble. And I'll come get you soon. Tomorrow probably, or else the next day . . . Right . . . Love you, too. Good night, Matty. Talk to you tomorrow."

He put down the phone. He turned unsteadily in Ali's direction and gave her a boozy hug. "Thanks so much for coming," he mumbled. "After what I've been through the past few days and hours, it's good to see a friendly face."

"What's been going on?"

"The cops put me through hell today, that's what!" he said. "I didn't ask for an attorney at first because I didn't think I needed one. I thought they were just going to ask me a few routine questions like when did Reenie leave, what time was she supposed to get back, that kind of thing. And they did ask those things at first. But later on they came after me like gangbusters. They kept after me for hours on end, even though I told them I had an alibi, even after I offered to take a lie detector test—which I took and passed by the way—and even after that. From the way they treated me, I thought I was on my way to jail for sure. I was afraid I wasn't coming back."

"But you did," Ali interjected. "You're here."

"That's right. I am here! About an hour or so ago, they found Reenie's suicide note and suddenly everything changed to sweetness and light. Suddenly I'm no longer the scumbag husband/homicide suspect. Now it's 'yes, Mr. Bernard,' and 'no, Mr. Bernard,' and 'of course you're free to go, Mr. Bernard,' and all that happy crap.

"They found a note?" Ali asked.

Howie nodded. "In the car. Or in whatever's left of the car. They didn't find it until just a little while ago."

Ali felt numb. "What did it say?" she asked.

Howie shrugged. "That she couldn't face dragging it out. That this way would be better for all of us—that she wanted to spare us."

He paused long enough to wipe a tear from the corner of his eye, but Ali was having a hard time sorting out the conversation. Was Howie Bernard grieving for his dead wife or for himself. It was hard to tell. Maybe it was a little of both.

"So it really was suicide?" Ali asked.

"Of course it was suicide," he replied. "What else could it have been?"

A bottle of Oban single malt scotch sat on the coffee table in front of them. Howie reached over, poured another generous shot or two into a tumbler-sized glass, and nodded. "At least now I can go ahead and plan the funeral. It'll be Friday, by the way. Two o'clock. At Reenie's old Lutheran church down in Cottonwood. She'll be buried there, too, in the family plot."

He stopped and looked at Ali a little fuzzily. "I'm forgetting my manners," he said. "Can I get you something? A drink? Some of that chicken you brought?"

Ali shook her head. "I'm fine," she said.

For several seconds, he stared morosely into his glass. "It's good of you to drop by, Ali. I really appreciate it. As for the rest of my so-called friends, who needs 'em? Where the hell were they when the cops were busy accusing me of putting Reenie in a car and running her off a cliff to get rid of her? I mean, just because . . ."

Even drunk he must have realized that he was rambling on more than he should have. He stopped.

"Because what?" Ali prodded eventually.

"Nothing," he muttered. "Not important."

"It is important," she insisted. "Tell me."

Howie gave her an odd look. Finally he answered. "Reenie and I may have been having our little difficulties, but for them to think that I'd kill her . . . it's utterly pre . . . pre . . . preposterous." It took three tries before he managed to get his tongue around the word.

"What kind of difficulties?" Ali asked the question without really expecting an answer.

"Oh, you know," he said, waggling his glass. "The usual thing—a bit of a rough patch. We might have got through it, or it could be we would have ended up in divorce court, but then, when the bombshell dropped about her health . . . You know about that—about the ALS?"

"Yes," Ali said. "I know."

"Godawful stuff, ALS," he continued. "But what I can't understand is why she did it now. She wasn't that sick, at least not yet. She could still drive. She was probably just making a point."

Ali was surprised to hear Howie voice his own doubts about the suddenness of Reenie's departure.

"You thought she was going to stay to fight?"

"That's what she said," Howie replied.

"And what did you mean when you said she was making a point?"

"She was mad at me," Howie continued. "Furious. We barely spoke the last two weeks, but I had no idea . . ."

"You quarreled?" Ali asked.

"She was talking about going to Mexico to try out some new treatment. Something with supplements that the FDA hasn't approved yet and may not ever approve. It's expensive as hell and not covered under our insurance. I told her it was too risky and probably a waste of time and money."

"Risky?" Ali asked. "She was dying anyway. How risky could a treatment be, especially if there was even the smallest chance it would help?"

"Well, then, a rip-off maybe. I've heard of all kinds of quacks who've set up phony treatment centers. They take people's money. When it's gone, they put their patients either in a pine box or on a bus and ship them home."

So we're back to the money, Ali thought. *Reenie wanted to try some new treatment, and Howie said no—solely to keep from having to spend the money.*

"Do you know anything about this treatment center?" Ali asked. "Where it is? What it costs?"

"A one-time payment of eighty-thousand bucks," Howie muttered, staring into his almost empty glass. "And you know what you get for all that dough? Not a cure, that's for sure. Probably just the symptoms slowed down for a couple of months and a few extra months at the back end, but for part of that time she wouldn't even be here. She'd have to be in the treatment center."

"Where is it?"

"Down there someplace. In Mexico. Guayamas. Mazatlan. I don't remember, really. It's one of those little beach towns."

"Do you remember the name of the facility?"

"She didn't go there," Howie said very slowly and carefully as if explaining a difficult concept Ali was too stupid to understand. "She wasn't *ever* going to go there. I told her flat out that we couldn't afford it, and that was the truth. Besides, the whole thing was a rip-off and a fraud. Why should I remember the name?"

He was starting to sound surly, and Ali decided it was time to try a different approach. "I talked to Andrea Rogers," she said.

"I did, too," Howie said. "She's broken up about this, poor woman, completely broken up."

"Andrea says she talked to Reenie after her doctor's appointment on Thursday," Ali said. "According to her Reenie said she was planning to stop by the bank on her way home. Do you have any idea which one?"

"B of A," Howie managed. "The detective already asked me all about it. I tried to help. Called the bank to check, but there wasn't any activity on Thursday afternoon—not on any of our accounts or on any of our credit cards, either. That's not true. She was at a Hallmark store in Scottsdale, but that was before her appointment not after it. But as far as her doing something in a bank branch? *Nada!* Nothing! Zippo!"

He smiled wryly and poured himself another drink.

"Tell me about the note," Ali said. "What was it like?"

"I already told you . . ."

"I mean what kind of paper was it on?"

"Paper?" Howie asked with a scowl. "Regular computer paper."

"So it was done on a computer?" Ali asked.

"Didn't I just say that?" he asked irritably. "Yes, it was written on a computer and printed on ordinary computer paper. They found it folded up and stuck in a crack between the seat and the frame. How it kept from flying out, nobody knows. If it had fallen out into the snow it probably never would have been found because it was white, you see." He paused and then looked at Ali. "Why do you want to know?"

How long had Reenie and Howie been married? Ali wondered. *Ten years at least. So how was it possible that he knew so little about his wife? Reenie had been to a Hallmark store that day. She would have found a card, the perfect blank card, and used that to say her good-byes.*

"So she must have gone back to the office after all," Ali murmured. "After Andrea left for the day. Did they find the file on her computer?"

"No, Farris—that's the detective—said she probably deleted it after she printed it. They're sending the computer off somewhere. Phoenix, I think. He said something about scanning the hard drive for recently deleted files. But I'm sure that's why she did it the way she did. To show me. All I can say, though, is, thank God she left the note. If it hadn't been for that I'd probably be in jail tonight, instead of sitting here at home drinking scotch."

Ali had never liked Howard Bernard much. She'd tried to get along with him, for Reenie's sake. For friendship's sake. But it was hard to endure this rambling and maudlin exercise in self-pity especially since he was clearly far more sorry for himself than he was for Reenie. Or the kids.

A pair of headlights turned into the driveway, an engine switched off, and a car door opened and closed.

"Hey," Howie said, brightening suddenly. "Looks like somebody's stopping by after all."

Clearly pleased, he struggled to rise from the sofa, but before he had time to shamble across the room, a key turned in the lock and the overhead light switched on. To Ali's amazement, a young dark-haired woman stepped into the room, closing the door behind her as if she owned the place.

"Howie," she said, meeting him halfway across the room and giving him a kiss that was anything but neighborly. "Sorry I'm late."

Over Howie's shoulder, the woman must have caught sight of Ali. "Oh," she said quickly, extricating herself from Howie's drunken embrace. "I'm sorry. I had no idea you had company. I should probably go."

"No problem," Howie said. "No problemo! This is Ali Reynolds, an old friend of the family come by to pay a condolence visit and buck me up." His slur was worse now. "And this is Jasmine, Ali. Jasmine Wright. She's a student of mine—an excellent student, by the way—one of my doctoral candidates."

Jasmine's name registered in Ali's hearing and heart on the exact same frequency as April and

Charmaine's had. And the look on Ali's face was most likely something close to absolute fury.

A doctoral candidate with her own key to Reenie's house! Ali thought. *How very convenient!*

Jasmine Wright—Jasmine Wrong as Ali chose to think of her—was fairly tall and willowy, but curvy in all the right places. She had olive skin, dark eyes, and very white teeth. Her skintight Spandex top ended a good six inches above her equally tight and low-cut jeans. She didn't look like any history major Ali ever remembered meeting, and as a package she was way more than a balding, paunchy, and married history professor could have expected—or deserved.

"Ali Reynolds," Ali said. Plastering a phony smile on her face, she stood and extended her hand in greeting. "Reenie and I were friends from high school on."

Howie launched off into his own unnecessarily expansive explanation. "Ali was Reenie's best friend," he enthused. "Can you believe it? She came all the way over from California to help out. The kids are in Cottonwood with Reenie's folks, and since I didn't know for sure what was going to happen today—if they were going to let me go or not—Ali was kind enough to take the kids' cat home with her. Sam, you know Sam, don't you?"

Jasmine nodded.

Why the hell am I stuck with Sam? Ali wondered suddenly. Surely someone else—somebody with a key to the house, for instance—could easily have stopped by to feed and check on Samantha.

While an oblivious Howie droned on, the two

women regarded one another with wary speculation.

"How very nice," Jasmine said with a careful smile, but in a tone that clearly meant she didn't think it was nice at all.

"Under the circumstances," Ali said coolly, "it's the least I could do."

"The usual?" Howie asked, turning to Jasmine with an effusive smile. In return, Jasmine allowed him a curt nod. He headed for the kitchen, leaving the two women alone.

Entirely at home, Jasmine seated herself with casual grace on the hassock next to where Howie had been on the couch. The fact that she seemed totally comfortable and at ease in Reenie's house—in Reenie's living room, in a place whose every decoration Reenie had personally chosen and installed—sent Ali into a blazing fury.

"All of this has been very hard on him," Jasmine said.

"It's hard on everybody," Ali said pointedly. "Most especially Reenie."

Howie returned to the living room carrying a glass of white wine, which he handed to Jasmine, slopping the top third of it along the way. Then he sat back down heavily, picked up his own glass, and poured a little more scotch for himself. "There's chicken in the kitchen," he said. "Somebody must have brought it. Want some?"

Jasmine shook her head. Ali did a slow burn. Was Howie so drunk he didn't even remember who had brought the KFC?

"Funeral's Friday," he said to Jasmine. "Did I tell you already?"

She nodded. "You told me," she said.

"Oh," he muttered. "Sorry. And the kids are in Cottonwood?"

Jasmine nodded again.

She already knew that, too, Ali thought. *Long before she unlocked the door and came inside. That's why she's here, you dunce, for a quick roll in the hay while the kids are safely out of the way and so's your wife.*

Howie was drunk and repeating himself. If Jasmine wanted to hang around with someone that stewed, that was up to her, but Ali had reached the limit of her endurance. She rose to her feet. "Since you have someone here to keep you company," Ali said, "I should probably go."

"So soon?" Howie muttered, but he didn't bother trying to get up. Considering his condition, Ali knew that was just as well. Jasmine made no pretense of objecting to Ali's departure.

"I suppose I'll see you on Friday?" Ali asked her.

"Yes," Jasmine said. "I'll be there.

Ali hustled herself out the door before she could say or do anything more—before she slugged Howie in the kisser and knocked Jasmine Wright onto her curvy little butt. Neither was an acceptable option.

As Ali drove away, she seethed with anger. While Reenie was busy dying, Howie had been screwing around. *Do the cops know about this?* she wondered. But more than that, more than anything, she wondered if Reenie had known.

It would have been tough enough dealing with

a terminal illness, but if she had somehow discovered Howie's betrayal as well . . . With all that going on, maybe committing suicide wasn't such a stretch after all.

Ali remembered what Andrea Rogers had said. "Not that I could have done anything to help, but at least we could have talked. She wouldn't have been so alone."

"Reenie, Reenie, Reenie," Ali whispered under her breath as she drove. "If you didn't call Andrea, why didn't you call me?"

Chapter 10

Back at the hospital, Ali learned that with Bob out of surgery and safely in the recovery room, her mother was ready to head back to Sedona. Ali offered to walk her out to the car.

"Are you all right?" Edie asked. "You look upset."

"I am upset," Ali said. "I just met Howie Bernard's girlfriend."

"Oh, that," Edie said.

Ali was shocked. "You mean you knew about it?"

"There were rumors floating around," Edie responded.

"How long?" Ali asked. "Since before Reenie was diagnosed?"

Edie nodded. "Long before that," she said. "I think I heard about it sometime last fall. From Jody Sampson, one of the ladies in Garden Club. Jody claimed one of her friends had run into him at a hotel down in Phoenix when she went there for a flower show. Howie was there with one of his students. According to Jody, what the two of them were studying had nothing to do with history."

"Did Reenie know about it?" Ali asked.

"Did you know about what Paul was doing?" Edie asked, effectively turning the question back on her daughter.

It was far too easy for Ali to put herself in Reenie's place. Easy to see how, with two small children in the picture, Reenie might have chosen to turn a blind eye on her husband's infidelity in order to protect Matt and Julie; in order to keep from rocking the boat. But once it was so blatant that she couldn't ignore it any longer, she had gone looking for an attorney. And, according to Andrea, Reenie had canceled the appointment as soon as her diagnosis was confirmed.

"See you tomorrow," Ali said without answering. "Drive carefully."

With Chris there to look after his grandfather, Ali left the hospital shortly thereafter as well. All the way home she stewed about the fact that Edie had known more about what had been going on in Reenie's life than Ali had.

What about the cops? Ali wondered. *Did Detective Farris know about Jasmine Wright? Was that one of the reasons the interview with Howie had taken the better part of the day?*

In the end, though, Farris must have accepted the supposed suicide note at face value. He had let Howie go; let him come home. Maybe Howie had some kind of airtight alibi. *But does Jasmine?* Ali wondered. *And isn't the female of the species deadlier than the male?*

And now that Ali knew about Jasmine, what was she going to do about her? In the blog, Ali had openly discussed the various aspects of Reenie's situation, but she couldn't very well add Jasmine into the mix.

Ali already knew that Matt had read the newspaper account of his mother's death and had come up with the information that Reenie had most likely committed suicide. Wasn't it possible that Matt was computer savvy enough that he might stumble upon Ali's blog as well. That meant she had to avoid making any mention of what she had learned this evening, including the existence of Howie Bernard's mistress. Ali was determined that, if Matt and Julie were ever to learn about their father's infidelity, the information would have to come from someone other than Ali Reynolds.

She was still half mad about being unnecessarily stuck taking care of Sam when she let herself into the house and found the cat draped comfortably across the back of the sofa as if she owned the place. Sam blinked her one eye, but she didn't move from her perch, and Ali left her undisturbed.

Ali undressed and went to bed but not to sleep. She was still too wound up by everything she had learned. Besides, her body had spent decades living on the night shift. A sleepless hour and a half after going to bed, Ali finally gave up, crawled back out of bed, and busied herself at the computer, writing the next morning's post.

cutlooseblog.com
Wednesday, March 16, 2005

Yesterday's Ides of March wasn't a whole lot better for me, my family, and for my dead friend's family than a long-ago Ides of March was for Julius Caesar. It started out with me visiting Reenie's children.

It ended with my father in the hospital undergoing multiple surgeries to set broken bones after a serious snowboarding accident. Dad's going to be fine, but he's also going to be off work for the foreseeable future.

My parents have owned and run the Sugarloaf Café in Sedona, Arizona, for as long as I can remember. My father is in charge of the kitchen. My mother does the baking before the restaurant opens, then she switches roles and waits tables. Since my mother is standing in for my dad, someone has to stand in for her.

When I was in high school and college I waited tables at the Sugarloaf. Since they're in desperate need of a pinch hitter at the moment, I've volunteered. That means I'm going to have to rise and shine very early in the morning, and I don't know how well I'm going to do. Check with me tomorrow afternoon. Make that THIS afternoon. And if I don't have enough energy left over to log on to cutloose in the foreseeable future, don't be surprised.

Posted 12:05 A.M. by AliR

She went back to bed after that and still couldn't sleep. Lying there her mind mulled over all she had learned. From what Howie had said, it sounded as though the investigating police officers were more than happy to latch on to the suicide theory and be done with it. But Ali wasn't.

The very fact that Reenie had been exploring the treatment program in Mexico—fraudulent or not; effective or not—only served to reinforce what Ali already believed: Reenie's determined intention had been to fight ALS with everything she had and with every weapon at her disposal.

Regardless of whether or not Reenie had known about Jasmine Wright's cozy relationship with Howie, it must have been galling for her to have Howie tell her that they simply couldn't afford the proposed treatment.

Parsimonious bastard! Ali thought. Howard Bernard was looking out for Howard first and foremost. What was good for his bank account was good for him, regardless of what was good for Reenie. It would leave him that much more to spend on Jasmine later on.

And who the hell is Jasmine Wright anyway? Ali wondered. *Where does she come from? And how much of a proprietary interest does she have in Howie Bernard's future?*

That brought Ali back to the note. The printed note. A note with no corresponding document file on Reenie's computer. If it was printed, that meant it wasn't signed. Anyone could have written it, printed it, and concealed it in Reenie's car. Two people stood in the way of that note being automatically accepted as the gospel—Andrea Rogers and Ali Reynolds. But Andrea had already tried stating her objection only to be soundly ignored by Detective Farris. *That means he probably won't listen to me, either,* Ali thought.

Eventually, Ali drifted off to sleep. But she didn't sleep well. In her dreams Howie and Jasmine were getting married, and Ali was the matron of honor but the flower girl came down the aisle tossing out handfuls of bread-and-butter pickles instead of rose petals. That dream was still close to the surface of Ali's consciousness when the alarm sounded less than three hours later. Even though it felt like the middle of the night and she was more tired now than when she went to bed, Ali couldn't help laughing as she made her way into the shower. The last time she ever remembered dreaming about pickles, she had been pregnant with Chris.

Dressed, showered, and determined, Ali pulled into the Sugarloaf at six on the dot. Clearly Edie had made it up at four since the first thing Ali noticed as she stepped out of the Cayenne was the enticing aroma of freshly baked sweet rolls.

"You made it," Edie said with a smile as her daughter entered through the back door. "Extra sweatshirts are in the locker in the employee rest room."

Two minutes later, dressed in a sweatshirt two sizes too large for her, Ali picked up her order pad and a coffeepot and walked through the swinging door into her past—a past she had never expected to revisit.

By nine o'clock in the morning, her feet were killing her. That was about the time Detective Dave Holman slipped onto the end stool at the counter. "Heard about your dad," he said, as Ali poured coffee into his cup. "Is he going to be all right?"

"Eventually," Ali said. "But he's got bones broken in one ankle and in the other leg, too. In other words, he's going to be off work for some time."

"And you're pitching in?"

Ali nodded.

"Isn't that a bit of a come-down for you?' he asked.

Ali bit back a sharp remark. "No," she said coolly. "I believe it's called stepping up. What'll you have?"

Ali had thought that she might mention what she had learned about Howie and Jasmine Wright to the detective the next time she saw him. Once he made that comment, however, she wasn't about to tell him anything. If the cops didn't already know Howie was screwing around on Reenie, too bad. As Dave had pointed out the previous day, he and Ali were on opposite sides of the fence and unlikely to be either friends or allies.

It turned out to be a very long day. By the time Ali got home at three in the afternoon, she was dead tired. She lay down on the bed, planning to put her feet up for a few minutes. She awakened to a ringing telephone two hours later. In order to answer the phone Ali had to reach across Samantha, who was cuddled up next to her.

"I'm headed up to Flag to see your father and to give Chris a break," Edie said. "Want to ride along?"

Ali laughed. "Obviously you're a whole lot tougher than I am," she said. "My feet are killing me. I came home, dropped onto the bed, and fell sound asleep."

"I'm used to it," Edie told her. "That makes all the difference."

"Do you need me to ride along?" Ali asked. "I'll come with you if you want me to."

"I'm perfectly capable of driving myself back and forth to Flagstaff," Edie told her. "I've been doing it for years. Besides, you sound beat. You should probably stay home."

Feeling guilty, Ali allowed herself to be convinced. Once off the phone, she forced herself off the bed and into the shower. Only then, did she go near her computer:

> Today has been a day for going back to my roots and for remembering any number of things that I didn't know I'd forgotten. There's the light, fluffy texture of my mother's award-winning sweet rolls and the aroma of bacon, eggs, and hash browns cooking on a hot grill. There's the heady smell of coffee when the hot water first hits the grounds. There's the feeling of relief when the last customer has finally walked out the door, the cash register has run off the day's receipts, and the last bag of trash has been hauled out to the Dumpster.
>
> But the main thing I had forgotten was just how hard the work of running a restaurant can be. Waiting tables in even a small-town diner is hard on your feet and on your back. It's also hard on your spirit. Doing it again after all this time has given me a whole new appreciation of what my parents and their former partner, my aunt Evie, have done all their adult lives, keeping alive the restaurant my grandmother started more than fifty years ago.
>
> Working in the Sugarloaf today has also made me value anew the work done by countless people in the food service industry all over this country. They're the men and women who every day, morning and evening, greet their customers cheerfully and

courteously. In the process of serving whatever food has been ordered, they also serve up something else. Along with bacon and eggs and hash browns, they dish up human connections and spiritual sustenance.

Being in the restaurant today was going back to my roots in another way, too. I was there as Bob and Edie Larson's daughter and not as some distant member of the media elite. Sedona is a small town. People who came in today gave me a break when I was slow to deliver their food. They understood and forgave the fact that my waitressing skills are more than a little rusty. Somehow they all knew that my father's been hurt, my mother needs help, and I was there to give it. I think my mother thought I'd consider the work beneath me. I know at least one of my customers thought so as well. But I'm comfortable being "daughter" at the moment. It suits me, and I'm glad I can be here to help.

Posted: 5 P.M., by AliR

With Samantha beside her on the couch, Ali began reading through the e-mailed comments that had come in since she had last checked.

Dear Ali,

When I used to see you on the news, I always thought your life was perfect. Now I know it isn't. Mine isn't either. Take care.

NoName

Dear Ms. Reynolds,

I was five when my dad took off and left my mother with three kids to raise on her own. I remember her telling me, "A woman without a man is like a fish without a bicycle." I never understood quite what that meant back then, but I do now. And she was right. We got along just fine. You'll be fine, too. By the way, we have the same name except I have two Ls and you only have one.

Allison

Dear Mrs. Reynolds,

I married my husband in the Temple, for now and all eternity. He has a girlfriend, too. I cry myself to sleep every night. I don't know what I did to cause it, but I won't give him a divorce, not ever. And you shouldn't either. What God has put together, let no man put asunder.

Rhonda

It's not just men. My wife had an affair with her professor. When she told me about it, she was laughing like she thought it was funny. I got so mad I put my fist through the wall. She called the cops and told them I was going to hit her. I wasn't, but she filed a restraining order against me. Now she has the house, and I can't even see my kids. I'm back home and living with my parents.

Alan

Ali paused a long time over that one. Was it possible that Jasmine Wright was married and this was a message from her husband? No, Ali decided, finally. That would have been too much of a coincidence, but it was interesting to have Alan's point of view and to realize that male victims of infidelity suffered just as much as their female counterparts did. The big difference for men was that they had fewer places to go to unload their troubles. They were expected to tough it out no matter what.

He gets to unload here, Ali thought, and shipped Alan's comment to The Forum.

Dear AliR,

Once you're unfortunate enough to step into the world of ALS you'll find it's a very small one. It's like you get on a road that only runs in one direction. When you start out, you meet others who are following the same path. You ask them for directions and suggestions, so you'll know what to expect along the way. Some people travel the road faster than others, so someone who started out late may leapfrog ahead of someone who was diagnosed earlier.

You don't know me, and I don't know you, but my sister, Lisa Kingsley, knew your friend Reenie. They met in an ALS chat room. At the time Reenie's diagnosis hadn't been confirmed, but she was looking for options. She wanted to know about the treatment Lisa was taking. It was very expensive, but I believe it helped Lisa for a while and I think she was encouraging Reenie to try it.

Lisa is gone now. I know you're grieving over your lost friend, but I can't help but think that perhaps Reenie made the right choice—for her, anyway. Living with ALS is hell. So is dying of it.

You and Reenie's family have all my best wishes and sympathy.

Louise Malkin
Lubbock, Texas

Ali read through that one several times, blinking tears from her eyes as she read. Finally, rather than posting it, she simply wrote back.

Dear Louise,

Thanks for being in touch, and thanks for your kind wishes. And please accept my condolences on the loss of your sister.

I'm curious about the kind of treatment Lisa was receiving and where. Can you tell me anything about it? I asked Reenie's husband but he wasn't able to tell me much other than he thought it was based somewhere in Mexico.

Regards,
Ali Reynolds

The next e-mail had no salutation and no subject line.

You are a bitch. Why would anyone want to hear what you think about anything? You want other women to be just like you and the one who threw her poor husband's remotes into the water. You must think that was a cute trick even though her husband probably had to work a long time to earn that equipment and she wrecked it just like that. I wouldn't let my two-year-old get away with that let alone my wife.

How dare you print such crap? How many women, with good, caring husbands, read your stupid blog and decide it's time to take their children and run? If my wife ever did that, I would beat her within an inch of her life.

Speaking of my wife. I know she has been visiting your site and you are putting bad ideas in her head. If she tries to leave me, I swear I'll come looking for you. Someone needs to pull the plug on you just like they did on your friend.

Watching

A chill passed over Ali's body as she read the words, and the fear she felt must have communicated itself to Samantha. The cat stopped purring abruptly, raised her mangled head, and peered warily around the room.

Ali read through the message again. This wasn't the first time she had received a written threat. You couldn't be in the news business in this day and age without people sending threats filled with vulgar language and simmering hatred.

For years Ali had driven home late at night, traversing LA's freeways at a time of day when there were plenty of nutcases on the road. She had taken the course work necessary to be given a license to carry, and she had her own slick little Glock 26 stowed in the bottom of her bright pink Coach handbag. It was there primarily because, at the time she and Chris were loading the Cayenne for the trip to Sedona, she hadn't taken the time to sort out the contents of her purse. Right now, though, she was glad it was there, and she was grateful that she'd spent time at a shooting range learning how to use it.

Ali glanced around the room and wondered about the thickness of the walls in Aunt Evie's manufactured home. *Would they stop a bullet?* she wondered. *And what about the hollow core metal door?* It had once seemed substantial enough, but now it looked lightweight and vulnerable. Would it be strong enough to withstand the charge of someone trying to push his way into the house?

It was one thing to receive that kind of threat when you were housed in a television station with security guards stationed all around and with cement bollards blocking the sidewalk entrances. And you didn't worry that much when you lived behind the tall electronically controlled gates of Paul Grayson's wall-enclosed mansion on Robert Lane, either. But when you and your son were staying alone in a mobile home parked at the very edge of town, high on an Arizona mountainside . . .

Ali understood that some of the people issuing those threats were nothing more than harmless kooks venting their spleens in a media world destined to ignore them. But others were definitely dangerous. Ali hadn't the slightest doubt that Watching was one of the dangerous ones.

Her next thought was to delete Watching's message and simply let it go, but after a moment of consideration, she didn't do that, either. Somewhere in the blogosphere was a defenseless woman with a two-year-old baby who was living with a very dangerous man—a man who was busily tracking the websites she visited and the messages she sent and received in the presumed privacy of her personal computer.

Through the years Ali had done numerous special appearances for YWCA events and for organizations dedicated to helping victims of domestic violence. As a result she had learned far more about the subject than she wanted to. Ali knew, for example, that the most dangerous time for abuse victims is just before or just after they make the decision to leave. That's the moment when, valid protection orders be damned, women are most likely to be slaughtered by their abusive mates.

And the mother of that two-year-old, deep in the misery of her awful marriage and desperately weighing her options, would have no clue that her husband knew exactly what she was doing, down to the last betraying keystroke.

That left Ali no real choice. She had no idea what the woman's name was or where she lived. Ali had no way of knowing if the woman in question was one of the blog correspondents whose words she had posted on the Web. Even though Ali knew the woman's e-mail address, writing to her directly would be far too risky. If Watching found something from Ali in his wife's incoming mail, he'd probably go berserk. On the other hand, if she posted Watching's e-mail to The Forum, there was a chance that perhaps the woman would read it and recognize it for what it was—a direct threat to her and to her child.

Ali shipped Watching's e-mail to The Forum and posted her own accompanying comment:

> On the day we take our wedding vows, most of us naively assume that our marriage really will last forever. We truly believe that whatever traps and problems that befall other couples and lead them to divorce courts won't happen to us. Because we're different. Because we REALLY love each other. Sometime later reality sets in and things go wrong. And what we thought didn't matter to us—staying out late with the guys, keeping in touch with old flames, becoming surly and controlling—turns out to matter a great deal.
>
> And once things do go wrong, bad marriages can be divided into two subcategories—survivable and deadly. Survivable bad marriages are where you come out with your kids, maybe some child support, and—hopefully—a shred of self-respect. The deadly ones are just exactly that—deadly. That's because one of the partners isn't prepared to let the other one go. One of these twisted individuals would rather see his (and yes, most of the people in this category are male) mate dead than see her living happily ever after with some other person.
>
> That kind of possessiveness exists in a world where everything is "my way or the highway." Men like

that enforce their iron will with ugly words and iron fists or else with knives or loaded weapons.

There are places where women in marriages like that can turn for help. You can find them listed under social services in your local phone book or on the Internet or at your local library. If you suspect that your husband or partner is tracking your computer keystrokes (The way the guy in the previous post is doing!), use the telephone. If he checks your outgoing cell phone calls, use a pay phone. And then, leave. Don't pack a bag. That might tell him in advance that you're planning on going, because that's the most dangerous time for you and your children. Once you make up your mind, he'll do whatever he can to stop you—and I do mean the most appalling of whatevers!!!

You'll be a refugee—a displaced person. In order to start over, you'll need documents. Stuff your important papers (children's birth certificates and shot records, marriage license, driver's license, social security cards, and divorce decrees) into your purse and then get the hell out. Trust me. Nothing you leave behind will be worth coming back for—NOTHING!! Go and don't look back. It'll be better for you and far better for your children.

Posted 7:52 P.M. AliR

Ali Reynolds had been reporting murder and mayhem for years, but always from a distance. Always from behind the camera with no personal involvement. Now, in a matter of days, that distance had dissolved. Suddenly she was drowning in other people's lives, and not just Reenie's suicide, either. The malevolence in Watching's message left her almost paralyzed with fear—and not just for herself, for the man's unsuspecting wife and child as well.

Within minutes, she heard the familiar announcement, "You've got mail." There were two new messages. The first one was harmless enough:

Dear Ali,

I'm sorry for your loss. You were lucky to have Reenie for a friend, and she was lucky to have you. Please take care.

barbaram

The second one was almost as chilling as Watching's had been:

Dear Ali,

Your post made me so sad. It reminded me of my lost friend, only her husband killed her. She was trying to get a divorce and had a protection order and everything, but he busted down the front door and shot her in front of her two little kids before she could get away. He's in prison now, but that doesn't make me feel any better.

Louise in Omaha

In Omaha, Ali thought. She had somehow envisioned that all the responses were coming from southern California and were a direct result of her having left TV news. That fact that someone from Omaha was reading her blog was surprising. And the message, such a striking counterpart to Watching's threat, left Ali feeling cold, alone, and very much afraid.

Chapter 11

Some time much later, a car pulled up beside the house. Ali, having dozed off with the computer on her lap, was startled awake when a car door slammed. When she hurried over to the window and peered out through the blinds, she was relieved to see her father's familiar red-and-white Bronco parked just behind her Cayenne. Chris was already jiggling the locked front door by the time she got there to open it.

"Since Grandma's there at the hospital visiting Gramps, I decided to come home long enough to shower and change clothes," Chris said. As soon as he stepped into the living room, Samantha leaped off the couch and disappeared behind it. "And who's that?" he added.

"Sam," Ali answered. "Matt and Julie Bernard's cat. She'll be staying for a while."

"She?" Chris asked.

"As in Samantha."

At first Ali had planned on telling Chris about Watching's threatening e-mail, but now she decided against it.

When he goes back to California, he'll be studying for

finals. Then in his last quarter of school, he'll need to concentrate on his studies rather than worry about me.

"What's the word on Grandpa?" she asked, as he prowled through the refrigerator, settling at last on Edie's leftover pot roast.

"They'll probably let him out tomorrow," Chris answered. "Grandma's not too happy about that. She thinks it's way too soon. He's going to be in a wheelchair—at least initially—and she has no idea how they'll manage. I don't either. Their house is tiny. The restaurant may be wheelchair accessible, but their house isn't. I can help for tomorrow, but the day after that I'm going to need to head home and start studying for finals. I ran into a guy up in Flag who's driving to LA on Friday. He offered me a ride, but that's the day of Reenie's funeral, so maybe I should stay on—"

"No," Ali said briskly. "You don't need to stay for the funeral, and you've already been a huge help. Take the ride and go. Your finals come first. Grandma and I will manage."

"But how?" Chris asked. "It's hard enough getting him in and out of the bathroom at the hospital. The one at their house is way smaller than that. There's no room to maneuver a wheelchair, and it doesn't have rails."

"We'll figure it out," Ali said.

The idea of her hale and hearty father suddenly stuck in a wheelchair and needing a handicap rail in order to use the bathroom took her aback. Bob and Edie Larson were the ones who were always delivering help to others. Now, through force of circumstance, they'd have to be on the receiving end. As disconcerting as it was to Ali, she knew it would be far worse for them.

Chris nuked a plate of food in the microwave and then disappeared into his room. A few minutes later he was back for seconds. While the second plate was heating in the microwave, he came over to the couch and sat down beside her.

"I looked at the site, Mom," he said seriously. "What are you going to do about Watching?"

"Nothing," Ali said. "I'm sure he's harmless."

"What if he isn't?" Chris asked. "With all your talk about Reenie and the Sugarloaf, it would be easy for him to track you down if that's what he decided to do."

"He won't," Ali said with more assurance than she felt.

"You probably should have used pseudonyms for the people in your blog," he said quietly. "That way, if someone goes off about something, it wouldn't be quite so easy to find you. Not only that," Chris added, looking around the room. "This place doesn't even have an alarm system."

"Aunt Evie never needed an alarm system," Ali told him.

"Aunt Evie wasn't writing a blog attracting nutcase readers," Chris countered.

"I'll look into it," Ali said. "I'll talk to someone and see how much an alarm system will cost."

It was no coincidence that she didn't mention the Glock in her purse. After all, Chris was her son, her baby. There was no reason to worry him.

After he left to return to Flagstaff and his hospital vigil, Sam emerged from her hiding place behind the couch and cuddled up next to Ali while she finished providing answers to Helga Myerhoff's e-mailed interrogatory. After that, she sat for a long time, thinking about Chris's concerns and some of her own as well. Finally she turned once again to her computer.

cutlooseblog.com
Thursday, March 17, 2005

Welcome to a brand-new day at cutlooseblog.com.

Cutloose is one of those tricky English language terms that has more than one meaning. On one side of the coin, cutting loose can mean going out and having fun—acting wild and crazy. On the other side, being cut loose means you've been shoved out of or away from something (a job or a marriage, maybe) when you didn't really want to go—like being shoved kicking and screaming out of an airplane, for example, with no real belief that the parachute somebody strapped on your body will actually work.

I worked in the news industry for a number of years. Now after passing the magic forty-year mark, I'm being "cut loose" for being too old. Simultaneously, I'm being "cut loose" from a decade-old marriage, it turns out, for exactly the same reason—I'm seventeen years older than the new light in my husband's life.

"Cut loose" from my previous life, in what's often called the "mainstream media," I have decided to try my hand at the "new media." I've been told that bloggers usually put on their pajamas and take up their keyboards because they feel passionately about something. That's certainly true for me. I've started cutlooseblog.com at a time when I'm still mad as hell about what happened to me.

At first I tried writing about what had happened to me according to the old news-media model—as in "monologue." But along the way, something strange happened to my monologue routine. I found out I wasn't alone—far from it. It turns out a lot of other people have been "cut loose" in much the same way and for many of the same reasons I was. That's where the "conversation" part of this process started.

Cutlooseblog.com has morphed into a real conversation. If you don't believe me, check out The Forum section and see what people are saying back. It has also become my own personal parachute at a time I didn't even know I needed a parachute. It allows me to continue to have a voice after the powers that be shut me down and turned off my microphone.

People tell their stories to me and to the other people who log on. We compare notes. I've decided, however, that due to possible legal complications, real names are no longer allowed, not for me and mine and formerly mine or for people who want to add their own posts to the site.

On the blog, I've decided to be "Babe." (Hey, I may be too old to cut it on television news in LA, but in my mind and the place where I'm living now, my self-proclaimed babeness is just fine, thank you very much!) For the purposes of this discussion, my ex—bless his pointed head, and with sincere thanks to one of my mom's favorite comediennes, Phyllis Diller—is referred to as "Fang." His new future wife is "Twink" as in, well . . . you fill in the blank. His other girlfriend, who may not know about Twink I will be Twink II. Or maybe I should call them Tweedle Dum(b) and Tweedle Dee. (No, I think I like Twink I and II better.)

My son, who was and is blameless in all this, is Tank. When he started crawling as a baby he went through or over whatever obstacles got in his way. He never went around them. He's still like that, so Tank it is.

If you're sending me pieces of your own story, you'd be well advised to choose your own pen name. Otherwise, as editor, I'll be obliged to choose one for you. Posts can be sent to me at Babe@cutlooseblog.com. If you don't want what you send posted on The Forum, all you have to do is say so.

So welcome aboard www.cutlooseblog.com. There are parts of my story of which I'm not very proud. That may be true for others as well. See the post listed several stories above this one, which I like to call "The Case of the Sinking Clickers." In that one someone named Tami found her own special way of "cutting loose."

Send me your stories. I'm sure you'll be just as amazed as I am at what comes back—sometimes advice, sometimes a version of "can you top this." But remember, from now on, names must be changed to protect the innocent, because some people *are* innocent in all this—most especially our kids.

Posted 11:55 P.M., by Babe

The alarm dragged Ali out of a deep sleep at five A.M. Her feet were still sore when they hit the floor, and as she limped into the shower she was questioning her sanity in offering to wait tables. Slower moving than she had been the day before, she trudged into the Sugarloaf at five past six to find the first breakfast rush already well underway.

Sedona is a tourist town—a town where wealthy retirees from California and elsewhere have built multimillion-dollar houses designed and situated solely to capture the vivid red rock views. It's a place where busloads and carloads of tourists arrive daily to browse through the high-priced fine art galleries and the low-priced curio shops. Few of those—the upscale residents or the Bermuda shorts–clad tourists—ventured into the Sugarloaf Café.

Tourists occasionally stepped inside, but it was the local working stiffs—the construction workers and the linemen, the hotel clerks and maintenance men—who came in before and after their shifts each day to drink coffee and wipe out that day's supply of sweet rolls. By 6:30 each morning the same rowdy crew of television cable installers usually took over the big corner booth. They all wore wedding rings, and they all flirted outrageously with Jan and Edie. Now that Ali was there, they flirted with her as well.

"Come on, Edie," one of the installers called to Ali's mother when she delivered an order to the kitchen service window. The name sewn on his shirt pocket was Sean. "Give us a break. Put Jan back behind the counter and give us a shot at Ali for a change."

"I'll give you a chance at Ali, all right," Edie called back. "But I'll lend her one of my rolling pins first."

Jan showed up at their table and slammed a coffeepot down in front of them. "What's the matter, Darlin'?" she demanded of Sean. "I always used to be good enough for you."

Her good-natured response was greeted by hoots of laughter.

The cable guys were still there and just finishing up a half hour later when an outsider showed up. Over the years Ali had learned that it was easy to spot wintertime visitors and guess their place of origin.

In the early spring when it was still brisk in Sedona, natives would be hunkered down in utilitarian jackets and sweaters while people from back East and from the Midwest tended to show up in shorts. Like the natives, visitors from California dressed for warmth, but with more style.

The out-of-towner who came in that morning and grabbed the end stool at the counter was of the latter variety. His designer sweats weren't something available from the nearest Wal-Mart. Neither were the running shoes, which had probably set him back to the tune of several hundred dollars. He clutched a razor-thin cell phone to his ear while he perused the menu. Ali came by with the coffeepot and a questioning look, but he waved her away and continued with his call.

Everything about him rubbed Ali the wrong way—the clothes, the phone, the attitude. For years she'd been embarrassed by similar behavior on Paul's part. Caught up in phone calls, he'd resort to pointing at items on menus or making his way through a checkout line without ever interrupting his conversation or even acknowledging the overworked clerk who was trying to wait on him.

With that in her background, it wasn't surprising that Ali bristled when he waved her away, as though her offering to pour coffee for him was an unwelcome intrusion. *That's once*, she thought.

When he was done with the call, however, he expected instant attention. As Ali added up the bill for the two people seated next to him, he drummed his fingers on the countertop.

"What kind of a joint is this?" he asked. "Anybody here ever hear of a latte? They're not listed on the menu."

Ali resented the guy's automatic assumption that the Sugarloaf was a lowbrow hangout full of dim-witted rubes. *That's two*, she thought. To their credit, the roomful of rubes fell obligingly silent, waiting to see how Ali would handle the interloper.

"Lah tay." She repeated the word wonderingly, as

though it was entirely foreign to her. "Never heard of one of them," she drawled. "What is it?"

"My God, woman!" the man exclaimed. "Haven't you ever heard of Starbucks?"

Starbucks was just down the road, but Ali was enjoying herself. "Sure," she replied, managing to keep a straight face. "StarMart gives 'em out as coupons every summer. You can use 'em for rides and stuff at the county fair."

The guys in the corner howled with laughter. Shaking his head in disgust and without placing an order, the man turned and headed for the door. He got as far as the cash register where he stopped abruptly, turned around, and came back.

"Wait a minute," he said, gesturing toward Edie's gallery of publicity shots. "I thought you looked familiar. I've seen you before on TV. On the news in LA. That's you, isn't it."

Ali was dressed in her Sugarloaf sweatshirt and a pair of jeans. She wore minimal makeup and her hair was pulled back into a scrunchy-held ponytail. Carrying two plates that were part of one of Jan's orders, her current situation bore little resemblance to the glamorous creature featured in those black-and-white glossies. Not only that, with Watching's threatening e-mail still reverberating in the back of her head, she didn't much want to be that other version of Ali Reynolds, either.

"Nope," she declared. "That would be my twin sister, the smart one in the family. She got the brains; I got the looks."

Shaking his head, the guy headed for the door, reaching for his cell phone as he did so. Once the door closed behind him, the whole front of the restaurant erupted in applause and raucous laughter, but the next time Ali picked up an order from the service window, the expression on her mother's face was grim.

"What if that had been our buyer?" Edie demanded. "And for your information, we do too have lattes, three kinds in fact—vanilla, mocha, and hazelnut—at three bucks a pop. We make 'em in the back, because there wasn't room enough to put the new equipment behind the counter. And they're not on the menu because your father thinks they're a pain in the butt, but we *do* have them! And the customer is always right."

"Got it," Ali said, feeling chagrined. "I remember now . . . You don't really think that was your buyer, do you?"

"No," Edie relented. "Probably not. The buyer's coming in with a business broker. Those guys never go to work until after nine."

At 8:30, Detective Dave Holman took his usual spot at the far end of the counter. He seemed particularly downcast. A little embarrassed by the curt way she had treated him the previous morning and newly reminded of her customer-relations failings, Ali offered him a good morning smile as she poured his coffee.

"Are you all right?" she asked.

"Not really," he said with a shrug. "My ex just told me that she and her new hubby are taking my kids and moving to Lake Havasu, of all the godforsaken places in the universe!"

Ali had been to Lake Havasu on occasion. One

of Paul's friends owned a palatial mansion on a bluff overlooking the Colorado River. The town hadn't seemed that bad to her at the time, but it didn't seem like a good idea to mention that to Dave Holman.

"Sounds tough," she said. "How old are your kids?"

"Six, ten, and fourteen," he said. "Two girls and a boy. Rich is the one I'm worried about—the fourteen-year-old. There's a whole lot of stuff going on over there on the river—drugs, cars, gangs—you name it—and I don't want my son getting caught up in that stuff. Don't get me wrong. It's not all sweetness and light here, either, but at least I can keep an eye on him and know what's going on. Over there, I'll have no way of knowing whether or not he's hanging out with the wrong crowd, which is exactly where his slimeball stepfather fits into the picture, by the way."

As the man railed on, Ali remembered what she'd said in the blog about customers coming to restaurants for more than just the food. Dave Holman came to the Sugarloaf Café every morning looking for food and human contact. On this particular morning he needed sympathy and understanding far more than he needed his ham and eggs.

"Fourteen is about how old my son Chris was when I married my slimeball," Ali told him. "And Chris has turned out fine."

"You're right," Dave agreed. "I met him the other day. He's a nice kid."

"With you for a dad, I'm sure Rich will be, too," she said. "No matter what your ex and her new husband do."

Dave looked up at her with the smallest glimmer of hope in his eyes. "You think so?" he asked.

Ali nodded. "I'm sure of it," she said. "Now what can I get you?"

"The usual," he said. "Ham and eggs, over hard. Whole-wheat toast."

Ali was busy for the next while. She waited until she brought Dave's order and his second cup of coffee before saying anything more to him.

"I talked to Howie Bernard the other night," she said casually.

"He's another piece of work," Dave replied.

"You know he has a girlfriend, then?" Ali asked.

"Pretty much everybody knows about her," he said.

So they know about Jasmine, Ali thought. *But are they really looking at her?*

"Everybody but Reenie?" she asked.

Sipping his coffee, Dave nodded thoughtfully. "Probably," he said. "The wife is usually the last to know. Or the husband," he added.

"He told me about the suicide note."

"We're lucky the note stayed in the car when everything else went flying," Dave said. "A miracle, really. If it had been thrown out into the snow, it never would have been found."

"Is it possible that Reenie didn't write the note?" Ali asked. "I mean, it wasn't signed, was it? Anyone could have written it."

Dave gave Ali a searching look. "What do you mean?" he asked.

Ali shrugged. "This will probably sound really lame, but I don't think she'd type a note like that. She'd use a card."

"A card?" Dave returned. "Somebody's started a line of suicide note cards now?"

"Reenie always sent cards," Ali explained. "For as long as I can remember. And she always found just the right one for whatever occasion. A piece of computer paper wouldn't have done it for her. She would have found a note card—a pretty blank one—and used that to say good-bye to her family, especially her kids."

"A card," Dave repeated, but he sounded unconvinced.

"If you don't believe me, go look in her office up in Flag," Ali said. "One whole wall is covered with cards—the ones people sent to her over the years, and she kept them all. But I'm sure that during that same period of time she sent out way more cards than she received."

"What are you saying?" Dave asked.

"What if Reenie didn't write the note?" Ali asked. "What if someone staged the whole thing? What if they murdered her and made it look like suicide?"

Dave didn't answer.

"Reenie sent me a note that day, too," Ali continued. "She sent it by regular mail and on a cute little card. I didn't get it until after she died, and it didn't say a word about suicide. Not a word. We were friends, Dave, good friends. Since she went to the trouble of sending the card, don't you think she would have said something to me about what her intentions were?"

"What did she say?" Dave asked.

Ali's next order was up. After delivering it, she hurried into the employee's restroom and retrieved

Reenie's card from her purse. She brought it back to the front counter and handed it to Dave. He read through it and then handed it back.

"Have you showed this to Detective Farris?" he asked.

"No," Ali said. "I didn't think he'd be interested."

"He might be," Dave said. "You're right. It doesn't sound like Reenie's referring to the bumps on Schnebly Hill Road. How about if I have Detective Farris give you a call?"

"Thanks," Ali said.

"What's your number?"

Ali gave it to him. "Hey," Edie called to her from the kitchen. "No hanky-panky with the customers while on duty."

Blushing, Ali turned away, but when she went back to clear Dave's place a few minutes later, she found more than double the usual tip shoved under his coffee cup.

The remainder of the morning went by quickly. The potential buyer and the business broker showed up exactly when Edie had predicted—9:30 on the dot. They were both dressed in suits and ties, which made it easy to separate them from the rest of the Sugarloaf's khaki- and jeans-wearing clientele.

It had been another chilly morning during which the sweet rolls had disappeared at an alarming pace. Edie had put two aside, just in case. As soon as the buyer bit into his, a look of pure ecstasy passed over his face.

That would be fitting, Ali thought, *if one of Myrtle Hansen's sweet rolls helped start the business and another one helped end it all these years later.*

The two men were seated in one of the booths in Jan's station, so Ali didn't wait on them, but she kept a close eye on the progress of their breakfast. From the kitchen, Edie Larson did the same. Only when they were finished did Edie, now sporting a clean apron, emerge from the kitchen to chat with them. Her arrival at their booth was followed by handshakes and introductions all around. Al Sanders, the taller of the two, was the business broker. Kenneth Dobbs was the potential purchaser.

Dobbs's praise for the food was nothing short of effusive. "That was by far the best sweet roll I've ever tasted in my life. Do you make them yourself?"

"Every day," Edie answered.

"I thought your husband would be here too," Sanders said, glancing back toward the kitchen.

"Our grandson is here visiting from California," Edie returned without missing a beat. "Bob decided to take a few days off. But you can talk to me," she added. "My husband and I are equal partners in this place. Talking to one is like talking to both."

"Mr. Dobbs is considering making an offer," Sanders continued. "But before he does, he'd like to bring in a restaurant consultant to have a look at the place. Would you mind?"

"No," Edie said. "That would be fine."

"What about tomorrow?"

"Sure," Edie said with a reassuring smile. "That would be great."

Her smile lasted only long enough for Dobbs and Sanders to pay their bill and walk out the door.

"A restaurant consultant. Just what I need," Edie grumbled on her way back to the kitchen. "By tomorrow, your father will be here, either in a wheelchair or on crutches. He'll be doing his best to run the place by remote control while I'm stuck with a restaurant consultant who'll want to turn the Sugarloaf into some kind of trendy glass-and-brass monstrosity."

"It'll be all right, Mom," Ali said. "I'm sure it will."

"I hope so," Edie murmured. As she walked away, she used a corner of her apron to brush a tear from her eye. The strain was beginning to show. Ali knew Edie Larson was tough as nails, but with everything that was going on, Ali wondered how much more her mother could take.

Chapter 12

Right in the middle of the lunch rush Chris showed up at the restaurant, pushing his newly released grandfather in a rented wheelchair. They were followed by a grubby-looking and gaunt stranger with dirty clothes and even dirtier hair. From the reek of woodsmoke and body odor, it seemed likely that he was homeless. He was missing several teeth, and his nose seemed to have been broken several times and from several different directions. Despite his scrawny appearance, however, the man single-handedly lifted Bob's considerable weight out of the wheelchair with an air of practiced ease.

Bob pointed to a spot behind the cash register. "Put the damned wheelchair over there so it's out of the way, then sit, both of you, and let's order some decent grub. The stuff they call food in the hospital isn't fit for man nor beast."

The grimy newcomer quickly folded the wheelchair and stowed it, then he and Chris eased their way into the booth on either side of Bob Larson. As Chris walked past her, Ali gave her son a questioning look as if to say, *Who's that?* Chris merely shook his head and said nothing.

Ali motioned to Jan that she'd take over serving that booth. She emerged from behind the counter, coffeepot in hand.

"They let you out, did they?" she asked her father, pouring coffee into his cup.

"Finally," Bob said heartily. "And not a moment too soon. They claim the swill they serve there is coffee, but it's worse than the food. Decaf, too. I had a headache that wouldn't quit until Chris here was good enough to go out and bring me back some real coffee." He sipped the coffee Ali had poured and gave a contented sigh. "Wonderful," he murmured. "Ambrosia."

She filled Chris's cup and then turned to the newcomer who, after glancing nervously around the room, was trying unsuccessfully to hide behind his open menu.

"Coffee?" she asked.

"Please," he said. As soon as she poured some for him, he loaded up with cream and several spoonfuls of sugar.

"Here's my beautiful daughter, Ali Reynolds," Bob beamed enthusiastically, making introductions as though what was happening wasn't the least bit out of the ordinary. "This is Kip Hogan, Ali, an old buddy of mine. He and I were corpsmen together in Vietnam for the 82nd Airborne. Do you believe it? Somebody told him I was living here in Sedona, and he came looking for me. Chris and I happened to run into him on our way down from Flagstaff. It's a good thing, too. Like I was telling him on the way here, I happen to be in need of a good corpsman at the moment."

A corpsman, Ali thought. That explained the businesslike way he had stowed the wheelchair, to say nothing of the way he had hefted Bob out of it.

"Glad to meet you," Ali said.

Knowing her father's penchant for rescuing strays, Ali had no doubt that he had chosen grubby and, to put it bluntly, stinky Kip as his next rehab project. Out in the kitchen, Edie Larson was busy slamming pots and pans.

"That's my wife, Edie, back there rattling those pots and pans. Edie's a hell of a good cook if I do say so myself. So what'll it be, Kip? Order whatever you like."

The ominous noises emanating from the kitchen made Edie's opinion about the situation perfectly clear. A few of the Sugarloaf's regular customers cast their own wary looks in Kip's direction. They didn't seem thrilled, either.

"I'll have huevos rancheros," Chris said.

"Bacon and eggs for me," Kip said softly. "Over easy on the eggs. And maybe one of those sweet rolls."

"Ah, the sweet rolls," Bob agreed. "Good choice. Very good choice. If there are any left, I'll have one of those, too, Ali. And some extra butter."

"It's lunchtime," Edie called from the kitchen. "We ran out of sweet rolls hours ago. And you need extra butter like you need a hole in your head."

"Okay, okay," Bob grinned at his wife. To Kip he said, "Don't worry about her. Edie's bark is a whole lot worse than her bite. We'll both have biscuits, then, Ali. Biscuits and gravy or biscuits and honey?"

"Gravy would be nice," Kip said longingly.

Something in the way he said the words made Ali realize that in addition to being dirty, Kip Hogan was also very hungry. Edie must have figured it out as well, because the plate of biscuits and gravy that was waiting at the service window a few minutes later was more than a double order. And, even though nothing more had been said, Bob's biscuits came complete with honey and several extra pats of butter.

"Maybe I won't have to kill him after all," Edie grumbled the next time Ali was within earshot. "His cholesterol will do the job for me."

"Kip's been hanging out at one of the camp sites up along the rim," Bob Larson explained when Ali returned with the rest of their order. "I told him we'd be glad to have him stay in the motor home for a couple of weeks. It's not much, but it sure beats living in a tent."

Years earlier, as a favor to a friend, Bob had bought an old used Lazy Daze. At the time Bob had still harbored the dream that some day he'd be able to talk Edie into hitting the road as an RVer. The decrepit motor home had seen better days before Bob had bought it, and time hadn't improved its condition. Over the years, the tires had more or less melted into the ground. Ali doubted the engine would even turn over anymore, and God only knew what kinds of creatures had taken up residence, but if Kip Hogan had been camping out in this kind of weather, he most likely would be more than happy to share four flimsy walls and a floor with any number of creepy-crawly vermin.

"Great," Ali said, trying to sound enthusiastic.

While the three men ate, several people stopped by to give Bob get well wishes. Around one or so, Kip and Chris loaded Bob back into his chair and then wheeled him out the door to get him settled into the house. Edie watched them go.

"Good riddance," she grumbled. "I don't need him sitting out there like King Tut and ordering free food for every Tom, Dick, or Harry who steps inside the place."

As they finished up the last of the orders and started the cleanup, though, Edie was still muttering under her breath. By the time Chris came over to help carry out the last of the trash, however, she was in a somewhat better mood.

"That Kip guy looks like he needs a shower and a haircut and a clean set of clothes," Jan Howard told Chris as he tied up the garbage bags. "But it'll be good to have him helping out for the next little while. It's lucky you ran into him."

Chris looked uncomfortable.

"Hah!" Edie barked from the kitchen. "Luck had nothing to do with it. You didn't fall for that old 'soldier's together' malarky, did you?"

Jan looked puzzled. "I thought that's what Bob said, that they'd served as corpsmen together in Vietnam."

"Bob was a corpsman," Edie corrected. "And maybe Kip was, too, for all I know. Or maybe he was doing first-aid on helicopters."

"But Bob said . . ."

"I don't care what Bob said," Edie told her. "He's a proud man who's laid up and can't work. He's also a big man who's going to need help getting in and out of bed and chairs and cars and other things it's probably best not to mention. And my guess is he'd rather die than have to ask me for help. Instead, he comes dragging home with this stranger who may or may not murder us in our beds. Right, Chris?"

Her grandson nodded. "When we left the hospital, I thought we'd come straight here," Chris admitted. "But he made me pull off the road, right there at the turnoff to Schnebly Hill Road. We stopped at a parking lot that was still so full of snow I was afraid we'd get stuck, but then a guy showed up. Walked right out of the woods. He came up to the car and greeted Gramps like they really were long lost friends. Then the first guy went away, and the next thing you know, Kip shows up. He came out of the woods, dragging a duffle bag. He threw the bag in the back of the truck, climbed in, and we came straight here. That's the whole story."

"See there?" Edie said triumphantly. "I told you it was bogus. Until this morning, Bob Larson didn't know Kip Hogan from a hole in the ground, but if Bob had told me he wanted to hire someone to help him get around so I wouldn't have to do it, I never would have stood for it. So there you are. He pretends they're old friends. I pretend I believe him, and everybody's happy. Got it?"

Jan Howard sighed and shook her head. "Whatever floats your boat," she said.

As Ali and her mother were leaving the restaurant, Edie caught Ali in a hug. "You raised a great kid," she said.

Ali knew it was true. Life on upscale Robert Lane could very well have turned Chris's head and wrecked him, but it hadn't. One of the things that had helped keep him on track had been the month or so he spent with his grandparents in Sedona each summer.

"Thanks," she said. "I seem to remember having lots of help from you and Dad."

"I'm sorry he has to leave tomorrow," Edie added. "I don't know how I would have made it through this without him holding down the fort at the hospital."

Ali was almost to the car when she remembered the next day was Friday. "What about tomorrow? Reenie's funeral is at two, so I'll need to get off by noon."

"No problem," Edie told her. "If you can come in for breakfast, that'll be fine. One way or another we'll manage."

"But what about the restaurant consultant?"

"We'll manage," Edie repeated. "Don't you worry about it."

"And what's the deal with Dave Holman?" Ali asked.

"Deal? I'm not sure I know what you mean."

"Come on, Mom," Ali said. "Out with it. You knew about Paul and me. You knew all about Howie Bernard having a girlfriend. I'm sure you have a very good idea about what's going on with Dave."

Edie sighed. "He's still in the Marine Reserves,"

she said. "His unit was called up for active duty and he got shipped off to Iraq for six months. While he was gone his wife, Roxie, took up with a guy named Whitman, Gary Whitman, a slimy timeshare salesman from up at the resort. Roxie served Dave with divorce papers on the day he came back, and she married Whitman the day after the divorce was final."

"Roxie and her husband are getting ready to move to Lake Havasu."

"I know," Edie said. "I was worrying about how he would handle it."

Edie walked away across the parking lot, leaving her daughter standing in stunned amazement. *How does she* do *that?* Ali wondered. Because one way or another, it seemed that there was very little that went on in northern Arizona without Edie Larson's full knowledge.

After leaving the Sugarloaf, Ali stopped by the florist and ordered flowers for Reenie's funeral—a spray of two dozen yellow roses to be delivered to the church in Cottonwood. Yellow roses had always been Reenie's favorite. Then Ali went home to do cat-litter duty. She noticed that she wasn't nearly as tired as she had been the day before, but her feet and back were still mad at her.

With the sky outside a brilliant azure blue, Ali thought she'd be able to sit outside on the deck and soak up some sun. Within minutes of sitting down on the patio, however, she realized that the sunlight was deceptive. There was still a decided chill in the air, so she went back inside, settled down on the couch with Samantha at her side, picked up her computer and logged on. Her new mail folder was brimming with correspondence.

> Give me a break. The poor little rich girl is actually having to lift a finger at real work for a change? Sitting in front of a TV camera and reading the news is not work. Your whining makes me sick.

> I found this site by accident. I Googled Sedona because my wife wants to go there on vacation. If it's full of people like you, why bother? I could just as well save my money and stay in southern California.
>
> Brad

Yes, Ali thought. *Why don't you stay in California?* But she posted Brad's comment anyway, just to be fair. The next one was even worse.

> Wow. No wonder they fired your ass. You're such an ugly broad. Maybe if you invested in some decent plastic surgery, it would fix your disfigured glare. In the meantime, I hope you're using a paper bag to cover your ugly face when you're out in public. And whatever you do, do NOT post a picture on your blog. Better people should never know what you really look like.
>
> Much love,
>
> Melissa G.

Two for two, Ali thought. *What is it, a full moon?* Making an effort to not take the writer's malice personally, Ali posted that comment as well. After all, hadn't she just claimed that cutlooseblog was supposed to be a conversation? And conversations generally came with more than one side and more than one opinion.

As Ali opened the next e-mail, however, she was feeling more than a little gun-shy.

Dear Ali,

I never expected to be writing to you, but now I am. I hated you for a long time, but now I realize that they've done the same thing to you that they did to me. I guess what goes around really does come around.

Ali skipped to the bottom of the message to the signature part: *Katherine Amado Burke*. Katy Amado had been Ali's immediate predecessor at the station in LA, the woman Paul Grayson's influence had bumped out of the news co-anchor chair.

My last night on the air, the news director came to me just before the broadcast and told me I'd been axed. He said I should sit in front of the camera and tell my viewers I was leaving to spend more time with my family, and I did. That was a joke, of course, because I had a husband who already had both feet out the door. (I have a different husband now, a much nicer one.)

It's not easy being shown the door and tossed on the scrap heap of life when you still think you have a lot to offer. I went into a long downward spiral with the help of drugs and booze. When I finally hit bottom, I ended up in the rehab facility where I'm now on the board of directors.

I'm writing to say thank you for not just sitting down and shutting up when they told you to. I've read through the material posted at cutlooseblog.com, and I think you're providing a real service for people going through tough times. Being busy is helping you, and it's also helping others, so keep it up. And please accept my condolences on the loss of your dear friend.

Katherine Amado Burke

P.S. Feel free to post this if you wish.

For a long time after she finished reading the note, Ali sat staring at the words. Katherine Amado was the last person Ali would have expected to offer her either kindness or encouragement, and she found the letter touching. The next one intrigued her:

Dear Ali,

I wish I knew more about the treatment Lisa was receiving, and I'd certainly tell you if I did. It was evidently some kind of experimental protocol and part of her being admitted to the program was signing a confidentiality agreement.

I know it was expensive. She sold her house and took a prepayment on her life insurance proceeds in order to fund her care. She said it was an investment. That what she was doing might not help her, but that maybe it would help the people who came behind her.

Lisa was unmarried and had no children. I'm her only heir. The boxes containing her personal possessions are all out in my garage. I've put off going through them because the thought of doing it makes me incredibly sad. But it's a job I need to tackle before it gets any hotter. If I find out anything more, I'll let you know.

Sincerely,
Louise Malkin

Ali puzzled over that one for a long time, too. If Lisa had used both the equity from her home and an advance on her life insurance policy to pay for the medication, it had to be expensive—similar to the unattainable $80,000 price tag Howie Bernard had mentioned.

Ali sent an immediate reply.

Dear Louise,

Cleaning out garages is no fun, but if you do happen on any information regarding Lisa's course of treatment, I'd really appreciate knowing about it.

Ali

The next message was utterly chilling. There was no salutation and no signature. It consisted of only two words:

She's gone.

There was no need for Ali to scroll back through her old mail to know the sender had to be Watching. Regardless of whether or not Watching's wife had read Ali's post, she had taken Ali's advice and headed for the hills, hopefully taking her two-year-old with her. And Ali didn't have to consult his message to remember verbatim what Watching had said about that: "If she tries to leave me, I'll come looking for you."

Ali was thinking about that when the phone rang and startled her. It wasn't her cell phone—it was Aunt Evie's, the land line she paid for and hardly ever used. The phone that seldom rang unless it was a solicitor doggedly making his way through a list of numbers. Caller ID said it was a private call. Thinking about Watching and about the possibility of him being out there, looking for her, Ali almost didn't answer. Finally, on the fourth ring, she did.

"Ali Reynolds?" a man's voice asked. A real man this time, not Helga Myerhoff's smoking-induced baritone.

"Yes."

"This is Detective Farris from the Coconino County Sheriff's Department. Dave Holman suggested I give you a call. I understand from him that you and Ms. Bernard were good friends."

"Yes," Ali said. "From high school on."

"Dave also mentioned that she had been in touch with you shortly before her death and that you thought that communication might have some bearing on the case. What was it, a phone call, letter, e-mail?"

"A greeting card," Ali said. "Reenie liked to send greeting cards."

"And what did it say exactly?"

Ali retrieved her purse. Ignoring the Glock, which had somehow managed to rise to the surface, Ali pawed through the purse's contents until she located Reenie's card. "Here it is: 'I think I'm in for a very bumpy ride, but I'm not ready to talk about it yet. I'll call you next week. R.'"

"That's all?" Farris asked.

"Yes," Ali answered.

"And what is it about this card that makes you doubt the authenticity of the suicide note we found in the wreckage of Reenie Bernard's vehicle?"

"It's just that Reenie was a friend of mine," Ali said quickly. "Sending a typed suicide note just isn't like her. She wouldn't do it."

"You're saying your friend would commit suicide, but instead of typing the note, she'd write it out longhand?"

"I didn't say . . ." Ali began.

"Look," Detective Farris said. "I don't mean any disrespect, and I'm sorry for your loss, Ms. Reynolds, but Mrs. Bernard's secretary over at the YWCA tried to tell me the same thing, that when we did find a note, it would be on some kind of greeting card, something with a pretty picture on it."

"Yes, but . . ."

"I'm a detective, Ms. Reynolds," he said. "A homicide detective. I've investigated any number of suicides over the years, and I have to say that as far as notes are concerned the results are about fifty-fifty, half typed and half handwritten. A few were done on typewriters. Most of the typed ones were computer generated and without benefit of a valid signature, but that didn't mean the notes weren't valid. And none of them—not a single, solitary one—ever showed up on a greeting card of any kind.

"Just to set your mind at rest, we've examined the printers from Ms. Bernard's office as well as the one they have at home. We're reasonably sure the note wasn't typed on either one of those. The truth is, however, Ms. Bernard was in the Phoenix area that day. She could easily have gone to a Kinko's somewhere to write and print the note."

"But . . ."

Farris went on without pausing long enough to listen to Ali's objection. "I know losing a loved one is difficult," he continued, "and the fact that someone has taken his or her own life is often particularly difficult to accept, but so far I've found nothing at all that doesn't point to the fact that Reenie Bernard committed suicide. We've been unable to find any legitimate reason for Ms. Bernard to be coming down Schnebly Hill Road in the middle of a snowy night. She was from around here. When she opened the gate at the top of the hill, I'm sure she knew how dangerous it was. I think she also knew exactly what she was doing.

"I'm probably saying more than I should, but I want you to understand where we are on this, Ms. Reynolds. The autopsy findings also bear out what I'm telling you. Her injuries are consistent with that plunge down the side of the mountain. There's nothing at all that indicates foul play."

"What about her trip to the bank?" Ali asked.

"Her intended trip to the bank," Farris corrected. "No banking slips or receipts were found in her vehicle or at the scene. We've already ascertained that there was no activity on any of the Bernard accounts that day. Now, if you have something more substantial to add, some kind of additional information, I'll be happy to look into it, but until then . . ."

The call-waiting signal beeped in Ali's ear.

"I have another call coming in and I need to take it," she said. "Thanks for being in touch. If I think of anything else, I'll be sure to let you know."

"Hi, Ali," Bree Cowan said when Ali clicked over to the other call. "I just talked to my mother. She and Dad are having a few people over tonight, but there's so much food at the house that they'd like more people to stop by and eat it. It'll mostly be friends and relatives from out of town, and you certainly qualify on that score. They could use the company, and so could the kids. I thought maybe . . ."

Going to visit the Holzers made a lot more sense than sitting around at home wondering what Watching might or might not be doing. "What time?" Ali asked at once.

"Sixish."

"I'll be there."

Once off the phone with Bree Cowan, Ali sat there holding Reenie's friendship card and letting the anger she felt toward Detective Farris wash over her. He had dismissed her concerns out of hand. He had given her the same kind of brush-off he had given Andrea Rogers.

His mind's made up, Ali thought bitterly. *Don't*

confuse the issue by asking him questions that don't necessarily agree with his pet theory.

Still looking at the card she realized that, for the rest of her life, whenever she saw one of those particular cards, she'd think of Reenie. And then she realized something else. Just because Detective Farris wasn't interested in her questions didn't mean she should stop asking them. Alison Reynolds was a journalist after all, someone trained to ask questions, and ask she would.

With that in mind, and with a whole new sense of purpose, Ali reached for her computer.

Chapter 13

It took hardly any time for Ali's search engine to track down Jasmine Wright—Jasmine and Timothy Wright, to be exact—with an address on N. Verde Street in Flagstaff. In other words, Howard's prize pupil and key-carrying side-dish was married—or had been—a short enough time ago that the phone company database had yet to catch up with any possible changes in address or marital status. Opening a new file on her computer, in a document she labeled simply REENIE, Ali pasted in both the address and the telephone number.

She did a public records search and found no references to either Jasmine or Timothy that included anything concerning divorce proceedings. Finally, she picked up the phone and dialed their number. Her heart skipped a beat when a male voice answered the phone on the third ring.

"Mr. Wright?" Ali asked that much but she had no concept whatsoever of what she would say next.

"Yes."

Ali's mind raced. "My name is Larson," she said, reverting to her maiden name. "Ali Larson. I hate to bother you. I'm sure you remember that terrible snowstorm we had a week ago. My car was parked on a street near campus. Someone skidded in the snow and creamed my poor Camry—took out all three panels on the passenger side. The problem is, it was a hit and run. I've been told that your wife sometimes parks in that same area, and I was wondering if she might have seen—"

"Jasmine's not here," Timothy interrupted. "She moved out months ago."

"Do you have any idea where I could reach her?"

"No," he answered. "None at all. Sorry." And he hung up.

Ali thought about Alan, the poor guy who had written to cutloose to express his devastation after learning that his wife was screwing around with her professor. *Poor Timothy*, Ali thought and meant it. The Wrights' divorce might not be final, but it was definitely in the works. And if Jasmine was clearing the marital decks to make way for Howie, was it possible Howie had been doing the same thing?

It would have taken a year or two, or maybe even longer, for Reenie to die of ALS. A divorce took six months to a year, depending. Murder was a whole lot quicker. So where had Jasmine and Howie been on Thursday night? Did they have an alibi for the time when Reenie was flying off the cliff? Detective Farris probably knew the answers to those questions, but he wasn't going to tell. Ali would have to find out about that on her own.

So who would be her allies in this project? Andrea Rogers, for sure. Bree and Jack Cowan. The Holzers. As for the cops? *Not a chance*. Knowing the

Cowans and the Holzers would be otherwise occupied, Ali picked up the phone and called Andrea.

"Can you do me a favor?" Ali asked.

"Sure," Andrea said. "What?"

"Jasmine Wright has split with her husband. Could you try to find out where she's living?"

"How come?"

"I talked to Detective Farris," Ali said. "He gave me the same treatment he gave you. As far as he's concerned, the typed suicide note stands. Case closed."

"You don't agree?"

"No," Ali said. "I don't."

"And it's not an accident?"

"No."

Andrea sighed. "Murder then," she said. "Who?"

"Since the cops don't suspect anybody, my position is to suspect everybody," Ali answered. "Starting with Howie and Jasmine Wright."

"I see," Andrea said. "In that case, I could just as well tell you that I've been doing some nosing around on my own."

"What do you mean?"

"You know Reenie," Andrea said. "She wasn't one for scrimping when it came to spending money on services or programs, but as far as the office was concerned . . . Six years ago, somebody donated a dozen or so computers. We used two of them, and Reenie put the rest of them away to use later. They're all dinosaurs now and not worth fixing, but they're perfectly reliable, right up until one of them quits."

"So?"

"The first one I used was the first one that croaked, and I didn't have all my files backed up the way they should have been. We installed flash cards so we could back up on a daily basis, but when we moved into the new office and set up a network, our IT guy fixed it so that Reenie's computer backed up to mine each day and mine backed up to hers as well. Sort of a fail-safe system."

"You're saying you have her files?"

"Yes," Andrea said. "All of them."

"Does Detective Farris know about that?"

"He didn't ask so I didn't tell him," Andrea answered. "And I know it's snooping and probably none of my business, but I've been going through her files anyway. I'm sure the police have been doing the same thing."

"And?"

"The last file Reenie worked on was a spreadsheet," Andrea said. "The file was saved on Wednesday night at eight o'clock. So she came back into the office after I left for the day."

"What kind of spreadsheet?"

"It lays out all her death benefits," Andrea said. "It lists all the insurance policies—group and individual."

"How much?" Ali asked.

"Almost five hundred thousand," Andrea answered. "There's twenty-five thousand of group insurance from here, an additional hundred in group insurance through Howie's work, a hundred from an individual policy. The rest is from their bank—one that will pay off the outstanding mortgage on their house. Then there's an additional twelve hundred a month from Social Security until Matt and Julie each reach their eighteenth birthdays."

Ali did some mental calculations. On the one hand, $500,000 sounded like a lot of money, but if you subtracted out $80,000 for the protocol and then whatever hospital expenses Reenie's final illness might have entailed, that money could have been eaten up in no time.

"So she was definitely putting her financial house in order," Andrea was saying. "I'm sure Detective Farris sees that as something else pointing to suicide, but I think she was trying to get a clear idea of how things would work once she was gone. I think she was just being responsible."

"What about her Internet account," Ali asked. "Can you access that? If we knew who she was e-mailing and what about, it might give us a big leg up."

"I know her e-mail address," Andrea said. "It's R.Bernard@FlagYWCA.org, but I have no idea what her password is."

"Do what you can," Ali told her. "And if you figure it out, let me know. What about her calendar. Is that there?"

"Yes."

"And what does it show for Thursday?"

"One appointment: two P.M., Dr. Clyde Mason, Mayo Clinic, Scottsdale."

"Phone number and address?"

Andrea gave it to her and Ali put that information into the Reenie file as well, and as soon as she got off the phone with Andrea, she dialed Dr. Mason's office. It wasn't easy talking her way around the gatekeepers—first the office receptionist and then the nurse—but eventually Ali prevailed. By the time Dr. Mason came on the line, he sounded none too happy.

"I've already spoken to the authorities on this matter," he complained. "As I told them, privacy rules limit my ability to comment on a patient's condition including whether or not someone is one of my patients. Who are you again?"

"Alison," she said. "Alison Larson. I'm a reporter with . . ."

"A reporter!" he bristled.

"And I was also Reenie Bernard's best friend," Ali put in quickly. "But my questions aren't about her. I'm assuming she wasn't your only ALS patient."

"I have several," Dr. Mason said.

"Supposing one of your patients, not Reenie, of course, happened to have heard about some new course of ALS treatment down in Mexico, would you advise them to try it?"

"No," Dr. Mason barked. "Absolutely not."

"I've been told that this supposed course of treatment is expensive—in the neighborhood of eighty-thousand dollars or so. I also understand that after Reenie left your office, she planned on visiting a bank."

"I advised her not to have anything to do with those crooks," Dr. Mason blurted. "I told her to go home and spend whatever time she had—whatever quality time she had—with her family, and not to waste financial and emotional resources on some kind of scam."

"So you think this treatment, whatever it is, is a scam?"

"No question." Mason quieted suddenly and Ali knew he had said more than he intended. She was afraid he might hang up on her.

"One more thing," she hurried on. "And this is strictly theoretical. From what I've been able to learn, some ALS patients, faced with what has to be a very dire future, choose to go out on their own terms."

"Yes," Dr. Mason agreed. "Some of them do, but not within the first week of getting their final diagnosis," he added. "Hardly anyone ever does that."

It took Ali a moment to assimilate what had happened. It sounded as though Dr. Mason had answered the question she hadn't asked, but she had to be sure.

"So you don't think Reenie committed suicide?"

Dr. Mason hesitated for so long that Ali thought he wasn't going to, but then he did. "In my experience," he said, "that would seem unlikely."

"Thank you," Ali managed, pushing her voice past the sudden lump in her throat. "Thank you very much."

"You're welcome," he said. "And please accept my condolences on the loss of your friend. From everything I learned about her through my dealings with her, Reenie Bernard struck me as a wonderful person."

"Yes," Ali managed. "She was certainly that."

Once Ali was off the phone, it took several minutes before she reached for her computer and turned her attention to the New Mail section of cutloose-blog.com.

Dear Babe,

And in my opinion, you are one. As far as I'm concerned, Melissa G. is walking around with a bag over her brain. Obviously her daddy never taught her the lesson Thumper's father passed along to his little ones. "If you can't say something nice, don't say nothin' at all!"

I miss seeing you on the news, but I think you're doing good work.

Randy

Dear Ali,

Why are some people so mean? They need to get a life.

Donna

Dear Babe,

From what you've said, it sounds as though you've never experienced domestic violence. Lucky for you. I have, and I really related to what's going on with Watching's wife. I spent eighteen years in an abusive relationship. My husband was a physician. He didn't beat me up physically, but he did mentally. He told everyone in town that I was a mental case and he told me that if I ever tried to leave, he'd kill me in a way that no one would ever detect. I'm thinking now of your friend's suicide. He also said that if I ever did get away, he'd track me to the ends of the earth and put me out of my misery.

My husband was an influential person in town—you'll notice I'm not saying which one. He made sure I didn't have money of my own and no credit cards, either. I wanted to leave, but I didn't know how. Then I heard about an organization called Angel Flight. Most of the time, they fly patients back and forth across long distances for chemo or dialysis treatments. But now they've started doing domestic violence escape flights as well.

Two years ago next month, I walked out of my house with nothing but the clothes on my back. A friend gave me a ride to the airport. A private plane met me there and away I went. If I'd had to pay for a ticket, I couldn't have afforded one, and since there were no tickets to buy, there were also no credit card receipts that he could use to find me.

I live somewhere else now. People here helped me establish a new identity. Starting over isn't easy. I'm waiting tables now, too, and I'm glad to do it. At least I'm safe. At least I'm alive. My parents and my sister know I made it out, but they don't know where I am because I'm afraid my ex-husband might brow-beat or threaten them into revealing my location. I love them and miss them, but for right now this is what I have to do for me. I'm better off safe and alone than dead.

I'm unwilling to come out of hiding. For that reason alone, I haven't divorced my husband and, as far as I know, he has yet to divorce me.

I pray that Watching's wife and baby stay safe. Unfortunately, due to liability issues, the organization that helped me is reluctant to be involved in situations that involve minor children. And I'm praying that you'll be safe as well.

Noname, notown, nostate.

While she was posting that one, Ali had reason to be grateful. Noname was right. Ali had never had to deal with domestic violence on a personal basis. She had money, credit cards (at least they were still working as far as she knew), food to eat, a place to live, and friends and family who loved her. Compared to Noname, Alison Reynolds was very, very lucky.

Dear Ali,

I bought your autographed photo from e-Bay for $4.67. I thought you'd want to know.

Your fan,
Sylvia

Her landline rang while she was posting the e-Bay message. The caller was none other than Paul, and he was furious.

"Did Helga tell you to do that?" he demanded. "Is that what this is all about?"

"I don't know what 'this' you mean," Ali returned.

"I mean pretending to wait tables at your folks's place in Sedona. What's that all about, looking for a sympathy vote? Poor Ali Reynolds. Lost her job at the news desk and now things are so bad that she's had to revert to her old standby, waiting tables. Except I happen to know you're still on the station's payroll at the moment even if you're not on the air."

"I'm not pretending," Ali returned, keeping her voice level. "Dad got hurt. I'm helping out."

"Yeah, right," Paul returned. "And you just happened to call up Lauren Masefield at the *LA Times* to give her the word along with what she assures me is a real cool picture."

Ali knew Lauren Masefield. She wrote a weekly gossip column covering local TV issues and detailing the comings and goings and detox adventures of various LA-area television personalities.

"What picture?" Ali asked.

"The one that's going to be in the paper in the morning. I understand it's a fetching one of you in all your Sugarloaf Café glory, packing around a couple of platters loaded with food. Lauren tells me the resolution's not too hot, but that's what you get for having whoever took the picture use a cell phone camera instead of a regular one."

That's when Ali remembered the latte guy in the designer sweats, the one who had recognized her, the one she had made fun of for the benefit of the locals. She remembered, too, that he had been carrying a cell phone. Now it seemed he had managed to get even with her. Worst of all, Ali knew she deserved it.

"I know who took the picture," she said coldly. "Believe me, he's no friend of mine."

"Whatever," Paul said. "It doesn't matter. The only reason I know about it in advance is that Lauren called me to see if I had a comment. I didn't. Not for her, but I have one for you. Playing the 'poor me' publicity card isn't going to carry any weight at all when it comes time to hammer out a property settlement."

"Wait a minute," she said. "What I'm doing has zero to do with you and nothing to do with a property settlement. It's about family, Paul, something you wouldn't recognize if it smacked you over the head."

In that moment, with Paul's rant ringing in Ali's ears, he sounded like a total stranger. It was difficult for her to grasp that she had been married to the man for seven years. Ali's mother was right. She had put herself in emotional neutral and had coasted. Now that her gears were fully engaged, it was time to fight back.

"And another thing," she added. "When we last spoke, it was all 'Honey Bunny this and that' and you were trying to talk me into coming back to you and telling me that we could work things out. Now you're talking property settlement?"

"That was before I knew you were going ahead with this boneheaded lawsuit," he said. "I won't be manipulated," Paul declared.

"Neither will I," Ali returned. "And incidently, you are being manipulated. Just not by me. So if you have anything more to say to me, I suggest you do it through my attorney. I'm sure you can find Helga easily enough. I would imagine her number is in the book."

Ali hung up the phone. Once her hands quit shaking, she went back to the computer.

Dear Babe,

Since I don't really know you, it feels weird to address you that way, but here goes. I, too, have recently been diagnosed with ALS. I've heard from several people about some new treatment program available in Mexico. Do you know anything about it? It seems to cost a lot of money. Does it work? Is it worth it?

Don Trilby
St Louis, MO

She wrote back to him immediately.

Dear Don,

I'm sure you're still reeling from your diagnosis. Learning you have ALS is a terrible blow for both you and your family. I'm in the process of trying to find out more about ALS treatment protocols that may be available in Mexico and not in the US. The one I've heard about requires an up-front commitment of $80,000 and may or may not offer any real or lasting benefits.

As I said, I'm attempting to investigate these treatment claims in order to learn whether or not they're bogus. If you were to send me whatever information you've gathered, I would be most grateful. In the meantime, you may want to contact Dr. Clyde Mason, a neurologist at the Mayo Clinic in Scottsdale, Arizona. His contact information is pasted below. I believe Dr. Mason is familiar with some of the Mexico-based treatment programs, and he would most likely be able to give you far better advice than I would be able to.

My very best to you and to your family in this difficult time.

Babe

Out of respect for Don's privacy, she posted neither his note to her nor her response. Now she posted a new comment of her own.

cutlooseblog.com
Thursday, March 17, 2005

I know that this blog has surfaced in ALS circles. I'm only just now beginning to understand all the heartbreaking ramifications of this dreadful disease—something many of you learned a long time ago.

I have reason to believe that my friend Reenie, who died last week, was considering participating in an experimental protocol of some kind, a Mexico-based ALS course of treatment that has yet to be tested or approved for use in the United States.

There are lots of people in this world who choose to prey on the unfortunate. They have no scruples about making dishonest claims to desperate people in search of answers. I'm worried that the treatment Reenie was considering—one that required an initial "investment" of $80,000—may be one of those bogus schemes, something created expressly to bilk money out of people who can ill afford to lose it.

My intention is to turn my training as an investigative journalist to this situation and see what I can do to ascertain whether or not the proposed treatment is legitimate. If it were found to be so, I would be among the first to shout its praises from the rooftops. If it's a fraud, I want to help put it out of business once and for all.

So if you know about this—if you've heard of or participated in something that sounds like the program Reenie was being encouraged to join—please let me know. You can write to me in confidence through the blog. If you don't want your comments publicly posted, all you have to do is say so. But I want to find out the truth about this. It no longer matters for Reenie because she's gone, but it matters to the rest of you, and if Reenie were alive, I'm sure this is exactly what she'd want me to do.

Posted 5:03 P.M., March 17, 2005 by Babe

Realizing it was almost time to head for the Holzers' gathering in Cottonwood, Ali closed her computer. As soon as she did, it beeped to say it was shutting down. Samantha immediately stirred from her sleep, got up, leaped off the couch, and headed for the kitchen. Despite all the turmoil in both their lives, Samantha was evidently learning to make sense of her changed circumstances.

"Is that a subtle hint that it's dinnertime?" Ali asked with a laugh. "And who says old humans can't learn new tricks?"

Chapter 14

The sun was just going down when Ali pulled up to Ed and Diane Holzer's place on their ranch outside Cottonwood. When she had stayed overnight with Reenie as a girl, the house had seemed incredibly spacious and luxurious besides. And compared to her parents' apartment behind the Sugarloaf it was. After living in Paul's Robert Lane mansion, the Holzers' house seemed to have shrunk.

The driveway was full of cars. As soon as Ali got out of the car, Matt and Julie came racing out of the house to meet her. "Do you know how come our dad isn't coming?" Matt demanded.

Ali was taken aback. "He isn't?" she asked.

"Grandma says Daddy's too busy," Julie put in. "I think he's too sad, and I don't blame him. Aunt Bree said to tell you to come on in. Dinner's ready."

Julie waltzed off in the direction of the house. Matt stayed with Ali. Of the two of them, Julie seemed in far better shape. Maybe she was too young to fully comprehend all that had happened. Matt, on the other hand, seemed to understand too much.

"I think he doesn't care about us anymore,"

he said bitterly, once his sister was out of hearing range. "I think he sent us here to get rid of us. He has a girlfriend, you know."

Shocked, Ali wasn't sure how to respond. "Who told you that?" she asked finally.

"Nobody," Matt said with a hopeless little shrug. "I'm not stupid, you know. Her name's Jasmine. She'd come to the house sometimes when Mom was at work or when she was out of town. I caught her kissing Dad in the living room once. I saw them. They didn't see me. Is that why Mom did it, do you think? Is that why she committed suicide, because of her?"

"I have no idea," Ali said.

That was the best she could do. She certainly was in no position to mention her own doubts about the official suicide call. Besides, if Reenie hadn't committed suicide, and Howie and Jasmine somehow ended up being implicated in her death, how much worse would that make things for the two children?

"Dad says she left us a note," Matt continued. "But why would she do that? Why would she leave just one? Wouldn't she leave a note for him and one for Julie and one for me?"

It was back to the note again. Everybody seemed to have a differing opinion about Reenie's note—opinions with no real answers.

"That's how it seems to me, too," Ali said after a pause.

The back door opened and Bree Cowan walked toward them. Before his aunt could reach them, Matt abruptly changed the subject. "How's Sam doing?" he asked.

"She's fine," Ali said. "But I think she misses you."

"I miss her, too," he said. For the first time, his eyes misted over, and he moved away, drifting off toward the house before Bree had a chance to speak to him.

"He's taking this very hard," Bree said, watching him go. "But then, we all are."

Looking at Reenie's sister, Ali wondered if Bree knew about Howie's ongoing affair with Jasmine Wright. There was no way to tell, and for the moment Ali decided to follow Matt's lead and say nothing.

"Come on," Bree said with forced cheerfulness. "Let me take you inside and introduce you to some of these people."

Throughout the evening it was clear that Bree and her good-looking husband, Jack Cowan, were in charge. They managed guests, food, and drink with the casual ease of people accustomed to doing a good deal of entertaining. Their efforts left Ed and Diane Holzer free to visit with people who had traveled long distances to comfort them. Watching the family dynamics at work, Ali couldn't help being grateful that with Reenie gone, her parents still had Bree and her husband to lean on during troubled times.

Much later, as things started to wind down, Ali noticed Ed Holzer sitting off by himself looking haggard and spent. She went over to him and sat down on a nearby footstool.

"How're you doing?" she asked.

"Not so hot," he said.

"I noticed Howie didn't show up," Ali said. "How come? The kids were upset that he wasn't here."

"Because I called him up and told him he wasn't welcome," Ed said shortly "For Diane and the kids' sake, I'll do my best to tolerate him at the funeral tomorrow, but I just couldn't face having him here tonight." Ed shook his head.

Ali gave Ed an appraising glance. "So you know about the girlfriend?" she asked.

He nodded miserably.

"Does Diane?"

"I haven't told her," Ed said. "But probably. It seems like everybody else does."

"Including Matt," Ali said.

"Damn!" Ed muttered.

It was the first bad word Ali had ever heard the man say, but she knew he meant it.

"She was dying," he added. "It was only a matter of time. Couldn't he have had the decency to wait?"

"Did Reenie know what was going on?" Ali asked.

"About him fooling around? I'm not sure," Ed replied. "Maybe, maybe not. If she did, she wouldn't have mentioned it to us. Wouldn't have wanted to worry us." He swiped at his eyes with the sleeve of his shirt. From across the room, Diane seemed to key in on his distress. Under her questioning look, Ed forced himself to sit up straighter and pull himself together.

"I've heard something about Reenie maybe wanting to be involved in some experimental treatment."

"I know she had been looking into several different things, even before she got the final diagnosis. Some of them were expensive, but I told her not to worry about that. If it came down to a matter of money, she could always come to Diane and me."

"Did she tell you anything about the various treatments?"

"Not really. She said she'd heard about an interesting one down in Mexico, but she was having a hard time getting enough information on it because everyone who signed up for it had to sign a confidentiality agreement."

"So she didn't mention who was sponsoring it or what kind of institution was behind it?"

Ed shook his head. "No. I don't think she knew. She might have found out more after she talked to me. But she did say that, regardless of what course of treatment she chose, and no matter whether or not it helped her, she'd do it anyway, just in hopes of helping the people who came after her. That was Reenie, of course," he added sadly. "Stubborn as all-get-out, but a do-gooder to the end, always looking out for the other guy. But that's why this whole thing is such a shock to her mother and me. First she says she's going to stand and fight. The next thing we know, she's gone and driven herself off the edge of a cliff."

Bree came across the room then, settled onto the couch next to her father, and rested her head on Ed's shoulder.

"How's it going?" she asked. "You look tired."

It had always been apparent that Ed Holzer, for some unknown reason, had preferred his younger daughter, Bree, to Reenie. His unabashed and inexplicable favoritism had been part of the family dynamic for as long as Ali had known the Holzers, and it had always been a source of conflict between the two daughters. Ali had long suspected that it had been one of the underlying reasons behind Reenie's getting involved with a bad boy named Sam Turpin during her senior year and her elopement only days after high school graduation.

Reenie had been smart enough, but she had delayed her entry into college until after the end of her first marriage. Bree, on the other hand, had gone straight from high school to college and, with no detours, had completed her MBA by the time she was twenty-six. She had started out working in her father's bank. When he sold out, she had gone to work for his fledgling property management company and had been there ever since. Now, as a full partner and in the face of Ed's declining health, she appeared to be running the show—the business end of things as well as taking charge of the evening's gathering.

Ed reached over and patted the back of Bree's hand. "Ali and I were just talking about some of the treatment options Reenie had been considering," he said. "I don't know much about any of them, do you?"

Bree shook her head. "Not really. To begin with, she was all fired up about some kind of holistic treatment that was only being offered in Mexico. The last time I talked to her, though, it must have been Monday or Tuesday, she said she had decided against doing any of them. She was going to live her life to the best of her ability and take her lumps."

"I hope it wasn't because of the money," Ed insisted. "We would have been glad to help."

Bree shrugged. "Don't beat yourself up about that, Dad. With all the stress Reenie had been under the last few months and especially the last week, you can't blame her for waffling back and forth about what she should do. When she finally made up her mind, she didn't bother talking about it; she just did it."

"But she should have called first," Ed objected. "She should have let us know. I hate to think of her out on the mountain all alone."

Bree nodded. "Yes," she said. "I'm surprised she didn't call."

This time, she was the one patting her father's hand, but Ed didn't seem at all comforted by the gesture. Moments later his sister and brother-in-law who had driven up from Mesa came over to say good night. Knowing her alarm would be going off at five A.M., Ali took that as a signal that she should leave as well.

Driving back to Sedona under the chilly light of a waning moon, Ali was struck by the fact that of all the people she had spoken to that night, no one else had expressed the slightest doubt that Reenie Bernard had committed suicide. Her family and friends all seemed to accept that as a given.

If it's so clear to everyone else, why isn't it clear to me? Ali wondered.

Back at the house on Skyview Way, Ali was relieved to see her father's aged Bronco parked in the driveway. That meant Chris was already home. Inside she found him sprawled on the couch watching the "Ten O'clock News" with Samantha curled up cozily beside him.

"I see you've won her over," Ali said.

Chris grinned. "It was easy," he said. "Grandma sent home some meatloaf, which I was willing to share. Where've you been?"

"Cottonwood," Ali said, sinking down on the couch beside him.

"With Reenie's parents?"

Ali nodded.

"I guess I'm glad I missed that one," he said.

"You haven't exactly been doing light duty," she said. "How are things with Grandpa and Grandma?"

"Better," he said. "Kip is a lot stronger than he looks, and he seems to know what he's doing as far as looking after Gramps. We found Kip some clean clothes and secondhand shoes down at the clothes bank. By the time Grandma got back to the house, he had cleaned up and was looking almost civilized. I was afraid she'd raise hell about him being there, but she didn't. She grumbled some, but that was about it."

"That's just how they are," Ali explained. "For some reason they have to *act* like they're fighting about it even though Dad knows he needs the help and so does Mom."

"Weird," Chris said. "Want something to eat?"

"No," she said. "Reenie's folks had more than enough food. What time does your ride leave in the morning and where do you meet him?"

"Noon, but Danny's picking up someone else in Phoenix along the way, so he'll come here to get me. Unless you've changed you mind and want me to stay longer."

"I haven't changed my mind," Ali said. "You've done more than your share. You need to get back to school."

Her computer was sitting on the coffee table with a business card on top of it. "What's this?" she asked, leaning forward to check.

"An alarm guy," Chris said. "You didn't call anybody, did you?"

"I forgot," she admitted.

"Well, I didn't. I called him myself and told him to get in touch with you next week to set up an appointment."

"Thanks," Ali said.

"By the way," Chris said, "once I get back to LA, I'm going to move out of the pool house. I'm not going to stay there if you're not there, not with the way Paul's treating you. I've done some calling around and I've already found some guys who need a roommate for next quarter, but what are you going to do?"

"I'm not sure," Ali said. "I'll help Mom and Dad for as long as they need me. After that? I really don't know."

"Do you think you'll stay here?"

"Maybe," she said. "Maybe not. Why?"

"Because I've been doing some checking around here for teaching jobs," Chris said. "There's going to be an opening for a welding teacher at the high school next year. They're always glad to have beginning teachers because they're so cheap. And that would give me a chance to work on my sculptures in the evenings and on weekends. If I'm going to make it in the art world, Sedona is as good a place as any to break in, but—"

Ali could barely contain her excitement. "That would be wonderful!" she exclaimed, leaning over to give him a quick kiss. "Have you told Grandma and Grandpa?"

"Not yet," Chris said. "I didn't want to get them

all wound up about it in case it didn't happen. The problem is, I've been checking on apartments just in case, and they're all so expensive, that I don't see how I'd make it."

"Apartment?" Ali demanded. "Why would you need an apartment? If you need a place to stay, you can stay here. How's that for a deal? If I'm not here, you can rent it for whatever you can afford. If I am here, we may end up being roommates."

"Sounds good to me," Chris said, grinning. "As long as you don't have too many loud parties and keep me from getting my beauty sleep."

As soon as Jay Leno came on, Chris wandered off to his bedroom. When he did, Ali put the business card to one side and opened her computer.

Dear Babe,

How come it's never the woman's fault? Do you guys all hate men or what?

Howard
Hammond, Indiana

Dear Ali,

Velma again. I just can't bring myself to call you Babe. You'll always be Alison Reynolds to me. Maybe that girl who bought your photo on e-Bay could send it in so you can post it. I still think you should have your picture here, no matter what that brat of a Melissa thinks. Don't pay any attention to people like that. Sticks and stones, remember?

Also, I'm still using my grandson's computer—I've

asked my daughter to get me one for my birthday next month—so I don't get to check every day. Please don't erase anything. For at least a week. That way I can go back and read what I missed.

By the way. My husband was a very nice man. He never hit me or anything. He always brought home his paycheck. From what I see here, I guess I was very lucky. We got married when we were both nineteen. He's been dead for eight years. I still miss him.

VelmaT in Laguna

PS I like having a pen name. I never had one of those before. And you can print what I write, but please check the spelling and punctuation. Will that make me a published author?

Dear Babe,

Pleese do not post this. My name is Corine Witherspoon. My husband is Ben Witherspoon, but when he rites to you he calls himself Watching. He is a dangrous man. I was his penpal when he was in prison for atttempted murder. He told me he was framed, but now I think he reelly did do it. I am in a safe house now. And this is a new e-mail address that he doesn't know. Thank you for warnning me. I think little Tony and I got out just in time. When I get a job, I will rite again and let you know how we are doing.

Corine and Tony

That one gave Ali goose bumps—twice over. For one thing she knew Corine and Tony were safe, but she knew Watching was really dangerous. She replied immediately.

Dear Corine,

Thank you for writing. I'm so glad to know that you and Tony are safe. I was worried about you.

Thank you, too, for warning me about your husband. Can you give me any information about him—about the kind of vehicle he might drive, where he lives, license plate number, that kind of thing? Having the information from you would be a big help as I work on figuring out how to deal with this. As you've probably noticed in the blog, I've put in a good deal of personal information. I'm afraid if your husband really does decide to come after me, he won't have any trouble finding me.

Sincerely,
Alison Reynolds

Dear Ali,

I've gone through Reenie's backup files. There's no sign there of any suicide note. None. I've also done my best to log on to Reenie's e-mail account but without any luck. It's possible she could have written it in there and printed it elsewhere.

I had better luck when it comes to Jasmine Wright, and some of it is very interesting. She was supposed to teach an evening American History class that night, but she didn't show up. I found that out from a friend who works in the NAU administration office. Jasmine lives with two other women down in Munds Park—which is very close to the turnoff to Schnebly Hill Road, by the way.

I wasn't able to get the exact address because they all get their mail at the post office, so tonight I did something I never thought I'd do. My friend told me which parking lot Jasmine uses. I waited there in the lot during her class. When she left, I followed her. Big surprise. She went straight to Howie Bernard's house. I waited around for an hour or so, but she still hadn't come out by the time I left.

Two things. How come she has a key? And if Reenie's parents were having a reception or something tonight down in Cottonwood, how come Howie wasn't there?

The YW's day care will be open tomorrow morning, but they're hoping to close early—at noon or so—so the teachers can come to Reenie's funeral. I've decided I'm not coming in at all. See you in Cottonwood.

Andrea

Dear Andrea,

Good work on the address thing. And you're right, Jasmine's proximity to Schnebly Hill Road is very interesting.

As far as Reenie's e-mail account is concerned, I'll forward the information to my son. Chris was a computer expert on the day he was born. He may be able to figure it out even if we can't.

Yes, see you at the funeral. Howie wasn't at the Holzers' place tonight for the very good reason that he wasn't invited. It seems the word is out on Jasmine, and Reenie's relatives are bent out of shape about it. I don't blame them. I'm bent, too. The other night Jasmine had nerve enough to tell me she'd see me at the funeral. I can't imagine she'll actually show up.

Ali

Ali pulled the information from the Reenie file and sent it on to Chris. If he wasn't studying, it would give him something to do the next morning while she was at the Sugarloaf and while he was waiting for his ride.

Dear Ali

Going through Lisa's stuff out in the garage made me very sad. One of the first things I found was a beautiful greeting card. The background is deep blue. The foreground is three lush pink begonias. There was no envelope so I don't have an address, but here's what the card said.

Dear Lisa,

Thank you for the information. I'm so sorry it didn't work for you the way you hoped it would. Please keep in touch.

Reenie

When I saw the card, I started to cry, for both Lisa and for Reenie. I couldn't help it.

And then I found something else—a receipt for a cashiers check for $80,000 payable to Rodriguez Medical Center, Mazatlan, Mexico. I hope this information is helpful. In the meantime, now that I've started the job of sorting, I'm going to keep on. Thanks for getting me going. Otherwise the boxes would have sat here for years.

Louise Malkin

The sound of a bugle on-line told Ali she had an instant message from Chris.

Dear Mom,

Reenie's password is Samantha. Duh!

Love,
Chris

Ali sent him an immediate thank-you. She was tempted to use it and log on right then, but she was tired. And she wanted to complete the next morning's post before she went to bed, so she worked on that instead.

cutlooseblog.com
Friday, March 18, 2005

According to some sources, bloggers supposedly sit around in their pajamas irresponsibly posting outrageous things on their computers. I strenuously object to the use of the word "irresponsibly." And I'm not convinced that anything I've said is "outrageous" either, although some of my readers may disagree with that assessment. But the pajama part? Absolutely! No question. I'm wearing them right now.

No matter how early I'm supposed to rise and shine, my interior body clock remains firmly stuck in the rhyme and rhythm of doing the late-night news. So even though I should have been in bed a long time ago, I'm not. Fatigue is going to set in big-time, probably right in the middle of the diner's breakfast rush.

I spent the evening with my dead friend's parents and with her two kids. Her husband, the children's father, was evidently preoccupied with other matters. He didn't attend. There was lots of food. No, make that mounds of food—although no one seemed interested in eating much of it.

While we all try to come to terms with having lost someone special from our lives, police agencies continue to investigate exactly what took her from us. And why. Most of the people who knew Reenie seem to have accepted the idea that she committed suicide in the face of her medical diagnosis. So far, I haven't been able to do that. I still want to know what was going on in her life—and in her heart and mind—during her last few hours on earth. I don't know why I want to know, but I do.

And so, although I still can't believe my friend is gone, today is her funeral. Don't be surprised if I don't post later today or maybe even tomorrow. I probably won't feel like it.

Posted 12:01 A.M. by Babe

She was about to sign off when there was New Mail click. When she checked, she recognized Corine Witherspoon's Hotmail address.

Dear Babe,

Ben works construction. Mostly drywalling. He drives a green Datsun 710 station wagon with Texas plates. We were living in Lodi when I left, but we were behind in the rent on the apartment, so he probally isn't there now. Take care.

Corine

Ali went to bed after reading the message. She didn't go to sleep, at least not right away, and when she did finally slip into slumber, nightmares came hot and heavy. Someone was chasing her through the snowy woods, firing at her with a machine gun. As the bullets whined around her, Ali dove for cover. But the cover wasn't there. She found herself tumbling and falling through the frigid air.

Even though the house was toasty warm, she woke up shivering.

Chapter 15

There wasn't enough time for the kind of makeup job needed to repair the ravages of Ali's lack of sleep. Her mother was kind enough to point that out as soon as she stepped into the kitchen at the Sugarloaf Café.

"What did you do last night, go out and tie one on?" Edie asked as Ali hurried into the locker room to collect that morning's clean sweatshirt. "You look like death warmed over."

"Gee, thanks, Mom," Ali returned. "You really know how to cheer a girl up."

"Well, you should be cheered, "Edie added. "I'm firing you."

"You're what?"

"Firing you. Laying you off. But not until nine o'clock or so. That's when Susan's due to show up."

"Who's Susan?"

"Jan's cousin, Susan Lockner. From Glendale. The Glendale by Phoenix, not the one in California. She retired from working at Denny's years ago, but Jan says she can still sling hash with the best of them. She and Jan talked it over last night and Susan's agreed to come up and help us out for a while. For as long as it takes is what Jan said, which I take to mean until your father's back on his feet. She'll be staying at Jan's place."

"Yup," Jan said, appearing in the service window. "I'm looking forward to it. It'll be like a perpetual sleepover. I'll bet I can still whip her butt at canasta."

"But . . ." Ali began.

"No buts," Edie declared firmly. "Dad and I talked it over yesterday. We decided it's not fair for us to impose our troubles on you any longer, especially since it's all due to your father's own foolishness."

"It's not imposing," Ali said, but Edie wasn't listening.

"And I'm sure you have plenty of other things to attend to," she continued undeterred. "Now let's get breakfast out of the way. I have no idea when that consultant is going to show up, most likely right in the middle of some disaster or other."

As Ali headed for the dining room, she felt more than a little bereft. That was surprising since it was over losing a job she had never wanted in the first place.

I'll probably feel the same way when it's time for Sam to go back to Flagstaff, she thought.

At first Ali kept a wary eye on all the customers coming and going, paying close attention to each stranger who came through the door and wondering if this one or that one might turn out to be Ben Witherspoon. Eventually, though, things got too busy for her to continue paying that kind of attention. By the time Dave Holman showed up at his usual 8:30, Ali, suffering from lack of sleep, was ready to admit defeat. She found herself watching the clock in anticipation of Susan's arrival.

"Will I see you at the funeral today?" Dave asked as she poured his first cup of coffee.

She nodded. "But not here anymore," she added. "I've been told my services are no longer required. It turns out I'm being replaced by a food-service professional."

"Sorry to hear that," Dave said. "I was just getting used to having you growl at me every morning. It was almost like being married again."

Ali was searching for an appropriately biting comeback when she saw the telltale twitch in the corners of his mouth and realized he was teasing her. "You should be so lucky," she said.

Susan Lockner showed up a few minutes later and a good fifteen minutes early. She marched straight into the kitchen and squeezed into the only 3X Sugarloaf sweatshirt to be had.

"Time to stand down, honey," she said, barreling up to Ali and bodily removing the coffeepot from her hand. "Reinforcements have arrived."

Ali obligingly walked around the counter and settled on the empty stool next to Dave.

"Hey, Edie," he called in the direction of the kitchen. "Since Ali's no longer hired help, can I buy her breakfast?"

"I wouldn't if I were you," Edie returned. "If her husband couldn't afford her, I wouldn't advise you to try it."

Ali blushed. She had done her best to keep her marital situation well under Sedona's gossip radar. Obviously Edie Larson felt no such compunction.

Dave looked at Ali in surprise. "Does that mean your marriage is on the rocks, too?" he asked.

"Looks that way," Ali said.

"I'm sorry," he said.

"It could be worse," Ali told him. "After all, I don't have young kids to worry about the way some people do."

Dave nodded. "Lucky for you," he said. "But still, if I had known, I wouldn't have given you such a hard time."

"It's okay," Ali replied. "I can take the heat, but in compensation, I will let you buy me breakfast. Besides, I need to ask you a couple of questions."

"Order first," he said. "Let's see what this new girl can do."

The term girl didn't exactly fit. After all, Susan was about as far into her seventies as Jan was. She was also pushing three hundred pounds, but once behind the counter, she knew exactly what to do, and she was more than capable of trading banter with the rowdy cable installers in the far corner booth.

Ali chose oatmeal and whole-wheat toast.

"What questions?" Dave asked when she finished ordering. "About Reenie? . . . Did you ever have a chance to talk to Lee Farris?"

"I did," Ali answered, "but nothing much came of it. As far as he's concerned, she committed suicide and that's it. Case closed."

"But you're still not convinced."

"Let's just say I have some concerns," Ali said.

"You think someone else is responsible?"

Ali nodded. "Maybe."

"Who?"

"Her husband has a girlfriend, for one thing," Ali said. "What about him? Maybe he got greedy. With half a million dollars in insurance proceeds there for the taking, Howie and his new pal are going to be left with a lot more money to throw around in view of Reenie's sudden death. Had her ALS had been allowed to run its course, Howie probably would have been looking at all kinds of medical bills in co-pays alone."

"Could have been," Dave corrected. "But that's only one concern. What else?"

"The supposed suicide note," Ali said. "The *alleged* suicide note. It was written on a computer. There's no signature on it. Anyone could have typed it, printed it, and planted it in Reenie's vehicle. And there's no indication Reenie wrote it on her own computer, by the way, at least not the one at work. There's no trace of it in any of her files."

"You know that for sure?" Dave asked. "My understanding was that Lee had taken charge of her computer."

"He did," Ali said. "But Andrea Rogers, Reenie's secretary, had a back-up copy of Reenie's files. So she looked. According to her there was no sign of any note."

"What about a home computer?" Dave asked. "She could have used one she had there."

"Detective Farris says not," Ali said. "His idea was that maybe she stopped off at a Kinkos and wrote and printed the note there while she was down in Phoenix, but I don't think so." Ali didn't bother mentioning the greeting card issue. That was a nonstarter. "And then there's the thing about possible treatments," she added.

"What treatments?" Dave asked. "I didn't think there were any treatments for ALS."

"There aren't any cures, that's for sure," Ali admitted. "There are some things that may help stave off symptoms for a while. And although there's lots of research going on, there've been no real breakthroughs. A lot of what's out there may be outright frauds—things that play on people's hopes and fears. One in particular has an initial entry fee of $80,000. What you get back for that amount of money, I have no idea."

Dave Holman whistled. "That much? Was Reenie involved in anything like that?"

"Maybe. I talked to her father about it last night. According to Ed Holzer, she was considering signing up for something. That he expected she'd fight ALS to the bitter end. I thought so, too. Which brings me to the bank."

"What bank?"

"I have no idea. Andrea Rogers says she talked to Reenie after she finished up with her appointment at the Mayo Clinic in Scottsdale. She told Andrea she would be stopping by a bank on her way home."

"So?" Dave asked.

Ali gave him a sharp look. "Why would she need to go to a bank at all if she was planning to drive off a cliff in a few hours' time?"

"Maybe she needed cash to buy gas for the trip home."

"I thought she might have been thinking about

signing up for one of the treatment programs," Ali said. "According to Detective Farris, though, there was no activity on any of the Bernards' Bank of America accounts that day and nothing at any of the branches."

"So Lee's already checked this out?" Dave asked.

"As much as he's going to," Ali conceded. "But what if there's another bank involved, one we don't know about?"

Ali's breakfast arrived. "If things were rocky at home," Dave mused after a pause, "maybe Reenie was starting a new account somewhere else. That's what my ex did," he added. "She left enough money in the joint account to keep it open, then she started a new account of her own, one that didn't have my name on it."

Ali thought about Howie Bernard and Jasmine Wright. "That is a possibility," Ali said.

"But doing that is bound to leave a trail of some kind," Dave said. "There'd be e-mails or phone calls or names in her address book. I know Reenie's cell phone was smashed to pieces in the wreck, but I wonder if anyone's taken a look at her phone records from her cell or from work, either one. If she was starting up a new banking relationship, we'll be able to trace it by tracking down the phone calls. And if we learn which bank she visited, we may start filling in some of the missing hours between the time she left the doctor's office and the time she went off the cliff."

"Detective Farris could look at the records if he wanted to," Ali said. "But I doubt he'll bother. I don't think he's interested."

"I might be able to take a look at them," Dave suggested quietly.

A wave of gratitude washed over her. "Would you do that?" she asked. "Really?"

"Glad to," he said. By then he had finished his breakfast while Ali was still working on hers. Dave stood up. "I've got a meeting to go to. See you this afternoon."

Ali had intended to ask him for advice about how to deal with Ben Witherspoon, but that hadn't happened. Coping with Watcher's threat had been pushed to the back burner by their discussion about Reenie. To his credit, Dave had listened thoughtfully to Ali's concerns about Reenie's case. That was far more than could be said for Detective Lee Farris.

"Thanks, Dave," Ali said. "For everything."

As Dave left, Bob Larson arrived. It took some maneuvering on Kip Hogan's part to get Bob's wheelchair up the ramp and in through the heavy glass door. Kip was aided in the effort by a suit-clad black man Ali had never seen before, who held the door open to allow the wheelchair access.

Once situated in the corner booth recently vacated by the second team of cable guys, Bob immediately began issuing orders to Jan and Susan. According to Bob there was a whole lot that wasn't right in the room. The stack of menus on the front counter wasn't straight. Two booths needed clearing, and no one had gotten around to sweeping up the sprinkling of Cheerios some restless toddler in a high chair had left scattered on the floor. Meanwhile the black man stepped up to the counter.

"My name's Rodney Williams," he said to Susan.

"I'm here to see Mr. or Mrs. Larson. I believe they're expecting me."

Ali groaned inwardly. Having the restaurant consultant blow in at exactly the same time as Bob Larson was a bad omen, and it was bound to provoke a battle between her parents. Glad Susan's ample presence made it unnecessary for Ali to hang around for the inevitable fireworks, she headed out the door.

Back at the house, she found Chris packed up and ready to go. He was sitting at the kitchen counter with his computer open in front of him.

"How come you're home so early?" he asked. "Is it already time to go to the funeral?

"The funeral's not until this afternoon," she told him. "I'm home now because Mom fired me."

"She fired you?" Chris repeated. "What did you do wrong?"

Ali went over and flopped down on the couch where Samantha immediately joined her. "I did nothing wrong," Ali said. "Jan convinced her cousin Susan to come up from Phoenix and take over my duties. Mom and Dad evidently decided they were somehow taking unfair advantage of me. They don't want to stand in the way of my getting on with my life and going out and looking for another job. Of course, they didn't bother asking me about it. If they had I would have told them I can't do any kind of real job search right now because of the noncompete clause in my contract."

"Bummer," Chris said.

Ali nodded. "That means that, by actual count, I've been let go twice in the space of a week. I'm sure I'm setting some kind of record, and it's very hard on the ego."

"Have you thought of podcasting?" Chris asked.

"What?"

"Pod-casting. It's kind of like a blog, only recorded—on video and/or audio. Instead of being posted as text—or in addition to text commentary, you read what you have to say into a video camera, just like you used to do when you read the news on TV. In podcasting, though, you'd be doing both the writing and reading. Once the segments have been uploaded, viewers can download them and watch or listen at their leisure."

"This sounds highly unlikely," Ali said.

"Don't be so negative," Chris countered. "You're getting lots of traffic on your site—more than I would have thought possible. Look," he said, pointing at the screen. "You may not have noticed, but there's a counter at the bottom of the page so you can see how many hits you're getting—more than three thousand in less than a week. I think that's pretty respectable. Between the domestic violence stuff and the items dealing with ALS, you've got a variety of interesting and powerful content, and, because of your work in LA, you already have an established audience. If you can attract enough readers, you might be able to find yourself some advertisers as well."

"As in advertisers who'd actually pay money?" Ali asked.

"I don't know how much, but I think so," Chris replied. "Maybe not enough to live on, but I'd guess you weren't making money hand over fist working at the Sugarloaf."

"What are you doing?" Ali asked. "Looking for a back door into the world of television news?"

Chris smiled. "Sort of," he said. "Except this time the only news director on staff would be you."

"I suppose it's worth looking into," Ali agreed. "How soon do I have to decide?"

"Whenever," he said. "If you want to do it right away, I can come back and help you set it up when I'm finished with finals. Otherwise, it can wait until after graduation."

Ali watched as he scrolled back to the top of the page. Just below the cutlooseblog.com header, there was now a photo of her, one she remembered Chris taking the previous year during Paul Grayson's annual pre-Christmas holiday bash.

"Where did that come from?" she asked.

"I had a jpeg of it downloaded on my computer," he said. "I read Velma's post about wanting to see your photo. It seemed to me she had a good point, so I posted one. In fact, that's what made me think about podcasting in the first place. Hope you don't mind."

"Melissa's probably not going to like it," Ali said.

"Melissa?" Chris asked. "Who's she?"

"The lady who thinks I should wear a bag over my head."

"Oh, her!" Chris replied. "If I were you, I never would have posted that one."

Ali's phone rang. "I can't believe it," Andrea Rogers said, her voice shaking in outrage.

"What's going on?"

"I drove by Reenie's house this morning on my way to have my hair done," Andrea said. "There's a whole stack of boxes on the front porch, like moving boxes or something. And Jasmine's car is still there, parked right in front of the house in the same spot where it was last night when I left. Reenie's not even buried yet, and Howie's having some tart sleep over? I swear, the man has no shame!"

"Neither does Jasmine," Ali pointed out. "They deserve each other."

"Doesn't he care about what people think or what the neighbors are saying?"

"Howie's so full of himself I doubt he's capable of taking other people's opinions into consideration," Ali said.

"But is he capable of murder?" Andrea asked. "Is she?"

Ali thought about her meeting with Jasmine Wright. "Maybe," Ali said. "That's why we need to find out where they both were last Thursday night and exactly what they were doing."

"I'm trying," Andrea said determinedly. "Believe me, I'm trying."

"So am I," Ali said. "Chris figured out Reenie's password. I'm about to log on and see what, if anything, I can find in her e-mail account. It bothers me, though. It seems disloyal to be prying into her private affairs."

"I know," Andrea agreed. "I felt the same way when I was going through her files last night. But if we don't look, who will?"

"Who indeed?" Ali returned.

Minutes later, armed with Samantha as the password, a conflicted Ali Reynolds was scrolling through the e-mails Reenie Bernard had sent and received in the last seven days of her life. The account had been set up to keep sent and previously read e-mails for a maximum of fourteen days. Reenie had been dead for a week. That meant that a full week's worth of correspondence had already been deleted from the files. It also meant that whatever information might have been gleaned from those messages had already been lost.

What remained intact was at once both mundane and surprising. Almost all the messages Reenie had sent dealt with the day-to-day realities of keeping the Flagstaff YW up and running. They concerned what was going on right then as well as in the future, when Reenie would no longer be in the picture. She had been in touch with several head-hunting agencies as well as with several other YWCA branches in search of someone who might be interested in taking over the helm in Flag. She had also sent out notes to any number of people—major donors most likely—telling them that her medical situation was changing rapidly and asking for their help in devising a suitable transition plan.

Reenie's notes, brimming with bad news, were written, however, in a matter-of-fact tone and without any discernable trace of self-pity. There was nothing in them that bemoaned her own personal situation or her declining health. Instead, in the days leading up to her death, Reenie Bernard had been totally focused on keeping her beloved YWCA afloat.

Reading through the correspondence, Ali remembered what Ed Holzer had said about his elder daughter, that she was "a do-gooder to the end." It was true.

Lots of incoming e-mails had arrived on that Thursday itself and in the days following Reenie's disappearance before people knew she was gone and before she had been declared dead. Those, along with e-mails that had arrived since Monday, had all been opened and then saved as new—presumably by Detective Farris.

Who gave him the password? Ali wondered. But then she remembered that Lee Farris was a detective after all. Surely he was every bit as smart as Chris and had figured out the Samantha bit all on his own.

Most were notes sent in reply to Reenie's earlier communications. In them people expressed their shock and dismay about what was happening and asked what they could do to help.

Then, as she sat there, Ali was surprised to hear the distinctive click that announced the arrival of new mail. With Reenie dead for more than a week, Ali opened the e-mail more than half expecting it to be meaningless spam:

Dear Reenie,

As you suggested, I've been in touch with the US Postal authorities. They're launching a fraud investigation of the way Rodriguez Medical Center does business. The people I spoke to aren't very hopeful that we'll ever be able to get back any of my mother's money, but thanks so much for all your help. I'll keep you posted. We've got to keep this from happening to anyone else.

Randy Tompkins

As the message sank in, Ali realized at once that she'd been wrong. She had supposed all along that Reenie had been going to opt for the high-priced treatment being offered in Mexico. Instead, she had ended up helping to expose it as exactly what Howie had thought it was—a rip-off. It meant that the unexplained trip to the bank Ali and Andrea had put so much store in counted for nothing. Dave Holman was probably right. Reenie had been busy establishing a banking presence somewhere else, somewhere apart from her joint accounts with Howie.

After switching over to her own e-mail for a moment, Ali retrieved Don Trilby's address. She forwarded Randy's note to him along with the following addition:

Dear Don,

I discovered the following e-mail among my friend Reenie's files. You may want to be in touch with Mr. Tompkins yourself before you make any permanent decisions on the course of your treatment. I haven't contacted Mr. Tompkins directly about this, but I suspect he'd be more than willing to discuss this with you.

My very best to you and your family,
Alison Reynolds

Finished with that, Ali returned to Reenie's mailbox where she glanced through Reenie's Favorites list and found a number of the ALS support sites Ali herself had visited in the previous days.

A sharp knock on the door compelled Ali out of Reenie's correspondence and back to the present. Samantha immediately abandoned her place on the couch in favor of a hiding place behind it.

"Danny's here," Chris announced, shouldering his backpack and picking up his single suitcase.

"Do you need help getting the Bronco down the hill?"

"No. Danny and I will caravan it down. I don't know why Gramps is in such a hurry to get it back. After all, I don't think he's going to be driving for a while."

Ali laughed. "He's had that Bronco since I was a kid," she said. "Driving or not, I'm sure he's lost without it. What about your skis?" she asked.

"They're down in the basement," he said. "And if you don't mind, I'd like to leave them there for the time being. That way, if I do end up getting that teaching job, it'll be one less thing to move."

"Your stepfather is going to be very annoyed when he finds out you're 'squandering' your education on being a teacher. He always thought you'd end up doing something in the entertainment world—building sets or something."

"Let's don't tell him, then," Chris said with a wink. "What he doesn't know won't hurt him."

Ali walked Chris as far as the door and kissed him good-bye. "Be careful," she said.

"Don't worry. We will."

Chris and Danny left a few minutes after twelve. As soon as they were gone, Ali abandoned her computer and hurried into the shower. After drying her hair, she sat down at Aunt Evie's dressing table. For the first time since she'd been in Sedona, she spent the better part of an hour carefully applying makeup. And it did help. The tricks of the TV trade ended up leaving her looking far better than she should have, considering the amount of sleep she'd had the night before.

For Reenie's funeral she dressed in the one good outfit she had brought along from California—a midnight blue St. John suit trimmed with a narrow band of gold thread with a matching pair of Bruno Magli pumps. Examining her reflection in the full-length mirror in the bathroom, Ali decided she looked fine. Adequate anyway. For someone her age.

Chapter 16

By the time Ali arrived at the church in Cottonwood at 1:35, the parking lot was already jammed with cars. So were the surrounding streets. She ended up having to park her Cayenne a block and a half away and walk the rest of the way.

Bree Cowan, waiting at the church entrance, hurried out to the sidewalk to meet her. "Thank God you're here," she said.

"Why? What's wrong?"

"Harriet Ellsworth is president of Reenie's board of directors. She had agreed to speak at the service, but her husband ended up in the hospital this morning. She called just now to say she can't come. Dad is having a fit. I told him I'd ask if you could possibly fill in. I know it's the last minute, but nobody knew Reenie as well as you do."

"Of course I'll do it," Ali said. "Let me go sit somewhere quiet so I can pull my thoughts together."

"There's a library off Pastor Bronson's study," Bree suggested. "Maybe you could use that."

Pastor Bronson was a round, balding, and disconcertingly jolly little man who directed Ali to a small book-lined room to the right of the pulpit. While Bree went to tell Ed and Diane that the difficulty had been handled, Ali scrounged through her purse in search of pen and paper.

Only one paper item came readily to hand—the envelope containing the friendship card Reenie had sent. Somehow, that seemed to be a fitting place to compose Misty Irene Holzer Turpin Bernard's eulogy. So Ali removed the card and wrote her notes on the back of the card itself.

Years earlier, Miss Abel, a speech instructor at NAU, had suggested Ali avail herself of Toastmasters to gain more experience in public speaking. Now, twenty years after spending a year attending weekly Toastmaster meetings, Ali found it unnecessary to write out everything she intended to say. Instead, she jotted down a few key words of reminder: 1. greeting cards; 2. high school; 3. makeup; 4. missing years; and 5. greeting cards again. Ali knew that, in order to be structurally sound, a good speech ends where it begins—that's how to make sure the speech has a point.

When it was time for the service to start, Ali entered the sanctuary from the front. She was happy to see that the church was crammed wall to wall. That was a tribute to Reenie, of course, but it also spoke well of Ed and Diane Holzer's standing in the community. Most funerals come with a pervading sense of sadness. In this congregation, however, Ali sensed an almost electric tension.

Howie, the two children, and an elderly couple Ali assumed to be Howie's parents sat in the front pew on one side of the church. Ed Holzer, arms folded on his chest, sat stone-faced directly across the aisle from him. Diane, already weeping, sat next to her husband with Bree and Jack Cowan seated next to her. It reminded Ali of a bad wedding where the bride and groom's feuding families line up on either side of the church. In that tradition, Ali chose a seat in the second row, directly behind Jack Cowan.

Throughout the proceedings, nothing at all was said about the manner of Reenie's death. It was as though, by mutual consent and diplomacy, everyone simply skipped over that part. In the program, however, there was a discreet announcement to the effect that remembrances in Reenie's name should be made to the church building fund or else to the ALS Research Foundation.

Ali's turn to speak came at the end of the service. It was only when she walked to the pulpit and prepared to make her remarks that she spotted Jasmine Wright seated on the aisle in the next to last pew.

Seeing her there was almost enough to derail Ali's concentration, but she pulled herself together. *This is for the kids*, she told herself fiercely. With her hands shaking from outrage rather than nerves, Ali smiled as believably as possible at Matt and Julie and held up the card.

"If you knew Reenie Bernard," she said, "you know who sent this. Reenie loved cards. She loved sending them and receiving them. She sent them at Christmas and Valentine's Day and Easter and the Fourth of July and Thanksgiving. Sometimes she sent them for no reason at all. This one happens to be a friendship card. You see, Reenie and I were friends.

"We met and became friends on our first day of high school, when we showed up in Mrs. Toone's algebra class and figured out that we were both scared to death."

Back in the fourth row, behind the Holzers, Dave Holman smiled and nodded knowingly as did several other people in the room. Some of them Ali recognized as classmates or schoolmates. Some she didn't, but clearly lots of the people in the room were familiar with the teacher in question. Mrs. Toone had been a daunting creature who took the position her students would learn algebra properly or else.

"We were both scared to be going to school with kids from all those other places. I was from sophisticated Sedona and imagined that kids from Cottonwood would be a bunch of country bumpkins. As for the kids from Verde Valley? Forget it."

A few chuckles rippled through the room.

"But then we got there and it turned out it was fine because we were all just kids. It seems unlikely now that a girl who grew up living in an apartment out behind a diner would become friends with a banker's daughter, but that's exactly what happened."

She talked about the things she and Reenie had done together—about school plays and pranks and organizations. And she talked about the missing years, when their friendship went dormant for a time but didn't disappear.

"We went our separate ways and lost each other for a long time after high school, but then I came home for our tenth high school reunion and there she was, the same old Reenie. We picked up our friendship again as easily as if we'd never been apart. We called each other often and wrote letters back and forth. That's when she started sending me cards again, an amazing collection of cards. My only regret is that I didn't keep all of them.

"If you've seen the YW's vibrant new facility up in Flagstaff, you've seen the works of Reenie Bernard's heart, hands, and mind. When other people said it was impossible to have a new building, Reenie ignored all the naysayers. She wasn't afraid to reach for the stars, and she built it anyway.

"I went to Reenie's office in Flagstaff yesterday," Ali continued. "One whole wall is covered, floor to ceiling, with greeting cards—the ones people had sent to her." Ali had to pause for a moment and compose herself before continuing. "It says in the Bible, 'As ye sow, so shall ye reap.' Reenie Bernard sowed greeting cards wherever she went, and she definitely reaped the same.

"Last night I heard from a woman named Louise Malkin who lives in Lubbock, Texas. Her sister, Lisa Kingsley, recently died of ALS. Lisa and Reenie met in an ALS chat room before doctors confirmed that Reenie, too, had been stricken with the disease. They became friends. I know that because last night, while sorting through her sister's belongings, Louise found a lovely greeting card. I don't think I have to tell you who sent it.

"Thanks for all the cards, Reenie. Thanks for giving all of us something to remember you by."

Ali resumed her seat then. As the organ began the

introduction to “Morning Has Broken,” she heard sounds of sniffling as people reached for handkerchiefs and tissues.

Miss Abel would be proud, she thought.

Outside, after the service, two black limos were lined up behind the hearse. Howie, his parents, and Matt and Julie rode in one. The Holzers along with Jack and Bree rode in the other while everyone else walked the three short blocks to Cottonwood Cemetery. If Jasmine came along to the cemetery, Ali didn’t spot her. There was no exchange of greetings or pleasantries between the two opposing sets of family members, not at the church or during the brief graveside service, either.

When it was time to return to the limos, Julie slipped away from Howie’s mother and ran over to Ed and Diane. She was crying and clinging to Diane’s waist when Howie stepped forward and drew her away to the limo for the ride back to Flagstaff.

So that’s how it’s going to be, Ali thought. *They’ve lost their mother and now they’re losing their grandparents as well.*

Back in the church’s basement parish hall, the tenor of the gathering seemed to have changed for the better. Yes, it was still sad. People were still grieving, but with Howie and his parents no longer present, most of the uneasy tension seemed to have drained away.

Ali was standing near the punch bowl when Dave Holman made his way over to her, coffee cup in one hand and a plate of sandwiches in another. “Good job,” he said. “Especially for a last-minute pinch hitter.”

"Thanks," she said.

"Do you have plans for later?" he asked.

Her first thought was that Dave Holman had a hell of a lot of nerve. How dare he try to pick her up at Reenie's funeral? But then he continued.

"I'm working at the moment," he added. "But I've been going over the phone records you were interested in. I've been tracking down some of those names and numbers. It occurred to me that you might be able to tell me about some of them."

"About the bank . . ." Ali began.

"Oh, it's there all right," Dave said. "I have a call in to the branch manager. He won't be back until tomorrow. Since you seem to know a good deal about all this, I thought maybe I should sit down with you and take an official statement . . ."

So he wasn't asking for a date—not exactly. "Sure," Ali said. "What time?"

"I could pick you up between six and six-thirty," he offered. "We could go down to the substation and maybe stop off somewhere for a burger afterward."

"That would be great."

Because there was no elevator at First Lutheran, Bob Larson had to wait upstairs in his wheelchair while his wife made a brief appearance at the reception.

"Great job," Edie said, as Dave Holman melted back into the crowd. "Reenie would have loved it. Especially the part about the cards. She always sent those lion and lamb ones at Christmas. I think I still have a couple of them. They were too cute to throw away."

"I wish I'd saved more of mine," Ali said. "So how'd it go with the consultant?"

"All right, I guess," Edie said, but she didn't sound enthusiastic.

"What happened?"

"Dad got along with the guy like gangbusters," Edie said. "I didn't like him much."

"Why not?"

"He wants your grandmother's recipes," Edie answered. "All of them. I thought we were just talking about selling the building, but the recipes? Your grandmother's sweet rolls?"

To Ali's amazement, her mother, who prided herself on not being the least bit sentimental and who ordinarily never cried at funerals, seemed dangerously close to tears.

"Mom, what's wrong?"

Edie shook her head. "I don't know what's the matter with me. It was my idea to sell the place, but now that it looks like it might happen, I don't know. The Sugarloaf's been my whole life. I don't know what I'll do without it."

Ali gave her mother a hug. "Don't worry," she said. "You'll figure it out."

Ali had planned on making a polite appearance at the reception and then taking off. That proved impossible. People she hadn't seen since high school—classmates, retired teachers, local business people—all wanted to stop and chat: It was such a shame about Reenie. Was Ali still doing the news in LA? Where was she living now? How long was she going to be in town? Did Ali's folks still own the Sugarloaf? How was it possible for her to stand up in front of all those people and speak off the cuff like that? It was all mundane chitchat, but some of the questions were more easily answered than others, and all of the conversations proved to be as difficult to escape as Br'er Rabbit's brier patch.

When Ali finally exited the church and headed back to the Cayenne, Andrea Rogers trailed after her. "I'm sure Harriet Ellsworth is devastated that she missed this," Andrea babbled. "But you're a much better speaker. By the way, I saw you talking to that Dave Holman guy. He's a detective with the Yavapai sheriff's department, isn't he? What did he want?"

"To go over some phone numbers with me," Ali said. "As far as I'm concerned, that's progress."

It was dusk by the time she finally drove up Andante and into the driveway on Skyview. The sun was sinking below the far horizon as she parked in the driveway. Tired after a long day and drained by the afternoon's storm of emotions, she barely paid attention as she unlocked the door and let herself into the house.

She was reaching for the light switch when something powerful slammed into her out of the dark. There was an explosion of pain inside her head, and she crumpled to the floor. She was out for a few seconds. When she came to, the spinning room was sprinkled with blinking stars. The overhead light was on by then, although she didn't remember actually hitting the switch.

Groaning, she pulled herself up onto her hands and knees. That's when she saw the boots—steel-toed work boots covered with an indelible layer of gray dust. She watched as one of the boots hauled back and took aim for a kick. The blow caught her in the midsection and sent her flying across the room. She landed against the end of the kitchen cupboard. She lay there like a rag doll, clutching her stomach, moaning, and gasping for breath.

"Where is she?" a menacing voice demanded close to her ear.

Ali could feel beery breath on her cheek and smell the man's sweat, but she didn't look at his face. Instead, she watched his feet, hoping against hope that he wouldn't kick her again; knowing he would. Without asking, she knew who he was—Ben Witherspoon—come looking for Ali and for his wife.

"I don't know where she is," Ali croaked. "I have no idea."

He kicked her again, harder this time. She heard the blow and felt it both. Her whole being roared in pain. She thought she screamed, but she wasn't sure. Part of her, oddly separated from her body, was suddenly asking a string of disjointed questions that were only remotely connected to what was happening. They seemed to come from somewhere nearby but not necessarily from inside her head. It was as though some outside observer was standing by, commenting on the play-by-play action: Is anything broken? How much more can she take? How long before he kills her? Is the phone still working? How did he get inside the house? Who let him in?

The pain found her again, dissolving the outside commentator as it roared back through her body. She rolled away from him, choking and coughing.

A rib, she thought. *He broke my rib.*

Ben Witherspoon was talking to her now, his voice low and threatening. Desperately she fought to gather her wits. She needed to know what he was saying. And planning.

"You're the bitch who sent her away, so she must have told you where she was going. Tell me!" he ordered. "I'm her husband, goddamnit. I have a right to know."

He kicked at her again. This time Ali managed to scramble far enough out of range that the bruising blow landed on her butt. It hurt, but it missed hitting anything vital.

Where's Samantha? she wondered now. *What the hell has he done to the cat?*

"I don't know where Corine is," she gasped. "She didn't tell me."

Witherspoon reached down and grabbed her by the arm, twisting it painfully behind her as he picked her up and flung her toward the couch. "That's your computer, isn't it? Open it and turn it on," he commanded. "I want to see how you do this crap!"

Ali's head was still spinning, but being upright helped. While she waited for the computer to boot up, she stole a look at the intruder. He was in his mid-thirties, wiry but strong. His hair was dirty blond and in serious need of washing. He had the bronzed leathery skin of someone who has spent too many hours working in the sun. With a sense of shock, she realized she had seen Ben Witherspoon before. He had come into the Sugarloaf for breakfast that morning just when Susan had been taking over for Ali. He had sat at one end of the counter. Ali and Dave had sat at the other.

What was it Dave had said just then? Hadn't he called Ali by her name? No wonder Ben Witherspoon knew who she was. Or maybe he had seen the Christmas photo Chris had posted on the blog.

"How did you find me?" she asked.

"It's none of your business," he said. "I'm the one asking the questions."

But Ali thought she knew the answer. He must have followed her up the hill when she left work.

Why wasn't I paying more attention?

She looked around the room. Her purse still lay by the door where it had fallen when he had knocked her to the floor. And since her Glock was in her purse . . . What was it Nancy Drake, Ali's self-defense instructor, had said to her about the uselessness of women carrying weapons in their purses.

Armed but not dangerous, she thought.

That was exactly where she was. Her Glock was there, all right, but totally inaccessible.

"The log-on's finished," she said when the interminable hour-glass finally disappeared from the screen. "What now?"

"You and I are going to do a post," he said. "Cutlooseblog's last post. We're going to do it together. I'll dictate the words. You write them down."

Ali's hands shook uncontrollably as she tried to work the keyboard. Her trembling fingers missed keystroke after keystroke as she attempted to type what he dictated. The implication behind his words was clear. This wasn't a suicide note because Ali Reynolds wouldn't die by her own hand. But she was going to die. Of that she was certain.

"Do you want me to post it?"

"Why not?" he said. "It's not going to make any difference."

Logging onto cutloose she could see that there were over a dozen messages waiting for her, but she made no attempt to open them.

This will be my last posting. I'm sorry for all the trouble I've caused. Good-bye.

Posted 5:52 P.M. by Babe

She looked at the time—5:52. What time had Dave said he was coming to pick her up? Sometime between six and six-thirty. She felt the smallest flicker of hope. If she could hang on long enough for Dave to arrive, she might make it. But could she last until then? Could she stall Ben Witherspoon that long?

"Is that all?" Ali asked.

"What do you mean all?"

"I already told you I have no idea where Corine is right now, but she sent me an e-mail. I could write to her for you. Is there something you'd like me to tell her?"

"What a good idea," he sneered at her. "Let's do that."

She had Corine's real e-mail address, but she didn't dare use it. What if Witherspoon stole her computer. If he logged on he'd have access to all of Ali's correspondence, including the e-mail from his wife. The guy was obviously computer savvy and knew how to find his way around the Internet. After all he'd been tracking Corine's computer movements for some time without her knowledge. If he ever gained access to her new e-mail address, Ali had no doubt that he'd somehow figure out a way to find her physical location as well.

Other than Corine, Chris alone knew everything about Watching's threat. Unfortunately he was probably in California by now. But then she remembered how her own cell phone had worked as they came across on I-10. If she managed to send him a message, would he understand what she was really trying to say? Holding her breath and praying he didn't have his phone turned off, Ali typed in Chris's e-mail address.

Ben came across the room and stood peering over Ali's shoulder as she typed. "CDR?" he asked, reading off the address line. "That's Corine's address?"

Ali nodded. "Her first initial followed by the initials of the shelter she's staying in. Daughters of the Revolution." It was the best Ali could think of at the moment. It sounded terribly lame to her, but Ben Witherspoon fell for it.

"Figures!" he snorted. "Of course, she'd take up with a bunch of commies. For all I know, they're probably lesbians, too—pinko, commie, lesbians."

"What do you want to say?" Ali asked.

"Dear Corine," he said. "You're a whore and a bitch . . ."

"I can't write that," Ali said.

"What do you mean you can't write it. You said you'd write what I wanted to say. What's the matter? Are your fingers broke?"

"I can write it," Ali told him, "but it won't go through. The spam filters will kick it out." Ali didn't know if that was true or not, but it sounded good. Again, Ben Witherspoon seemed to take her at her word. He studied her for a long minute with a somewhat puzzled expression on his face.

"Dear Corine," he began again. "I remember when we got married how you promised to love and obey. Obey, remember? I want you back. I want Tony back. You have no right to leave me like this and take my son. Babe is writing this. Remember her? I found her, and I'll find you, too. And you know what I'll do to you then. You'll be sorry. Ben."

He peered over Ali's shoulder the whole time, while she was typing and until after she punched Send. "Good," he said when she finished. He pulled the power cord out of the wall and handed it to her, then he returned to the couch. "Pack that thing up and bring it along. It's a lot newer than mine."

Ali's heart sank. It hadn't taken nearly as long as she had expected to send the message. Dave still wasn't here.

"Why?" she objected. "Where are we going? Besides, don't you want to see if she sends something back?"

"We're going for a little ride," he said. "Just me and you. In your cute little SUV instead of my Datsun. I'm trading that in, too."

"But . . ."

The land line began to ring. Instinctively, Ali reached for it.

"Don't," Witherspoon snarled. He reached for something on the couch beside him. When he picked it up, Ali saw it was a knife, most likely from the cutting block in the kitchen. He waved it casually in her direction. "Don't even *think* about answering it," he added.

They waited together until the phone stopped ringing. Moments later, the cell phone, still in her purse across the room, began to ring as well. "It's probably my son," she said. "I should probably answer. If I don't, he'll worry. He even might send someone over to check on me."

"Answer it then," Witherspoon snapped. "But not a word out of line. Not a single word, and no tricks, either. Got it?"

Nodding, Ali got off the couch and went to retrieve the purse. As she bent down to pick it up, she caught a glimpse of Sam's one yellow eye gleaming back at her from under the couch.

Thank God she's scared of strangers, Ali thought. *Thank God!*

Rummaging through her purse she spotted her Glock's blue-steel handle just under her pulsing cell phone, but she didn't try to pick it up. She didn't dare. Right that second, Ben Witherspoon was all the way across the room, far less than ten feet. That was something else Ali suddenly and belatedly remembered from Nancy's self-defense class—that within eight feet, someone with a knife can take out someone with a gun. The process of removing the gun from the purse and aiming it would take too much time. She'd be lucky to get off even one shot before Witherspoon and the knife were all over her.

Instead, Ali picked up the phone. Then casually, seemingly without thinking, she swung the purse's strap over her shoulder.

"Hi, Chris," she said. "How's it going?"

"Are you all right?" Chris demanded. "Is he there at the house with you right now or are you somewhere else?"

"You're already in Palm Springs?" she asked brightly. "Really? That's great. You guys are making good time then."

"Mom, do you want me to call the cops?"

"Yes," she said, "the funeral was very nice. Lots of people were there. Lots of them. One of the biggest funerals Cottonwood's ever had."

Please, God, she prayed. *Help Chris understand what's going on.*

His next words gave her hope. "Should I call Dave Holman?" he asked.

"Yes," she said at once. "Dave was there all right, along with everyone else."

"I'll call him," Chris said. "As soon as I hang up. Be careful."

"Good," Ali said quickly. "That's fine. Tell Danny to drive carefully." With that she ended the call.

"Come on then, Babe," Witherspoon said cheerfully. "Let's you and me go. Ladies first. But don't try anything stupid." He brandished the boning knife in Ali's direction. "I'd hate to have to use this here in your pretty little house. Wouldn't want to make that kind of mess. We'll share the load. You carry the computer. I'll pack the knife. And whatever you do, don't make a sound."

Chapter 17

Ali picked up the computer and started toward the door with her assailant right behind. She realized as she walked, that this might be her only chance. If he came close enough to her, maybe she could fire her 9 mm Glock at point-blank range in a way that would drop him like a rock and take the boning knife out of play. And maybe kill him.

That was the other thing Nancy had said: When you make the decision to buy and carry a deadly weapon, you've already made a moral decision as well. You've established that there's a point beyond which you will use that weapon to defend yourself, and you've drawn that line rationally and not in the blood-pounding heat of the moment.

Ben Witherspoon had crossed Ali's deadly-force line long ago. He had bet she wouldn't fight back, but he was wrong. Even so, she still hoped that when she opened the door, she'd find Dave in his patrol car parked outside, ready to come to her aid. But Dave wasn't there. If anyone was going to save Ali Reynolds, it was going to have to be Ali herself.

The night was cold, clear, and utterly silent. Ali's

breath puffed white in the frigid air, and every icy intake made her want to double over in pain. At least one rib was broken, maybe more. Overhead, the still, velvet-black sky was bright with winking stars. Ali had lost her shoes in the earlier scuffle. The cold gravel of the driveway bit sharply into the soles of her bare feet, making her limp, but the pain also helped her focus.

She glanced around hopefully, looking to see if any of her neighbors had spotted something amiss. Unfortunately, the laurel hedge around the backyard—the same hedge that gave the house its much prized privacy—now lent cover to the man who intended to kill her.

"You drive," Witherspoon growled at her. "But if you try to pull anything—anything at all—I'll slit your throat. Understand?"

Ali nodded. She understood all right. Absolutely. What's more, she knew he meant it. She also knew that, once she got in the car with him, she was as good as dead. Whatever she was going to do to save herself had to happen soon!

When she arrived at the front of the Cayenne, she stopped and made as if to put the computer on the hood. She felt the blade of the knife bite into her back.

"What the hell do you think you're doing?" he demanded.

She knew at once he'd cut her, not deep, but enough to hurt. Enough to make her bleed. Enough to let her know he meant business. "I need the keys," she hissed back at him. "They're in my purse."

"Get 'em then," he returned. "And be quick about it."

She had dropped her cell phone into her purse. It rang again just then, startling them both.

"Don't answer it," he snapped. "Let it ring."

She did as she was told, but the flashing light on the screen of the ringing phone provided an amazing amount of light inside her otherwise pitch-black purse—enough to see her car keys. Enough to see the gun.

Then something else happened. From far away down the mountain, Ali heard the faint wail of a siren. Witherspoon was standing right next to her, close enough that she felt him tense at the sound. Knowing this momentary distraction was her only chance, Ali wrapped her shaking hand around the handle of her Glock. Whirling, she spun around and faced him. She didn't even try removing the weapon from her purse. Instead, holding the gun inside, and with the leather of her Coach bag touching his belly, she pulled the trigger.

Nancy Drake's voice droned in her head. "Once you've made the decision to stop someone, you'd by God better carry through. Use hollow points. They're the ones that do the damage. And forget about target shooting. Go for the gut. Take out a guy's pelvis and he's going down."

With the first shot, Ben Witherspoon's eyes bulged as much in outrage as surprise, but despite Nancy's predictions, he didn't fall. "Why you . . ." he screamed.

In the aftermath of the shot, Ali's ears rang. She

couldn't hear what he was saying, but she read his lips. And his mind. He was enraged, and with the knife still in hand, his intentions were absolutely clear. So she let go of the purse and pulled the trigger again. This time the bullet found its mark and he did go down. Hard.

When Ali could hear again, she realized that her phone was still ringing. Or maybe it was ringing again. It lay where it had landed, a yard or so from her feet. Next to it, barely visible in the pulsing light, she caught the gleam of the car keys.

Just then, to her dismay, a steel-hard grip, like the jaws of a trap, locked around the base of her ankle. Witherspoon was down, all right, but he wasn't out. Ali reached for the door handle, trying to hold on to something to keep from falling. In the process, she slammed the Glock against the car door. The gun bounced out of her grip, fell to the ground, and then spun out of reach.

Ali hit the ground, too. When she landed, the jolting pain from her broken ribs was so excruciating it took her breath away. She felt a sharp stab of pain in her leg, too, and knew he had cut her at least once and that he'd do it again if she didn't get away. She kicked him then, hard, with her other foot. She felt the gratifying blow as her heel connected sharply with the bottom of his chin. The kick took him by surprise. His head jerked back and she heard his teeth knock together in his mouth. His grip loosened only slightly but it was enough. She squirmed away from him, scrabbling along the ground like an ungainly lizard, desperate to escape his reach.

The wailing sirens were much closer now, coming up the mountain, but they weren't nearly close enough or fast enough to satisfy her. If he came after her again, there was no guarantee anyone would reach her in time.

Nearby she heard the murmuring voices of worried neighbors who had emerged from their various houses in search of an explanation for the real-life gunfire that had suddenly drowned out the cops-and-robbers sound effects of their nightly police drama fare.

But Ali needed armed police officers right then far more than she needed well-meaning or curious neighbors. When her fingers chanced to encounter the familiar shape of her car keys, she did the only thing that made sense.

She grabbed them and pressed hard on the panic button and kept right on crawling.

The next thing she knew, Dave Holman was there beside her, kneeling on the ground.

"He tried to kill me," Ali heard herself blubbering. "He was waiting inside the house and . . ."

"Hush," Dave said, covering his lips with one finger. "Don't say another word. You're hurt. Let's get you to the ER."

cutlooseblog.com
Monday, March 21, 2005

First, please let me apologize for the long silence, especially after that post that said it was my "last" post. I know many of you have been terribly concerned. Some of you are already aware of what's happened. The rest of you are about to find out.

Twenty-two years ago, when I was pregnant with my son, I decided that when it came time to choose an OB-GYN to deliver my baby, I'd go looking for a woman. My reasoning was simple. Since men don't have babies, maybe a female doctor would be more in tune with what I wanted and needed. And I have to say, even all these years later, that Dr. Winona Manchester was perfect in every way. She had two children of her own. She was sympathetic and realistic. When she told me what I should or shouldn't do, I believed her. She'd been there and done that.

Since most of you know Tank is now twenty-two, you must be wondering why I'm telling you all this old news. I'm getting to that. And since this is a blog, and I don't have to say my piece in the forty-five seconds before the next commercial, I'm going to say it my way.

For years, in my role as a "public person" I've helped out with various social events. I've spent a lot of time raising money for cancer research for the simple reason that's what my first husband died of. I've also done a good deal of work for various women's groups, including organizations that deal with helping victims of domestic violence. But I did that more as a good citizen than because I really knew or cared that much about the issue. I was interested. I was involved. But like those male

OB-GYNs that I dismissed so long ago, I hadn't been there or done that—until now.

My last regular message was posted on Friday morning, the day of my friend's funeral. The night before I had received a second threatening e-mail from the estranged husband of one of my readers. You may remember the woman I advised to take her baby and run. I posted her husband's comment that if she left him, he'd come looking for me. She did run, and he made good on his promise. He found me. He broke into my home while I was attending Reenie's funeral and was waiting for me when I got back. (The cut screen and the broken window have both been replaced, and my new security system is being installed right this minute.)

Before Friday night, I never knew what it felt like to be kicked hard enough to break bones. (Two ribs, currently taped.) Or to be sliced by a kitchen knife. (Eleven stitches. Tetanus shot.) I also never knew that a life-and-death battle is just exactly that. In newscasts I've often been critical of "trigger-happy cops." But while I was spouting those views, it turns out I'd never been there or done that, either. I didn't know what it means to have your life turned upside-down in a him-or-me scenario.

I spent two nights at the hospital in Flagstaff, the same hospital where my father had his surgery last week. (My mother was there again, bless her.) I still hurt all over from the kicks that found their intended targets, and I'm grateful for the one that missed. One of the blows left a clear shoe-print-style bruise on my backside. Having that photographed for forensic purposes was not a high point of my existence, but I'll live.

I'm home now, and I'm alive. My assailant isn't. That's due primarily to the California concealed weapon permit I carry in my wallet and the Glock I had in the bottom of my purse when he attacked me. (If you are someone who thinks all handguns should be outlawed, you're more than welcome to write to me here, but I think you're going to have a hard time changing my mind.)

There's a lot more I'd like to say right now, but my lawyers (yes, that would be plural) won't let me. I've hired a local defense attorney in the event (unlikely, I've been told) that the county attorney decides to press charges against me. Arizona seems to be one of those states where people still have the right to defend themselves in their own homes and on their own property. The second attorney is due to the fact that the dead man's estranged wife, the abused woman who read my column and fled for her life, is now considering filing a civil wrongful death suit against me. (No good deed goes unpunished!)

After living for more than forty years with no attorneys, I now have four which, by my count, is approximately four too many.

Someone called a few minutes ago to let me know that a news team from my old station wants to come to Sedona to interview me. It seems that the LA area is "intense with interest" about my situation. I told them not to come. But if they show up anyway, I'll put them in touch with my attorney(s) and repeat my two new favorite words. "No comment."

Posted: 12:47 P.M. by Babe

Several hundred e-mails had come in over the weekend while she had been dark, almost all of them asking why Ali was abandoning cutlooseblog. Almost as soon as her post was up, she started hearing a barrage of clicks, as if people had been lurking in dark corners of the Internet, waiting for her to reappear. Not surprisingly, some of them were very familiar. Velma's message in particular made her smile.

Dear Babe,

Velma again. Okay, I finally did it. I called you Babe. Hope you're happy.

Thank you for putting up your picture. That was fun, but then all of a sudden you just stopped and nothing more came through. I checked every single day.

Last night they finally had something on TV about what happened to you. I'm so sorry, but I knew it all along. As soon as I saw that "last" post of yours, I knew something was terribly wrong. I even called information and got the long distance number for the police department there in Sedona. But the person I spoke to wanted to know what I was reporting, and of course, I had no idea of what or where or any of the other things she said she had to have in order to make a report.

I'm so glad you're going to be okay.

Velma T in Laguna

Sylvia's, too, was familiar.

Dear Ali,

This morning someone bought your autographed photo from me for $11.38. That means I more than doubled my money. As far as I'm concerned, you're a very good investment.

Your fan,
Sylvia

Some, however, were entirely new.

Dear Babe,

My name is Al Rutherford. I saw what happened to you on TV last night and it is amazing. I am a student at UCLA. Film studies. I need to write a screenplay, and I think your story would be awesome. Do I have to have your persmission to write it? If so, would you please send it. Also, when I finish I hope you will help me find an agent. Everyone says you have to have agents now although that didn't used to be the case.

Best,
Al (Short for Alvin)

When he was young, my father worked on the Chipmunk records

Dear Babe,

What happened to the cat? To Samantha? Is she all right? You didn't mention her and I'm worried that awful man may have hurt her, too.

Janelle

Ali immediately posted that one along with a response.

cutlooseblog.com
Monday, March 21, 2005

Sorry I forgot to mention it, but Samantha is fine. It turns out she's smarter than I am. As soon as the guy broke into my house, she evidently went looking for cover and didn't come out until after he was gone. While I was in the hospital, my mother came over to look after her. Thanks for your concern.

Posted 2:10 P.M. by Babe

Shortly after that the security system installer knocked on the front door to tell her he was finished. He came inside and spent the next half hour taking Ali through all the intricacies of her new wireless setup, including instructing her on setting the codes and tuning her television set to the proper channel so she could see who was outside knocking without having to open the door.

When he left, Ali wasn't at all surprised that she fell asleep on the couch. The doctor had told her the pain meds would make her sleepy, and it was absolutely true. During the day. At night, it seemed she couldn't sleep at all or, when she finally did, she was plagued by nightmares. In each of those, Ben Witherspoon was always back in her house, stalking her and menacing her, with a knife in one hand and a gun in the other.

A sharp knock on the front door startled Ali out of her afternoon nap. The security system installer had left her TV set tuned to channel 95. As Samantha scrambled to disappear, Ali checked out the television screen. On it, she saw Bob Larson's battered Bronco parked in the background. In the foreground stood Kip Hogan, Bob Larson's new right-hand man. An Arizona Diamondbacks baseball cap was pulled low over his eyes.

Seeing a man there, a relative stranger, caused an unreasoning fear to rise in Ali's throat. What she wanted more than anything right then was to have her Glock back and in her hand, but the weapon had been confiscated as possible evidence and was still under lock and key where it would remain until all legal wrangling had run its course.

Kip knocked again.

Straighten up, Ali told herself. She stood up, staggered over to the door, and opened it.

Kip took off the cap, bent down, picked up an ice chest, and then followed Ali into the house. "Afternoon, ma'am," he said politely. "Your mother sent over some food. Want me to put it in the fridge?"

Back on the couch, Ali laughed aloud at that and then stopped abruptly. The words 'it only hurts when you laugh' were no longer funny.

"If you can find a spot," she said. "There's already so much food in there, I don't know what I'm going to do with it all. People must think I'm starving. And if I eat it all, I'll turn into a blimp."

She had come home from the hospital to find her kitchen counter overflowing with platters of cookies, cupcakes, pies, and brownies along with plastic-wrapped loaves of banana bread. In all its carbohydrate glory, the place had looked more like a gigantic bake sale than a private kitchen. She found that the refrigerator and freezer both, too, had been stuffed to the gills with goodies. There were frozen casseroles stacked in the freezer while the fridge bulged with plates of fried chicken and covered bowls full of every kind of fruit salad imaginable along with two separate potato salads, one macaroni salad and a dish of very leathery red Jell-O.

While Ali watched, Kip worked with single-minded determination to cram this new load of foodstuffs into the refrigerator. "What about your friends up the mountain?" Ali asked, thinking in sudden embarrassment that only a week ago, Kip had been bunking in a snowy homeless encampment up on the Mogollon Rim.

"I'm sure they'd be most appreciative, ma'am," Kip said. "If there was any of it you didn't want," he added, "any you thought you could spare."

"Ask my dad," she said. "Tell him I have way more food here than I'll ever be able to eat. Maybe the two of you could come collect it tomorrow or the next day and take it up the mountain."

"I'll talk to him about it," Kip said nodding. "See what he has to say. Now, if you'll excuse me."

He exited then, scurrying away as if uncomfortable talking to her alone. Once he was gone, Ali limped out to the kitchen. The doctor had warned her that she'd feel worse in a day or two than she had in the hospital, and it was true. The many bruises on her body had gone from black to greenish purple. As they changed color they seemed to hurt more rather than less.

Ali picked through the goodies. Her mother had sent over a covered dish filled with potato soup. She dished up some of that and put it in the microwave to heat. She reached for a piece of chicken, to go along with the soup. But the chicken reminded her of Howie Bernard and the kids. She pulled the tin foil back over the chicken and settled for soup only.

Chris called while she was eating. "How are you?" he asked.

"Better," Ali said, making the effort to sound more chipper than she felt. "I'm doing fine. Really."

She'd had to talk like crazy to keep him from abandoning his finals and coming straight back to

Sedona. Her mother had helped with that one, or it might not have worked.

"You have enough to eat?"

She surveyed the mounds of food covering her counter. "Plenty," she said. "You wouldn't believe how much food there is."

Chris didn't sound like himself, though. "What about you?" Ali asked. "Are your finals going all right?"

"They're fine," he said without conviction.

"What's wrong, Chris?" she said at last. "I can tell by your voice that something's up."

"It's all my fault," he said. "I'm the one who talked you into doing the blog thing. If I had just left you alone, none of this would have happened."

"Yes," she said, "and then I wouldn't be sitting here gorging myself on your grandmother's delicious potato soup. Things happen for a reason, Chris. I was looking for a new direction, and you gave me one. Of course, neither one of us expected me to get the crap beaten out of me along the way. But what is it they say at the gym, 'No pain; no gain.' "

"Mom," Chris groaned. "Don't even joke about it."

"I'm not joking. Besides, what if Witherspoon had attacked someone who hadn't had a gun. What then?"

"But . . ."

"But what?"

"You killed someone, Mom," Chris objected. "My mother actually took another person's life. It's not a video game; not a movie. A real live person's life."

"Is that what's bothering you?"

"I guess," he said miserably. "I mean, the whole time I was growing up, I never thought you were that kind of person."

"You know what, Chris? Neither did I. All those years I lived with Paul Grayson, I was a mealy-mouthed namby-pamby. I put up with his bullshit and got along no matter what. I've spent a lot of time thinking about that the last couple of days and wondering why I did it, and I think I've finally figured it out.

"I did it because I was afraid something might change. Afraid something might happen. Afraid that if Paul dumped me I wouldn't be able to make it on my own. But I'm not afraid anymore, Chris, I'm not afraid of anything. And that includes Paul Grayson and cutlooseblog.com. Yes, you're right. The blog brought me Ben Witherspoon. So what? Facing him down brought me something I needed, something that had been missing from my life for a very long time—self respect. When push came to shove, when it was a choice of him or me, I had guts enough to choose me. Finally. And that counts for something."

Even as she said this, she realized it wasn't completely true. Because she had installed a security system. And she had felt that sudden sense of dread when Kip showed up on the doorstep. But it was mostly true, when it came to the big things, anyway.

"You're going to be all right, then?" Chris asked after a pause.

"Absolutely," she said. "I'm going to be more than all right. You can count on it."

She sat at the table for a long time after she got

off the phone with Chris, wondering if she had said too much or too little and whether or not her outburst had made any sense—to him or to her. He had asked her what time it was, and she had ended up telling him how the clock was made. *Too much information*, she thought.

Bored with watching a screen full of her empty front and back doors, Ali had switched over to a Phoenix channel where the evening news featured the story of a young fresh-faced man, Hunter Jackson, a 2003 graduate of Chandler High School who had died two days earlier in a mortar attack on his convoy in Baghdad.

Hunter hadn't seen the mortar that was destined to kill him, but suddenly Ali Reynolds had a whole new understanding of all those other young-faced kids who had gone off to do their duty and who had made the hard choices to kill or be killed; to kill or let their buddies or their allies or civilians be killed. She knew just as certainly that those young people came away from those decisions—those momentary life and death decisions—changed in the same way she was now changed as well.

"God bless them," Ali whispered aloud. "And bring them safely home."

Chapter 18

After dinner she fell asleep for a while again. By nine o'clock, she was wide awake and back reading mail at cutlooseblog.com.

Ms. Reynolds,

An eye for an eye makes the whole world blind. Shame on you.

David

Not very original, Ali thought. *He took that one straight off a bumper sticker.* And she didn't post it, either.

Dear Ali,

I don't know your regular e-mail address, so I'm writing to you through this. I'm sorry I haven't been in touch with you through all your troubles with your job and everything. And when I heard about you and Paul splitting up, I just couldn't believe it. You always seemed so happy.

Seemed, Ali thought. *That's the operant word.*

And then there was that picture of you that showed up in the *Times* last week. Please tell me that you haven't really been forced into waiting tables and that you're having to live in a trailer. If Paul won't give you enough money to live on, I could probably send you some.

So clearly whoever was writing this hadn't bothered to read any of the rest of the blog. Ali looked to the bottom. Roseanne Maxwell. Roseanne's husband, Jake, was one of Paul's so-called buddies and co-workers. So that's what this was—a thinly veiled political effort on Jake's part to get the goods on Paul and gain some corporate advantage.

And now I'm hearing that there was some kind of break-in last week at the place where you're staying and that you were hurt and somebody actually died. How awful! You must be falling apart. If you need a place to stay, our door is always open, and our lovely little *casita* has just been redone and it's totally available. Not only that, I'm sure Jake can do something to help you with the job situation. It can't be as hopeless as it seems. Chin up.

Love and Kisses,
Roseanne Maxwell

It didn't take Ali long to decide how to respond:

Dear Roseanne,

Thanks to both you and Jake for your kind offer. You're right. I'm living in the trailer . . .

She didn't say manufactured home with what was essentially two master suites. She didn't say that there was a Jacuzzi soaking tub in her spacious bath or an office alcove off her bedroom. Nor did she mention that the home had been placed on footings that allowed for a basement with wine cellar underneath.

. . . my Aunt Evie left me when she died. It has running water now, and air-conditioning won't be an issue until summer.

Don't worry about me. I'm in Sedona. If I just stay focused on my crystals, I'm sure everything will be fine.

Ali

It was a goofy enough response that Ali giggled aloud, but she didn't post either one. It wasn't necessary. Saying something like that to Roseanne Maxwell was as good as an Internet posting any day.

Then she went back to reading the mail. It was interesting to see that comments from gun-control advocates and gun-control opponents were fairly evenly divided and almost uniformly shrill. She posted some of them but not all, because many of them said the same things.

Dear Babe,

You sound like you're proud of yourself for taking another person's life. You shouldn't be. Because you had that gun, you didn't even *look* for other ways to end the conflict between you and the man who broke into your house. You just hit the trigger and went blam, blam, blam!!! The other guy's dead. End of story.

If there were fewer guns in the world, maybe we'd find other ways to solve the world's problems. Stories like yours make things worse instead of better.

Tommy F.

Ben Witherspoon wasn't interested in talking, Ali thought, *and maybe we should outlaw kitchen knives, too, while we're at it.* But she posted Tommy's remarks without any further comment from her.

Dear Babe,

The Bible says, "The meek shall inherit the earth." Guess you won't be on the receiving end.

Georgie

Guess not, Ali thought and posted that one, too. The next one gave her pause.

Dear Babe,

Twenty years ago, when my husband beat me up, I filed charges against him. He was tried, convicted, and sent to jail. As they were taking him out of the courtroom, he screamed that he'd get me when he got out. My friends told me to get a restraining order. I got a .45 instead.

When he got out, he broke into our apartment while I was asleep. He woke me up and said he was going to take our baby, my son, and throw him out the window. I got the gun out of my nightstand, followed him into the hallway, and shot him. He died and I went to prison. The cops said that yes, he broke into the house, but he didn't hurt me, and he wasn't armed at the time. They said it was my fault, that I should have called the cops instead of following him into the hallway and shooting him in the back. They weren't there, but they all said that showed premeditation.

And my public defender told me I'd better cop a plea to second degree or I'd go to prison for first, so I spent the next seventeen years in prison. DSHS took my son and the courts terminated my parental rights. I don't know where he is. He'd be twenty-two by now.

I hope this doesn't happen to you, and I don't think it will. You're white. I'm not.

Lucille

Ali didn't post Lucille's comment. Instead she wrote back.

Dear Lucille,

Thank you for your good wishes. Your letter is all too true. There's more than one level of justice in this country, one for those who can pay for quality representation and one for those who can't. I'm appalled by what happened to you. With your permission, I'd like to post your comment on cutlooseblog.com to see what kind of discussion it engenders.

Also, have you made any effort to locate your son? If I can be of any help in that regard, let me know.

Ali Reynolds, aka Babe

The phone rang. "Ali," Paul said. "I'm glad you're there. I need to talk to you."

It would have been nice if he'd asked how she was feeling or if she was okay, but he didn't.

"If this is about the station sending over that film crew tomorrow," Ali began, "I've already decided I'm not—"

"No, no," Paul interrupted impatiently. "It's nothing like that. It's April. I just found out she's pregnant."

So? Ali wondered. *What does this joyous news have to do with me?*

"The baby's yours, I assume," she said.

"Of course it's mine," Paul snapped back at her. "Whose do you think it is?"

No point in going into that, Ali thought. "Why are you calling me, then?"

"She wants us to be married," Paul said. "Right away. Before the baby gets here. That's what I want, too. This child is my future, Ali. This is the baby who will carry my genetic material forward. So what can I do to get this process started?"

Ali's first instinct was to simply burst out laughing. Wasn't this the same man, who, in the course of their last conversation, had declared that he wouldn't be manipulated? The ever-dependable pregnancy gambit had to be the oldest ploy in the book.

She also understood exactly why he was calling her directly. By going around Helga, he was sure he could negotiate himself a better deal. And he had reason to think so. After all, Ali Reynolds had gone along with his wishes for years. But with the death of Ben Witherspoon, the playing field had changed. Paul Grayson still hadn't figured that out.

"Well . . . ?" he pressed, pushing her to give him an answer in the same bullying voice he always used to get his way.

"When it comes to divorces," she said finally, "you have three choices—quick, cheap, and good. Pick any two. When you figure out which two you want, give Helga a call and we'll talk."

She hung up. The phone rang again almost immediately, but when caller ID showed it was Paul calling back, Ali didn't pick up. She'd already said her piece and had nothing more to add. Instead, she jotted off an e-mail to Helga.

Dear Helga,

Paul's girlfriend is pregnant and wants to get married—fast. I think he's ready to wheel and deal. Call him up tomorrow morning and see what you can do. I trust your judgment on this. The more we can stick it to him, the better.

Ali

She returned to cutloose.

Dear Babe,

As you suggested, I've been in touch with Mr. Tompkins. Based on what happened with his mother, I've made a determination not to pursue treatment with the Rodriguez Medical Center folks in Mazatlan.

According to Tompkins, the treatments consist mostly of stuffing the people full of overpriced but essentially over-the-counter supplements and then filling them full of a pain med cocktail that keeps them in enough of a pink haze that they don't know what's hit them. They keep them feeling better—right up until their money is gone. Then the patient is shipped back home to die, unless they conk out while they're still in Mexico. Bad idea.

The money we're not spending on them is almost enough to pay off our mortgage. I think I'll do that—stay home, take my lumps, and spend whatever time I have with my family.

Thank you again for your help.

Don Trilby

PS You're welcome to go ahead and post this. RMC has already filed suit against Mr. Tompkins for breaching his mother's confidentiality agreement, but I didn't sign any such thing, and I think other ALS patients and their families need to know how these creeps work. I'm glad I figured it out in time.

Ali was in the process of posting it when her phone rang. She was surprised when the caller ID readout said Howard Bernard. *Why's Howie calling me?* she wondered.

"Ali?" Matt asked. He spoke in almost a whisper.

"Matt!" Ali exclaimed. "Is something wrong?"

"Mom's stuff is gone," he said with a sob. "Her clothes and her jewelry and her coats and shoes and everything. It's all gone. They took it away. To Goodwill. While we were in Cottonwood."

Ali remembered what Andrea had said about the moving boxes stacked on the front porch. "They did what?" she exclaimed.

"Dad," Matt blubbered. "And I'm sure Jasmine helped. They packed up everything. It's like she was never even here. How could they do that? Didn't they know Julie and me would want some of her stuff? That we'd like to keep it?"

Sparks of anger lit up Ali's line of vision, but she didn't explode with the series of four-letter words that were on the tip of her tongue. She didn't want to add fuel to Matt's flame or any more hurt, either.

"Maybe they thought it would be less painful for you if you didn't have to deal with those things," she suggested.

"No," Matt said. "Dad wants to forget Mom, and he wants us to forget her, too. So he can marry Jasmine. Can I come live with you, Ali? Please? I wouldn't be any trouble, I promise. And Julie, too. We'd be good, the same way we are with Grandpa and Grandma down in Cottonwood. They always say we're not any trouble at all."

"I know you're not," Ali said quickly. "But it's not that simple. Parents can't just hand their kids off for someone else to look after."

"You mean like we did Samantha," Matt said.

"Well, yes," Ali agreed. "Kids are a little more complicated than cats. And parents get to have the final say."

"Shouldn't kids get to have some say, too? I mean, Jasmine pretends like she likes us. She's always saying nice things, but I know she doesn't mean them. She's just saying them to get in good with Dad. And with us. I don't like her, Ali. I don't want him to marry her."

Three days after his mother's funeral, Matt shouldn't have had to be worrying about his father remarrying. But then, Howie Bernard was a clod. A highly educated clod. He had always been one in the past and would continue to be one in the future.

Ali thought then about the note from Lucille telling her appalling story. The courts had terminated the poor woman's parental rights over a shooting that, with decent legal representation and any kind of justice, would most likely have been declared self-defense.

What if the remaining parent were charged and convicted of actual homicide? Ali wondered. *What if Jasmine Wright and Howie Bernard had plotted together and succeeded in murdering Reenie? What then?*

"They're not going to get married," Ali declared. "It's much too soon."

"Oh yeah?" Matt countered, and Ali had nothing to say in return.

"How's Sam?" he asked, abruptly changing the subject. "I keep asking Dad when we can come down and get her, but he says he doesn't know. That he's too busy."

"She's fine here," Ali said. "But I could bring her home if you'd like me to—tomorrow or maybe the day after that." She was stalling on going out of the house as much as possible. Her face and neck were still black and blue from the blow Witherspoon had nailed her with when she first walked in the door. And there were other cuts and bruises that she didn't remember individually but which made her look like she'd been in a serious fight—which she had.

"That would be awesome," Matt said, sounding suddenly much more cheerful. "I know Sam's ugly, but I really, really miss her."

"She's not ugly," Ali said. "She's interesting."

"Gotta go," Matt said suddenly. "Dad's home now." And he hung up.

As Ali hung up, she heard the New Mail click. At the top of the list was one from Helga@Weldon davisreed.com.

Dear Ali,

I'm on it. If it comes down to serious negotiations, we'll do a conference call. Hang on to your cell phone. If his sweet young thing has him by the balls, you can rest assured he won't be using his brains. We should be able to work a deal.

Talk to you tomorrow.

Helga

After reading that, Ali sat in front of the keyboard and tried to get a handle on everything she was feeling. She had every confidence that Helga would look out for her interests, but who was looking out for Matt and Julie Bernard's? Not their father. Not Howie, the unfeeling creep who was willing to send his wife's personal possessions off to Goodwill before his wife was even in her grave.

Ali remembered how she'd felt when Dean died. It had taken her months before she'd been willing to part with the last of his clothing. She'd kept some of it, just so she'd be able to press her face into it and still smell his scent and sense his presence. And Ali could imagine Matt and Julie finding the same kind of sensory comfort in some of their mother's things. But those were evidently lost to them now.

As for Howie? Was he so arrogant, so convinced of his own infallibility, that he didn't think anyone would notice the lack of respect he was showing for Reenie? Maybe he thought that, since she was ill, no one would bother looking beyond the official determination of suicide, that it would simply be accepted at face value.

But it won't! Ali vowed. *If he's responsible for what happened, I'll hound him until hell freezes over.*

With her fingers flying over the keyboard, she fired an e-mail off to Andrea.

Dear Andrea,

I just heard from Matt. It seems all those moving boxes you saw on Reenie's front porch were packed up to take her stuff to Goodwill. It's probably too late, but can you see if any of it can be tracked down?

Thanks,
Ali

Once that was on its way, she exited cutloose and logged on to Reenie's mailbox. By then, it was almost midnight—another day had passed. When the witching hour occurred, another day's worth of Reenie's correspondence would be lost forever. To keep that from happening, Ali went to the mail file and began making printed copies of everything that was there, starting from the oldest and working her way up to the most recent. When she finished with that, she opened and printed all the new messages as well, before resaving them as new. And then, just for completion's sake, she went through the spam folder—all 78 of them—one at a time, opening and checking them first before deleting.

When she saw one called Account Numbers, she expected it to be one of the usual spam gambits offering low mortgage interest rates or maybe a solicitation to help some poor unfortunate African heiress reclaim her fortune. Except this one wasn't spam. It was dated Thursday, March 17, 2005:

Dear Ms. Bernard,

Your inquiry from last week has been forwarded to me by Andrew Cargill, manager of our First United Financial branch in Phoenix. As you are no doubt aware, in the past few years there's been a good deal of consolidation in the banking industry. Each time a bank changes ownership, it results in changes in account numbers. Usually the account names remain the same although in some instances, secondary or tertiary names on the account may be dropped from the record.

I understand your concern that, in the case of your children's trust accounts, a substantial sum of money may be missing. However, I'm sure that by checking with the trustee and/or with the grantor should s/he be available, this matter can be sorted out with very little difficulty. Once we have been informed of the correct account name, it will be easy to come up with the account numbers.

Please let me know if I can be of any further service in this regard.

Lana Franklin

Vice President

Customer Relations

First United Financial

Fargo, ND.

A bank in Phoenix, Ali thought in triumph. *Yes!*

It wasn't what she had thought originally because now she was convinced Reenie hadn't gone there in search of money for treatment in Mexico. Instead it had something to do with her children's lost trust accounts. It could be as insubstantial as those old-fashioned Christmas Club things that you put money into each month so you'd have enough saved up to spend when next year's Christmas came around. The e-mail made it sound like the missing accounts amounted to more than that, but that could be a simple corporate hyperbole.

Regardless of why Reenie had gone to the bank, however, Ali had picked up her trail after everyone else had lost it. No one seemed to have any idea about her movements or actions between the time she left Dr. Mason's office and the time she went off the cliff.

Ali Googled the bank information and copied it into her Reenie file. The bank office was on Northern, near I-17.

I'll give Andrew Cargill a call in the morning. She thought about that for a minute. *No,* she decided, *I think I'll go see him in person.*

She went to bed then and, for a change, slept soundly. Now that she no longer had to be up bright and early for her shift at the Sugarloaf, she was, of course, wide awake well before sunrise and aching all over. The stitches in her back and leg precluded soaking in the tub, so she settled for a quick shower and went back to the computer.

cutlooseblog.com
Tuesday, March 22, 2005

My life is in limbo at the moment. Legal proceedings are moving forward in two separate states. Until those cases are concluded, it's difficult to see into the future and decide where I'm going.

The job I thought I'd do for my whole life is no longer my job. I've left the home I've lived in for the past several years. I thought my parents needed my help with their restaurant, but it turns out they seem to be able to get along fine without me. For twenty-two years I've been a mother, but my son is grown now and ready to be on his own, so I've worked myself out of that job as well.

It would be easy to sit around and worry about all those things, but I'm not going to. The best way to banish worry is to do something, specifically the job that comes most readily to hand.

My friend Reenie was buried last Friday. As far as I know, her death has been termed a suicide. Maybe it is—and maybe it isn't. But that's the job I'm assigning myself to do right now—to find out for sure—to ascertain, to my own satisfaction, whether Reenie Bernard did or did not kill herself and, if she did, why. We're not talking about legalities here. I'm not an attorney or a police officer. I don't have any vested interest in probable causes or chains of evidence. I want answers that carry weight in my heart rather than in a court of law.

In the past, I'm sure I would have accepted the "official" answer as the "real" answer, but circumstances change, and so have I.

And since all of you have been walking along the Reenie road with me, I'll keep you posted as well.

Posted 5:23 A.M. by Babe

Lucille had responded:

Dear Babe,

You can post my letter. I haven't looked for my son. I don't have the money, and I'm afraid of what I'd find. Maybe he's dead. Or like his father.

Lucille

Ali posted Lucille's first note, then she started to read the new stuff. The first one was from Andrea Rogers.

Dear Ali

Glad to know you're feeling better. Thank God! That maniac could have killed you.

I'll go to Goodwill first thing this morning, before I even go to the office. I know some of the people down there. When I tell them what's happened, I'm sure they'll do whatever they can to help. Some of Reenie's stuff is probably gone—some but not all. I'll do what I can.

Andrea

The next e-mail was a stunner.

Dear Mrs. Reynolds,

A friend of mine told me I could write to you here.

My husband was abusive. He used to beat me in front of the kids, but I stayed with him. Because of the kids. He finally got sick and died, praise the Lord!

But now my son is dead, too, and I keep wondering how much of it is my fault. I forgive you if you forgive me.

Sincerely,
Myra Witherspoon

Closing her computer, Ali went to get dressed.

Chapter 19

Myra Witherspoon's note stayed with Ali as she dressed and tried to make herself presentable. For both Lucille and for Myra, domestic violence had been a communicable disease, spreading its poison through their families from one generation to the next. And maybe even to the generation after that. Both of them had lost their sons. But obviously, both women had somehow plumbed the depths of their own heartbreak and found a measure of forgiveness for others. Otherwise they wouldn't have written.

It was humbling to realize that Myra was willing to forgive the person who had pulled the trigger and ended her son's violent existence.

If our situations were reversed, Ali wondered, *could I do the same?*

She rummaged through her closet until she found a long-sleeved turtleneck she had left in Sedona over Christmas. That covered the bruises on her arms if not the ones on the backs of her hands, and a pair of jeans did the same for the stitches from the cut on her leg and the scrapes on her knees from where she had scrambled away from her attacker in the gravel driveway. Her face was another matter entirely.

Working in front of the bathroom mirror, Ali soon discovered what many other women had learned before her—makeup can't do everything. No amount of Estee Lauder concealer camouflaged the ugly greenish yellow tinge of the bruise that spread from her cheekbone to the base of her neck. Eye-shadow only emphasized the cut near the corner of her puffy eye. Lipstick did the same for her cut and badly swollen upper lip.

Chris called as she was examining the final results in the mirror. "How are you feeling?" he asked.

"Medium," she told him.

"Maybe I should come back over this weekend," he offered. "My last final is over at noon on Friday."

"That's not necessary, Chris. Really. I'm fine. I've got more food here than I'll ever manage to eat. All I'm doing is hanging around with Sam and taking it easy."

"I just read this morning's post," Chris countered. "That didn't sound like you'd be taking it easy."

"Don't go all grown-up on me," Ali said with a laugh. "I just want some answers. That's all."

"And how do you plan on getting them?"

"By asking questions, I suppose," she returned.

"What kinds of questions?"

"My plan for today is to drive down to Phoenix and talk to the banker Reenie talked with the day she died. I just want to get a line on what she did after she left the doctor's office."

"That's all?"

"What do you mean, that's all?"

"I mean you won't be doing things you shouldn't."

"You mean as in not minding my own business? You really are starting to sound like your grandmother."

"And for good reason," Chris responded. "You just got out of the hospital, remember?"

"So you're worried about me!"

"You could say that," he agreed. "And from the sound of your post this morning, I should be, which is why, at the very least, I should come over and help."

"No," she said. "You definitely shouldn't do that. Finish your exams. Finish school."

"But you'll be careful?"

"Chris, I'm going to go talk to a *banker*," she said, not trying to conceal her exasperation. "How dangerous can that be?"

"In your case, who knows?" he returned.

Chris hung up abruptly after that. Ali and her son quarreled so seldom that their telephone tiff left her feeling uneasy. Had Chris started it or had she? And what did he expect her to do, just turn her back on Reenie and forget about it?

Sipping coffee, she reread the printed e-mail from First United Financial. This time her eyes stopped short on the words "the trustee and/or with the grantor." Who in Reenie's family would be best qualified to fill either one of those jobs?

Ed Holzer! Ali realized. *Of course. That made perfect sense.*

After all, the man had been a banker for years before selling out and establishing a property management firm in its stead. In fact, there was a good chance that Ed himself had established the trust accounts. Maybe these were things he and Diane had set up to benefit their grandchildren.

Ali had started making a to-do list to take with her. The phone rang just as she added Ed's name.

"Good morning," Bob Larson said. "How's my girl this morning?"

"Fine," she told her dad. "Still bruised and battered but fine."

"Your mother wants to know if you're coming down for breakfast. So do I, for that matter."

"I won't have time," she said. "I'm leaving for Phoenix in just a few minutes, and I thought I'd stop by and see Ed and Diane Holzer on the way."

"Our loss," he said. "Dave's, too."

"Dave?"

"Holman. He was hoping to talk to you, too."

Detective Dave Holman was the last person Ali wanted to see. She remembered Dave running to her side at the end of the Ben Witherspoon confrontation. And she had a hazy recollection of his worried face hovering in the background as the EMTs rolled her from the ambulance into the ER. She hadn't seen him again after that, and it was just as well. For one thing, Rick Santos, her criminal defense attorney, had told her to have nothing at all to do with law enforcement officers for the time being, at least not until the Witherspoon matter had been resolved, one way or the other. Before that, her attorney needed to be present at all times: As in anything you say can be held against you.

But Ali had a second reason for avoiding Dave Holman which, in her opinion, carried as much weight as her attorney's objections. If Chris somewhat disapproved of Ali looking into the Reenie situation, Dave was likely to be absolutely opposed.

"Tell him I'll be in touch," Ali said. She was about to hang up, but Bob caught her in time.

"Kip said something about your having extra food you want to donate?"

"Tons of it," she said.

"How about if I have him bring me up to your place later on this morning," Bob suggested. "I have a key. We can pick up your extra food and take it up the mountain. Kip's old neighbors will be glad to have it, and I imagine your mother will be thrilled to have me out from under hand and foot."

"Be advised," Ali said. "I have an alarm system now." She gave him the code. "And don't let the cat out."

"What cat?" Bob demanded. "Since when do you have a cat? You always hated cats."

In the crowded days between her father's snowboarding accident and Ali's own trip to the hospital, there hadn't been much occasion for visiting.

"Sam belongs to Matt and Julie Bernard," Ali explained. "It's only temporary. Samantha's the first cat I've ever really made friends with, and she's not half bad. Ugly, but not bad."

Bob laughed. "That sounds a lot like what your mother says about me on occasion."

When it came time to leave the house, Ali spent the better part of ten minutes fruitlessly searching for her purse. Baffled, she finally thought to look in the shopping bag her mother had used to bring her wrecked clothing home from the hospital.

Sure enough, there, zipped into a Ziploc bag, she found the remaining contents of her purse—wallet, MP3 player, three tubes of lipstick, a compact, nail file, a few paperclips, out of date credit card receipts, a plastic tampon container, and other assorted junk. The collection included an official-looking Yavapai Sheriff's Department document that notified her that her Coach bag had been kept as evidence and could be claimed at a later date.

Right, Ali thought. *A Coach bag with a bullet hole in the bottom.*

Ali paused long enough to write "buy purse" on her to-do list. She stuck that along with the print-out from Reenie's e-mail into her makeshift, see-through plastic purse and then set off for Phoenix by way of Cottonwood.

It was only a little past ten when Ali drove into the yard at Ed and Diane Holzer's place. She saw at once that their car was missing from the carport and no one answered her knock. Thinking Ed might have gone to his office, Ali drove on into town.

Holzer Property Management was located at the corner of Aspen and South Main in a block Ed had purchased and redeveloped. It was tucked into a small commercial complex that contained two dentists, an accountant, a chiropractor, a Mail-boxes, Etc., and a Subway sandwich shop. Ali was disappointed when she saw no trace of Ed's Buick in the parking lot there, either, but she went inside to check all the same.

The receptionist just inside the door was clearly troubled by Ali's appearance. "Ed isn't in today," she said, trying hard not to stare at Ali's cuts and bruises. "I believe he had a doctor's appointment this morning, but Bree is in. Would you like to talk to her?"

"Sure," Ali said. "Why not?"

Ali was shown into a conference room where she found Bree seated in front of an unfurled stack of architectural drawings. "My God!" Bree exclaimed, leaping to her feet and coming around to give Ali an effusive hug. "You look awful! I heard about what happened, but I didn't expect . . ."

". . . me to look like the wrath of God?" Ali finished with a pained grin. "Believe me, I'm a lot better now than I was two days ago."

"Grab a chair," Bree said, resuming her own. "What can we do for you?"

"I was looking for your dad."

Bree shook her head. "Sorry," she said. "You just missed him. Mom and Dad left about twenty minutes ago. They're on their way to Phoenix so Dad can see his cardiologist."

"Phoenix," Ali said. "That's where I'm going, too. Do they have a cell phone? Maybe I can catch up with them there."

Bree shook her head. "Sorry. Dad hates cell phones. Loathes them, in fact. Wouldn't have one on a bet. But this sounds urgent. Is there something I can do?"

Ali considered for a moment before deciding there was no reason not to ask Bree about the accounts. She was, after all, a managing partner. Presumably, whatever Ed knew Bree knew and vice versa.

"I'm doing some tracking on Reenie's movements the afternoon she died," Ali began.

There was a subtle shift in Bree's demeanor. "How come?" she asked, frowning. "As far as I know, it's all settled. At least that's what they told me—that according to Detective Farris the case was closed."

"It may be closed as far as he's concerned," Ali said. "Closing cases is what he gets paid for, but can you just accept that, Bree? Can you see your sister just giving up without a fight? I can't. She wouldn't turn her back on her kids that way. I still believe she'd stay and duke it out."

Bree took a deep breath. "The point is," she said, "this has all been terribly hard on my parents. They're starting to come to terms with what happened. It's only going to make things worse if you keep going over the same ground. Don't bother them with this, Ali, please. Let it go. Give them a chance to get past it."

Here was someone else telling Ali to drop it, to mind her own business. And in the old days the old Ali—the old please-everyone-but-yourself Ali—might have backed down.

"Hurting your parents is the last thing I want to do," she said. "But Reenie was my friend, Bree, and as a friend, I want answers about why she's dead—answers I can accept. Detective Farris may be right—suicide may well turn out to be the answer—but I still want to know why she did it, why she just gave up."

"So what are you doing about it?" Bree asked.

"Trying to find out what Reenie did after she left Dr. Mason's office in Scottsdale that Thursday afternoon. I have reason to believe she visited a bank, United First Financial in Phoenix. I believe she was trying to track down some trust accounts that had been established in her children's names, but the bank manager wasn't able to locate them."

"Oh, those," Bree said at once. "I'd forgotten all about them, but now that you mention them, I do remember. Dad and Mom set one up for Matt right after he was born, and they started one for Julie as soon as she showed up as well. I'm sure misplacing them is just a bookkeeping error of some kind. I can't imagine why on earth Reenie went to the bank directly instead of calling here."

"You have the records?"

"Of course we have the records. All it would have taken is a single call from Reenie to me to straighten this whole thing out, but then again, with everything that was going on in Reenie's life right then, she probably wasn't thinking straight."

"Probably not," Ali agreed.

"Anything else I can do, then?" Bree asked.

"No," Ali said. "Thanks for your help. I should probably be going. Give your folks my best, and when I talk to Andrew Cargill I'll let him know he should call you for information on those missing accounts."

"You're still going to talk to him?" Bree asked sharply. "I thought . . ."

"Andrew Cargill is the last person who saw your sister alive, Bree. Reenie may have mentioned something to him about where she was going and what she planned to do next."

"But—"

"It's what I have to do, Bree. For Reenie and for my own peace of mind."

Ali left then, without looking back, sensing rather than seeing Bree watching her exit from behind. Once back in the Cayenne, she programmed the address for First United Financial into her GPS and headed for Phoenix.

The sky overhead was a bright, cloudless blue. The winter rains had done their magic. Even with springtime weather only a few days old, there was already a hint of green everywhere as hardy high desert grasses poked their way up out of the ground. On I-17 traffic was heavy but moving and not at all slow. Spilling downhill from the Mogollon Rim and Arizona's high country, the freeway's long sweeping curves made the steep descent deceptively smooth. It was a stretch of highway where unwary truckers and motorists, oblivious to the force of gravity, could find themselves sailing along at speeds well above the 75-m.p.h.-posted limits.

It was also a part of the highway whose long vistas of distant mountains never failed to raise Ali's spirits. She passed the broad, grassy expanse of Sunset Viewpoint. As she started down the first steep grade that led to Black Canyon City and to the Valley of the Sun far below, her cell phone rang. Ali pressed the button, glad she had set her phone on hands-free mode.

"Ali?" the distinctively deep voice asked. "It's Helga."

"How are things?"

Helga Myerhoff laughed. "Couldn't be better," she said. "Never better."

"You've talked to Paul's attorney, then?"

"No," Helga said with a laugh. "I talked to Paul

himself. I have no idea why he seems to think he's qualified to do this on his own."

Ali was astonished. "He's trying to do this without an attorney?"

"Men who are used to running the show end up thinking they're smart enough to run all shows," Helga said. "And more the fool him," she added. "I believe your soon-to-be-former husband is what people in the real estate business refer to as a 'motivated seller.' He wants out of this marriage in the very worst way."

"And he's willing to pay for the privilege?" Ali asked.

"Apparently," Helga said. "I believe it'll be to our benefit if we can make the deal *before* some hotshot pal of his talks him into changing his mind."

"What's he offering?"

"Fortunately, he wants to keep the house. He's willing to buy out your half of the equity on both that and on the condo in Aspen, which was also purchased after the two of you married. The selling prices are to be based on the average of three separate and independent appraisals."

"Sounds fair," Ali said.

"That's what I thought," Helga agreed.

"What else?"

"He also wants to make a lump-sum payment for you to sign off on his pension. I'll need to look into that because I think there's a good chance he's screwing us on the pension's current valuation. Don't worry, though. I've got my favorite accountant bloodhound working that line of inquiry.

"Mr. Grayson is also willing to pay lifetime alimony, but only in the event you don't remarry," Helga continued. "That's standard, of course, but I told him the amount he was offering was a joke. I let him know that if he really wants us to sign off on this so he can make it to the altar before his kid gets here, he'd better get real in a hurry."

"I'm surprised he didn't hang up on you."

Helga laughed. "Frankly," she said, "so am I."

As she drove, Ali had been keeping a close eye on traffic, which had mostly slowed to the posted 60 m.p.h. limit. Glancing in her rearview mirror, Ali pulled out to pass two slow-moving trucks, one driving on the paved shoulder and the other in the right-hand lane. She was easing around them when a vehicle—a bright iridescent red SUV of some kind—suddenly emerged from around the obscuring curve behind her and charged forward.

"Ali," Helga said. "Are you still there?"

Ali knew the red car was coming way too fast. "Just a minute," she said. "Let me get out of the way of this nutcase."

Ali pressed down on the accelerator, and the turbo-charged Cayenne shot forward. Even so, by the time she had overtaken the trucks and was ready to move back into the right-hand lane, the red car was right on her bumper. Once Ali returned to the right lane, however, the red car didn't pass after all. Instead, it slowed and stuck—right in Ali's blind spot.

"Oh, for God's sake," Ali muttered under her breath. "Why the hell don't you just pass?"

"Ali?" Helga asked. "Are you talking to me?"

"This jerk behind me won't . . ."

Just then something slammed into her back left-hand fender. For what seemed like an eternity, as metal screeched against metal, the front end of the Cayenne swung sickeningly toward the left. As the median rushed toward her, Ali gripped the wheel and desperately twisted it to the right. Too late she realized that by then the other driver had veered away. Without the pressure against the rear of the Cayenne, the front of the vehicle suddenly snapped straight again. Ali knew instantly that she had overcorrected.

With terrible clarity, Ali saw the Cayenne swerve back to the right, aiming dead-on at the steel guardrail that lined the right-hand edge of the pavement. Invisible beyond the pavement was a sheer two-hundred-foot drop-off.

Wrestling the wheel, Ali tried to compensate for the overcorrection, but there wasn't room enough. Or time. Instead there was a sudden grinding explosion of steel on steel. Lost in a blinding curtain of air bags, Ali felt the disorienting sensation of spinning. Then, with the Cayenne still astonishingly upright, it came to a sudden stop.

The driver's side air bag had blown Ali's hands free of the steering wheel. Side-curtain bags had protected her head. But now, as the passenger space filled with smoke and dust, Ali sat stunned and gasping for air, trying to piece together what had happened.

Off in the distance, hidden somewhere in the wreckage, she heard Helga's voice. "Ali! Ali! What in God's name happened? Are you all right?" Then, there was a sudden sharp pounding on the car window next to her ear.

Fighting her way through the empty air bags, Ali saw the face of a bearded man peering in the window. Behind him, parked on the freeway, sat a gigantic idling semi.

"Lady, lady," he shouted through glass. "Are you all right? What the hell was the matter with that woman? She tried to kill you."

"I think I'm all right," Ali managed, but since she could only summon a whisper, he probably didn't hear her.

"Can you unlock the door?"

Eventually Ali complied, and the man wrenched it open. "Come on," he said. "My buddy's stopping traffic. He's calling the cops, too. If you think you can walk, let's get you out of there in case something catches on fire."

Once Ali was upright, the good Samaritan took one look at her battered face and backed away in horror. "My God, woman, you really are hurt! I'd better call an ambulance."

Ali laughed at him then. She couldn't help it. She laughed because, no matter how awful she looked, she wasn't dead and she should have been. She laughed so hard she finally had to sit down on the pavement to keep from falling over.

An Arizona Highway Patrol car showed up while Ali was still laughing.

"I think she needs an ambulance," the truck driver told the officer. "She's gone hysterical on us. Maybe she's in shock. Did you catch the woman in the other car?"

"We're working on it," the officer replied. He turned to her then. "Are you all right?"

"I'm fine," she said. "No problem."

"License and registration?"

But she wasn't fine enough to retrieve the paperwork herself. For an answer, Ali pointed back to the wrecked Cayenne. "In there," she said. "Registration's in the glove box. My cell phone's in there somewhere, too. If you could find it . . ."

The cop reached into the vehicle. He emerged a few seconds later, holding a piece of paper and the cell phone along with the loaded Ziploc bag she was using for a purse. To her amazement the bag was still fastened.

"This?" he asked dubiously.

Ali nodded, and then she began to laugh again. "Those Ziploc bags are something, aren't they?" she asked before dissolving in a spasm of giggles. "Maybe they could use this in a commercial."

When the EMTs from the Black Canyon City Volunteer Fire Department arrived, none of them was prepared to take Ali's word for it that she was fine. Instead, they loaded her onto a gurney, strapped her down, stuffed her into an ambulance, and took off. The ambulance hurtled forward for what, in Ali's disoriented state, seemed like a very long time. Suddenly it slowed almost to a stop, but still it kept moving forward, siren blaring.

"Are we there yet?" she asked the young attendant at her side.

He shook his head. "Not yet," he said. "There's a problem on the freeway. We'll get through it, though. Don't worry."

Don't worry, Ali thought. *That's what I told Chris.*

I've got to call him. But she couldn't. Someone had taken her phone.

Eventually they arrived at the John C. Lincoln Hospital in Deer Valley. For the second time that week, a no-nonsense ER nurse, armed with a scissors, came in and began snipping off Ali's shirt and bra.

"Do you have to do that?" Ali asked. "I'm going to run out of bras pretty soon."

Shaking her head, the nurse went right on snipping. It took three hours of poking, prodding and X-raying, before the ER physician finally shrugged and shook his head.

"Okay," he said. "I think you really are fine, but I'm keeping you until this evening for observation. Now what about the cops? There are at least three of them out in the lobby waiting to take a statement. Think you can handle talking to them now?"

Ali nodded. "Send them in."

To her amazement, a grim-faced Dave Holman led the way, followed by two uniformed officers and another in plain clothes.

"What are you doing here?" she demanded. Her first thought was that the county attorney had decided to prosecute her after all.

"The incident occurred inside the Yavapai county line," he said. "It's our jurisdiction."

"She tried to run me off the road," Ali said. "It's a miracle I didn't go right over the edge. What was the matter with that woman . . ."

"You saw her?"

"No," Ali said. "All I saw was the car, but that's

what the truck driver told me, that the driver was a woman. You did catch her, didn't you?"

Dave shook his head. "No," he said. "I'm afraid we didn't."

"Why not?" Ali demanded. "She was right there on the freeway. What happened? Did she just disappear into thin air?"

"She's dead," Dave said.

"Dead?"

Dave nodded. "DPS had reports about the incident with you and that the perpetrator was headed southbound. They put up a rolling roadblock just north of Black Canyon City. She tried to go around and went off the highway and off a cliff. She didn't make it."

"So was she drunk?" Ali asked. "On drugs? What?"

"No," Dave said. "It doesn't look like drugs or alcohol, at least, not at this time."

"But she tried to kill me," Ali objected. "Why?"

"That's what we hoped you'd tell us."

Ali was mystified and becoming slightly annoyed. "A total stranger—a maniac—tries to run me off the road, and you want me to tell you why? How on earth would I know?"

"Because she wasn't a stranger," Dave answered quietly. "I believe you knew her quite well. We've tentatively identified the victim in the second vehicle as Breezy Marie Cowan, Reenie Bernard's sister."

"Oh," Ali said. And for the moment, that was all she could say.

Chapter 20

The interview took the better part of the next two hours. Ali told them everything she could remember about her meeting with Bree Cowan as well as what she'd gleaned from reading through Reenie's accumulated e-mails, including Reenie's fruitless meeting with the manager at First United Financial's Phoenix branch.

About noon, Dave Holman's cell phone rang. "We've located Mr. and Mrs. Holzer," he said grimly, once the call ended. "I need to go talk to them."

He left, taking one of the uniformed officers with him. Ali was still answering questions from the other two when Edie Larson bustled into the ER followed by Kip pushing Bob in his wheelchair. The two officers stepped aside to let them through.

"What have you done this time?" Edie grumbled, leaning down to kiss her. "It's becoming very tiresome you know. All I seem to be doing these days is driving from one ER to another."

Ali was surprised to see either one of her parents right then, to say nothing of both of them. "I didn't call on purpose," she said. "I knew you were working and . . ."

"Dave Holman called us," she said. "And don't worry. Everything at work is under control. We borrowed a cook from Tlaquepaque to finish up the day. The manager there owed us from when we helped him out last Christmas." Having said that, Edie Larson heaved herself into the chair next to Ali's bed and promptly burst into tears. "You've got to quit scaring me this way, Ali. I just can't take it."

Bob patted his wife's hand. "Come on now, Edie," he soothed. "Dave told you she was fine, and you can see for yourself that it's true." He looked at Ali. "Do the Holzers know what's happened?"

Ali nodded. "By now they do. Dave left a little while ago to go tell them."

"But why?" Edie asked, drying her tears. "Why would Bree come after you that way? It makes no sense."

"Dave thinks it may have something to do with some trust accounts that were set up for Matt and Julie. Bree has evidently been looting them. He thinks Reenie was starting to figure it out. Fear of being exposed must have pushed Bree over the edge."

"And Reenie, too," Bob interjected. "What kind of car did you say Bree was driving?"

"A Lexus," Ali said. "A bright red Lexus. Why."

After parking Bob's chair next to the bed, Kip Hogan had retreated to a spot near the door and as far away as possible from the two officers still standing inside the curtained alcove. With some difficulty, Bob turned and gave Kip a meaningful look.

"Tell them, Kip," he said. "Tell them what you told Edie and me on the way down."

Kip looked at the cops warily and then cleared his throat. "There was a Lexus on the mountain that night," he said. "The night Ali's friend died. Two cars came through onto Schnebly Hill Road, a white SUV and a red Lexus. The white one, a Yukon, drove down the mountain. Pretty soon the man came walking back up the road, got in the Lexus, and they drove away. Me and a couple of my friends saw the whole thing, but when the cops came around asking questions, we didn't want to get involved, so we more or less melted into the woods. But now . . ." He shrugged. "I guess I am involved."

"Who was in the red car?" Ali asked.

"A man and a woman."

"What did they look like?"

"The woman had dark short hair," Kip answered. "The man was dark-haired, too. Little bit of a goatee."

All this time, in the back of Ali's mind, she had imagined that somehow Jasmine Wright and Howie were responsible for what had happened to Reenie. But the people Kip Hogan had just described could be none other than Bree and Jack Cowan. They had motive and opportunity and had been seen at the scene of the crime.

"Does anyone have Dave Holman's cell phone number?" Ali asked. "We should probably give him a call."

cutlooseblog.com

Wednesday, March 23, 2005

I'm not sure why emergency room personnel insist on cutting off perfectly good clothing instead of letting patients take their clothes off over their heads. But they do, and I'm running low on bras. Yes, that means I've paid a visit to yet another emergency room—a different one this time. That's twice in one week. I'm beginning to think being a freelance blogger is a risky occupation.

Because that's how I ended up in the ER—by being a blogger. The questions I was asking about Reenie brought me up close and personal (way too close it turns out) with the people who most likely killed her. The same questions also brought me far too close to a guardrail overlooking a sheer two-hundred-foot drop.

Yes, I know for sure that my friend was murdered. So do the police officers who have now, reluctantly, reopened her case. She was most likely unconscious when she was placed in a vehicle that was then driven off a cliff.

Most people are murdered by someone they know and love, and that is true in Reenie's case, as well. All along I suspected her husband might have had something to do with what happened, but it turned out I was wrong. It is now believed Reenie was murdered by her younger sister. And what was the motive? What else? The root of all evil—money.

Police believe that Reenie somehow discovered that her sister, Bree, was possibly looting trust accounts of monies that had been set aside to benefit Reenie's children. Rather than having the embezzlement exposed, Bree, with the help of her husband, allegedly turned to murder.

It's possible that money missing from the trust accounts is only the tip of the iceberg. Bree has worked in her father's company for years. Recently, due to her father's ill health, she's been in charge. It appears she also had been siphoning money out of the business without her father's knowledge or consent. How much damage she's done to him remains to be seen.

Bree has already answered for her crimes. She went off a cliff while trying to elude a police roadblock. She's dead. Her husband is in jail, being held without bond on suspicion of homicide.

That means Reenie's parents will be having yet another funeral this week—a second funeral for their second daughter. The first one, for Reenie, was an outpouring of public grief. The second one will be a private affair—family members only—as two fine, upstanding people try to come to terms with their own nightmare version of Cain and Abel.

It makes me wonder? How do parents cope with a tragedy like this where one of their children stands accused of murdering another? How do they find the courage to go on?

I don't know, but I'm sure they will. They have to. Because their grandchildren, Matt and Julie, are coming to live with them while the children's father goes off on a yearlong sabbatical.

Taking his girlfriend with him, Ali thought, but she didn't put that in the post.

Which means Sam will be staying on with me. And that's all right. Neither one of us liked being together much to begin with, but I think we're going to be friends.

Speaking of parents, mine have decided not to sell the Sugarloaf—or rather the buyer decided against making the deal. I guess his restaurant consultant advised him against it. My father is bummed about it; my mother is delighted, so I guess they'll work it out.

As for me, will I stay in Sedona? I don't know. But I think I will keep blogging. Dangerous or not, I'm beginning to like that, too.

Posted 12:28 A.M. by Babe

Here's a sneak preview of

J. A. JANCE'S new novel

JUDGMENT CALL

Coming soon in hardcover from

William Morrow

An Imprint of Harper Collins*Publishers*

Late on a Thursday afternoon, Sheriff Joanna Brady sat at her desk in the Cochise County Justice Center outside Bisbee, Arizona, and studied the duty roster her chief deputy, Tom Hadlock, had dropped off an hour earlier.

Her former chief deputy, Frank Montoya, had been lured away from her department with the offer of a new job—chief of police in nearby Sierra Vista. Looking for a replacement, Joanna had tapped her jail commander to step into the job. Tom was well qualified on paper, but he had found Frank's tenure as chief deputy to be a tough act to follow.

When Frank had been Joanna's second-in-command, he had handily juggled several sets of seemingly unrelated responsibilities—media relations, routine administrative chores, and information technology issues—with unflappable ease. Now, after more than a year in the position, Tom was finally growing into the job and had a far better handle on what needed to be done than he had in the beginning. Unfortunately, he still wasn't quite up to Frank Montoya standards.

After months of struggle, Tom had finally tamed the duty roster monster, handing Joanna a flawlessly executed copy of the upcoming month's schedule two days before she absolutely had to have it in hand. At this point, he was hard at work preparing a first go-down of the next year's budget. Joanna knew that he had placed several calls to Frank asking for pointers on both the budget and IT concerns, and she was grateful Frank had been willing to help.

The one place where Tom was still sadly lacking was in media relations. Faced with a camera or a reporter, the former jail commander morphed from your basic macho tough-guy into a spluttering, tongue-tied neophyte. Six months of participation in a Toastmasters group in Sierra Vista had helped some, but it would take lots more time and effort before Tom Hadlock would be fully at ease in front of a bank of microphones and cameras.

When the phone on Joanna's desk rang, she glanced at her watch to check the time before picking it up. At home her husband, Butch Dixon, was battling a tough copyediting deadline on his latest crime novel. As a consequence, Joanna was on tap to pick up the kids. Her nearly sixteen-year-old daughter, Jenny, worked three hours a day after school as an aide in a local veterinarian's office. With equal parts anticipation and dread, Joanna was looking forward to the day, coming all too soon, when Jenny would have a driver's license of her own. Once that happened, driving her back and forth to work and school activities would no longer be a necessity.

Joanna and Butch's two-year-old, Dennis, spent five hours each afternoon at a preschool that operated in conjunction with their church in Old Bisbee. Dennis was a gregarious kid. When the older members of what Joanna termed the "gang of four"—Jenny and the housekeeper's two grandsons—had gone off to school in the fall, Dennis had been lost on his own. When a spot had opened up in the preschool program at Tombstone Canyon United

Methodist, they had signed him up for a half-day program four days a week.

Joanna's first thought was that the phone call would involve some hitch in picking up the kids. Or maybe Butch needed her to stop by the store to pick up some last-minute item for dinner before she went home to High Lonesome Ranch. When she answered, however, it turned out that the call had nothing to do with the home front and everything to do with work.

"Jury's back," Kristin Gregovich said.

Kristin was Joanna's secretary, and the returning jury in question was only a few steps away from Joanna's office at the Cochise County Justice Center, a joint facility that not only housed the sheriff's department and the jail, but also the Cochise County superior court offices and courtrooms. The case currently being tried there was one in which Joanna Brady had played a pivotal role.

More than a year earlier, an elderly woman named Philippa Brinson had gone AWOL from what was supposedly a state-of-the-art Alzheimer's group home near the Cochise County town of Palominas. Sheriff Brady had been one of several officers who had responded to the original Missing Persons call on Philippa Brinson.

But Caring Friends had turned out to be a far worse can of worms than anyone expected. For one thing, arriving officers had been dumbfounded by the appallingly unsanitary conditions in what was supposed to be a health facility. The kitchen had been a food handler's nightmare, and they had found evidence that helpless residents had been routinely strapped to beds and chairs and left, trapped in their own bodily filth, for hours on end. A subsequent investigation had brought evidence to light that several Caring Friends patients had died as a result of serious infections that started out as bedsores.

It was while Joanna and her deputies were at the crime scene that they had been confronted by Alma DeLong, the owner of Caring Friends as well as several other Alzheimer's treatment facilities. Outraged to find police officers on the premises, she had launched a physical attack against them and had been hauled off to jail in a Cochise County patrol car.

Hours later, Philippa Brinson had been found safe. Confined to a chair in her room, she had managed to use nail clippers to cut away her restraints. Out on the highway, she had hitched a ride into Bisbee and had made her way to the old high school building. According to her thinking, she had been on her way to work in her old office, a place from which she had retired some thirty-five years earlier. After that misadventure, she was placed in the care of a niece and had gone off to a different facility—hopefully a better one—in Phoenix, while Joanna's department had been left to clean up the mess revealed by Philippa's brief disappearance.

Alma DeLong, arrogant and utterly unrepentant, had brought in high-powered attorneys to fight the charges lodged against her. For years, Joanna had held a fairly low opinion of Arlee Jones, the local "good old boy" county attorney, and that antipathy went both ways. The county attorney didn't approve of Joanna any more than she approved of him. Arlee was a political animal—well connected, smart, and lazy. Everyone knew that whenever possible, he preferred plea bargains to the work of actually going to trial.

When Arlee had offered Alma a plea bargain of a single count of negligent homicide that would have resulted in less than four years of jail time, Joanna hadn't been happy; but Alma had turned that option down cold, choosing instead to take her chances with a judge and jury. Annoyed and galvanized, Arlee Jones had gone after Alma DeLong with a vengeance, charging the woman with three counts of second-degree homicide, which in terms of seriousness, was two whole steps up the felony ladder from negligent homicide. DeLong was also charged with assaulting a police officer and resisting arrest.

After more than a year of legal maneuvering and stalling on the defense's part, the case had finally come to trial. Because Joanna had been a part of that initial investigation, she had been called to testify. She had spent a day and a half on the stand being grilled first by Arlee and later by Alma's defense attorney. Now, a full day after beginning their deliberations, the jury was finally back.

Because Alma was a well-known Tucson-area businesswoman, the trial had attracted a good deal of media attention. Rather than throw Tom Hadlock up against what was likely to be a mob of reporters, Joanna ducked into the restroom long enough to check her hair and lipstick before leaving the office and walking across the breezeway to Judge Cameron Moore's courtroom.

Once inside, Joanna slipped into an empty seat

next to Bobby Fletcher. His mother, Inez, was one of the Caring Friends patients who had died. Bobby's sister, Candace, had been more interested in winning a financial settlement than anything else. She had been notably absent throughout the criminal trial. Bobby, on the other hand, had been in the courtroom every day, observing the testimony with avid interest. Bobby was a man with plenty of deficits in terms of social skills and education and some criminal convictions of his own. When he had finally straightened up, Inez had taken him in and had been his unwavering refuge. A guilty verdict wouldn't bring his mother back from the grave, but it would go a long way toward giving her grieving son a measure of justice.

As the jury filed into the courtroom, Bobby said nothing. Looking for reassurance, he reached out and took Joanna's hand.

"Madame Forewoman," Judge Moore intoned. "Have you reached a verdict?"

"We have, Your Honor."

The piece of paper was passed to the judge. While the judge perused it, the defendant, flanked by her attorneys, rose to her feet.

"How do you find?"

"On the first count of manslaughter in the first degree, we find the defendant guilty."

Bobby Fletcher shuddered and covered his face with his hands, sobbing silently as the jury forewoman continued: "On the second count of manslaughter in the first degree, we find the defendant guilty. On the third count of manslaughter in the first degree, we find the defendant guilty. On the charge of assaulting an officer of the law, we find the defendant innocent. On the charge of resisting arrest, we find the defendant guilty."

The last two struck Joanna as incomprehensible hairsplitting. How could someone be innocent of physically assaulting an officer—something Joanna had witnessed with her own eyes—while, at the same time, be guilty of resisting arrest? But Bobby Fletcher had heard the single word he needed to hear. Alma DeLong was guilty of killing his mother. She had been free on bail. Once the judge granted the prosecutor's request to rescind her bail, a deputy stepped forward to lead her across the parking lot to the county jail where she would be held while awaiting sentencing.

Walking side by side, Joanna and Bobby Fletcher moved toward the courtroom door, where Bobby came to a sudden stop. "I want to wait here and talk to Mr. Jones," Bobby said. "I want to thank him."

Not eager to face the media throng that was no doubt assembled outside, Joanna waited, too, but she was also amazed. Bobby had spent huge chunks of his adult life as a prison inmate. The idea of him having a cordial conversation with any prosecutor on the planet was pretty much unthinkable. But then, to Joanna's astonishment, when Arlee Jones appeared, she found herself in for an even bigger shock. The county attorney approached Bobby Fletcher with his hand outstretched and a broad smile on his face.

"We got her," the county attorney gloated, pumping Bobby's hand with congratulatory enthusiasm. "We still have the sentencing process to get through, but one way or another, Alma DeLong is going to jail, starting today. Her bail may yet be reinstated, pending an appeal, but for now she's a guest in your establishment, Sheriff Brady. Unfortunately, the accommodations there will be somewhat better than her victims experienced at Caring Friends."

"Thank you, sir," Bobby Fletcher said.

"You're welcome, Mr. Fletcher," Arlee replied. "I'm not sure I ever mentioned this, but back when I was a kid, I used to deliver newspapers to your folks' place over on Black Knob. Even when times were tough, your mom always made sure I got a tip when I came around collecting. Depending on whether it was winter or summer, she also offered me either hot chocolate or iced tea. Inez Fletcher was a good woman. Sending her killer to jail is the least I can do."

The unguarded sincerity in that statement caused Arlee Jones to move up several notches in Joanna's estimation. She usually dismissed Jones as being a pompous ass in a mostly empty suit. Now she momentarily reconsidered that opinion. And that was the thing that Alma DeLong hadn't realized, either. Bisbee was a small town. The invisible spiderweb of connections running from one person and one family to the next was another reason Arlee Jones had tackled this case with unaccustomed zeal.

"So are you ready to talk to some reporters?" Jones asked.

"Who, me?" Bobby asked. A look of dismay spread across his face. "Are you kidding?"

"Yes, you," Arlee said, placing a guiding hand

on Bobby's shoulder. "And I'm not kidding. As far as people following this trial are concerned, you're the living face of the victims. You're the stand-in for every family that ever made the mistake of placing a loved one in a Caring Friends facility. You and the other families did so expecting that their father or mother or grandmother would be well cared for, even though we know now that wasn't the case.

"Having you speak to reporters tonight serves two purposes. It shows families that they can't just drop their loved ones off at one of these places and then not monitor what goes on once the doors slam shut. They have to be vigilant. And it also serves to show people like Alma DeLong that if they deliver inadequate care, there will be consequences. Can you do that?"

"All right," Bobby said uncertainly. "I guess."

Witnessing this, Joanna's approval needle on Arlee Jones dipped back down a bit. No doubt the man would make plenty of political hay from this incident. Having Bobby standing beside him during the press conference would provide a compelling segment on the evening news, and it would probably allow him to bank any number of sound bites that would work well the next time Arlee had to stand for election.

Joanna followed the two men out onto the covered outdoor breezeway. Content to be on the sidelines for a change, she stood next to Arlee Jones and listened in while a number of reporters piled on with a bombardment of questions. To Joanna's surprise, Bobby Fletcher answered all of them in the unassuming but straightforward manner that had made him an effective prosecution witness during the trial. He hadn't just dropped his mother off at the facility. He had seen the quality of care going down the tubes, and his attempts to rectify the situation had come to nothing.

All Joanna had to do was listen and smile and nod. The press conference ended without her having been asked a single question. That was exactly how she liked it, but her makeup had been on straight and her hair had been combed properly. Things didn't get any better than that.

Once the press conference was over, however, a glance at her watch told Joanna she was running late. When the day care facility closed at six, she had exactly five minutes of grace time to pick Dennis up. After that, she would begin accumulating late fines to the tune of twenty-six dollars for every additional five-minute period. Being late was not an option.

Joanna raced out through the back door of her office, jumped into her Yukon, and headed for Dr. Millicent Ross's veterinary office in Bisbee's Saginaw neighborhood, calling Jenny's cell as she went.

"I'm on my way," she told her daughter. "Meet me outside. Then I'll drop you off at the church so you can go in and sign Dennis out. If I have to mess around with finding a parking place there, we're not going to make it on time."

As directed, Jenny stood by the entrance to the clinic's driveway, leaning against a gatepost with one strap of her backpack flung over her shoulder. A stiff breeze blew in from the north, and Jenny's long ponytail fluttered like a blond flag in the turbulent air. Back in high school, Joanna had been a tiny redhead who had often been referred to as "cute." Jenny, on the other hand, was beautiful in a tall, slender, blue-eyed way that would never be considered "cute."

It came as no surprise to Joanna that Jenny, an accomplished horsewoman, would be a natural choice for the title of Bisbee High School's Rodeo Queen at some point in the course of her four years there. The surprise had been in the timing. Joanna had expected it to happen later on. Being rodeo queen as a senior would have been just about right, but Jenny had won the crown as a mere sophomore, leaving Joanna as the mother of a rodeo queen earlier than she'd ever thought possible.

Once she had made the mistake of mentioning all of that to her own mother. Eleanor Lathrop Winfield had responded with a singular lack of sympathy.

"It's one of those surprises that comes with being a parent, and you don't even have time enough to dodge out of the way," Eleanor had told her. "Besides, you're better off as the youngish mother of a rodeo queen than being an underage grandmother."

The implications in her mother's statement were quite clear: As in, your daughter's a sixteen-year-old rodeo queen. Mine was an unmarried, pregnant seventeen-year-old. Which do you prefer?

Guilty as charged, that was pretty much the end of Joanna's taking issue with the rodeo queen situation.

"Hey," Joanna said as Jenny dropped her backpack on the floorboard, scrambled into the passenger seat, and fastened her seatbelt. "How are things?"

"Good," Jenny said.

"And work?"

"Okay."

The older Jenny got, the harder it became to get her to reply to any given question with something other than a single word.

"School?" Joanna ventured.

"School was weird."

That was more than a one-word answer. It was long on worrisome implications but short on meaning. "What do you mean weird?"

"When the buses were leaving this afternoon, the parking lot was full of cops."

"Really?" Joanna asked. "How come? Did something happen? Was the school on lockdown?"

And if it was, she asked herself, why didn't I know about it?

"Mrs. Highsmith is missing or something."

Debra Highsmith, the high school principal, was someone with whom Joanna had crossed swords several times, most notably when Joanna had been invited to speak at Career Day and was notified that, due to the school's strict "zero tolerance of weapons" policy, she would need to leave both her Glock and her Taser at home. Joanna had gone to the school board and had succeeded in obtaining a waiver of that policy for trained police officers.

"Mrs. Highsmith is missing?" Joanna asked.

Jenny shrugged and nodded. "She wasn't at school this morning. When I took the homeroom attendance sheets down to the office, I heard Mrs.

Holder talking to Mr. Howard about it—that Mrs. Highsmith hadn't come in and that it was odd that she hadn't called in to let anyone know. After that, I didn't hear anything else until we were going out to the buses. That's when all the cop cars showed up."

Wondering what had happened but not wanting to grill her daughter, Joanna changed the subject. "How was Driver's Ed?"

"Mr. Forte is having a hard time finding a stick shift vehicle for me to practice on."

Jenny had won her local rodeo crown, but there were other titles to conquer. If she intended to run for or win any of those, both Jenny and her horse needed to attend the far-flung competitions, a reality which had underscored the fact that they needed suitable horse-hauling transportation.

With that in mind, Butch had gone on Craigslist and found a bargain basement, used dual cab Toyota Tundra pickup, complete with a heavy-duty towing package. It was a good enough deal that he had snapped it up on the spot. The only sticking point was that the Tundra came with manual transmission, and all the vehicles used for Bisbee High School Driver's Ed classes were automatics.

"If Butch finishes his copyediting, maybe he can take you out for a spin tomorrow since you don't have school."

"I'm working tomorrow," Jenny said. "We're planning to do the driving thing on Saturday."

Faced with severe budget shortfalls, the school district had switched to four-day weeks, leaving the schools shuttered on Fridays and weekends. It cut down on utilities and transportation costs, but it left working parents scrambling for something to do with their kids each Friday when school was out and the parents still had to work. Joanna was fortunate. On those days when extra kids had to be accommodated at the church-run preschool and day care, Dennis was usually able to be at home with Butch. When Butch wasn't available, they could call on Carol Sunderson, their part-time housekeeper, and her two grandsons.

Joanna pulled over to the curb, and Jenny dashed inside to get her brother. While she was gone, Joanna called Alvin Bernard, Bisbee's chief of police. She was still on hold when Jenny came out with Dennis in tow. As Jenny strapped her little brother into the car seat that was a permanent fixture in Joanna's patrol car, Alvin finally came on the line.

"Sorry to make you wait so long," Alvin said. "I'm busier than a one-legged man at a butt-kicking contest."

Like Arlee Jones, Alvin Bernard was a good old boy of a certain vintage. When Joanna was first elected sheriff, Alvin hadn't exactly welcomed her to the local law enforcement community with open arms. Over time, however, they had buried the hatchet and learned to work together.

"What's the deal with Debra Highsmith?" Joanna asked.

"Sorry, I suppose I should have given you a call about this," Alvin said, "but it's been crazy. When she didn't show up at school this morning and didn't call in, we sent out officers to do a welfare check. They found nothing—zip. Her purse and cell phone were there, but her car keys and car are missing. And there's a pair of shoes on the floor beside the door, as though she kicked them off as soon as she came inside. There was no sign of forced entry. No sign of a struggle. It's as though she went home after school yesterday afternoon and then both she and her vehicle simply vanished into thin air. We've checked with all the neighbors. No one admits to having seen or heard anything out of the ordinary with her or with her dog."

"She's got a dog?" Joanna asked.

"A big Doberman," Alvin replied. "The neighbors tell us she's only had him a couple of months, but he's gone, too. Dog dishes and doggy doo-doo are everywhere. No dog, but with the car and keys gone, it's unlikely that she's on foot, and chances are the dog is with her. All the same we're searching the neighborhood in case she went out for a walk with the dog. It could be she suffered some kind of medical emergency and ended up in a ditch where no one can see her. Or else she's in a hospital. I've got someone calling hospitals in the area just in case."

"Where does she live?"

"Out in San Jose Estates, so there's some distance between the houses. I've had uniforms out canvassing up and down the street. No one remembers seeing her out and about on foot or otherwise. However, we did find something pretty interesting."

By then Joanna had put the Yukon in gear and was driving down Tombstone Canyon with Dennis jabbering happily in the backseat. His brand of non-stop talk was pretty much lost on everyone but his sister, who seemed to understand his every word. Neither of them appeared to be paying the slightest attention to Joanna's side of the conversation.

"What's that?"

"Remember when she gave you all that crap over her zero tolerance of weapons at school?"

"Yes," Joanna said. "I remember it well. Why?"

"I knew she had applied for and received a concealed weapons permit. After her giving you so much grief about bringing a weapon to school, I guess I never thought she'd go the distance, but she did. Guess what we found in her purse? One of those two-inch Judge Public Defenders loaded with five four-ten shotgun shells."

A Public Defender loaded with shotgun shells certainly wouldn't have been Joanna's first choice of weapon. It was designed to do serious damage, and it wasn't something that lent itself to harmless practice shooting on a firing range.

"You've got to be kidding. She had one of those in her purse?"

"Yes, ma'am," Alvin said. "Big as life. Considering her very public attitude toward firearms, I thought you'd get a kick out of that."

As far as Joanna was concerned "kick" wasn't exactly the word that came to mind.

"Sounds like she was worried about something," Joanna said. "You don't go around with a handgun in your purse, especially one loaded with shotgun shells, if you haven't a care in the world."

"Who has a gun in her purse?" Jenny asked.

If Jenny was tuning in, that meant that Joanna's part of the conversation was over. "Keep me posted if you learn anything more," she said. "I need to get my kids home to dinner."

Alvin took the hint. "Okay," he said. "Talk to you later."

"You still didn't say whose gun," Jenny objected.

"Police business," Joanna said.

In her family those two words carried a lot of weight, just as they had years earlier when her father had used them with Joanna. It was a conversational DO NOT CROSS line that was every bit as effective as a strip of yellow crime-scene tape. It meant the subject was off-limits and any further discussion forbidden.

"I'm not a baby, you know," Jenny complained.

"No, you're not," Joanna agreed. "Which means that you understand I'm not allowed to discuss an ongoing investigation with anyone."

"I'll bet you'll discuss it with Dad," Jenny said.

Joanna's heart did a tiny flip. She and Butch Dixon had been married for years, but this was the first time she ever remembered hearing Jenny refer to him as "Dad" rather than "Butch." Although the whole idea gladdened her heart, she didn't want to screw it up by overreacting. Besides, there was always a chance that, in this case, Jenny was deliberately zinging her mother.

"What do you want to bet?" Joanna asked.

"Never mind," Jenny said. "I didn't want to know anyway."

With that Jenny lapsed into a brooding silence that lasted the rest of the way home. Joanna tried not to take any of it too seriously. When it came to parenting teenagers, bouts of surly silence were par for the course. When they got to the house, Jenny grabbed her backpack, darted out of the car, and slammed her way into her bedroom before Joanna managed to drag Dennis and all his toddler gear into the house.

"What's up with Jenny?" Butch asked.

From the complex aroma in the kitchen, Joanna could tell that dinner was all but cooked. Butch was busy setting the table.

"Nothing five years won't fix," Joanna said with a laugh.

"Oh, that," Butch said, giving first her and then Dennis quick pecks on the cheek as they walked by. "Wash hands, Little Man," Butch added to Dennis. "Dinner's almost ready."